Carole,

To a good friend —
all the best to you —

Will H R

Oct. 11, 2010

The Treasure of San Miguel Island

William White

ℰ

Eloquent Books

Durham, Connecticut

This is a work of fiction. Names, characters, places, and incidents either are a product of the author's imagination or are used fictitiously, and any resemblance to actual persons, living or dead, business establishments, events, or locales is entirely coincidental.

Eloquent Books
An imprint of Strategic Book Group
P.O. Box 333
Durham CT 06422
www.strategicbookgroup.com

ISBN: 978-1-60860-844-7

Book Design: Bruce Salender

Printed in the United States of America

Dedication

It is appropriate that there are two people worthy of this dubious honor. The first would be Freddie Steele, who I am almost certain has moved on from this life. He was in his mid-40's in the year of 1959 and would be in his mid-90's at this writing. I have not seen nor heard of him, nor known of his whereabouts, since that magical summer, but he still lives in my memory. He was a man from the past even in 1959, and it is hard to imagine him doing anything for a living other than abalone diving. It was a dying vocation even back then, and it remains so today. Freddie always pushed the boundaries of legality with everything he did, and we were totally awed by him and his brash behavior. I would find out much later that there were many life lessons graphically presented by Freddie to my friend Bobby Landers and me. Those lessons still remain embedded in my memory to this date. I am also compelled to point out that most of those lessons were good ones.

The second person worthy of this dedication is Bobby Landers (deceased), who was with me every step of the way and shared all the adventures of that summer equally with yours truly. We drifted apart through the years, as most childhood friends seem to do, and I was saddened when I head about his passing. He was a man who came from a humble beginning, who did everything he could to better himself while raising a family in rural California. It has been said that most people live their lives in quiet desperation, and such could be said about Bobby Landers. He struggled for everything he achieved and died young from heart failure. Only the good die young, while the ones like me seem to live forever.

Acknowledgments

I want to offer a special thank-you to John and Marilyn Bush for their technical critique on sailing terminology. I have been away from the sailing regimen for a number of years, and the world had passed me by. Then there was my son, Dustin, who gave me continuous encouragement after reading my rough-drafted chapters: Thank you, son, for all your kind words. Finally, where would the world be without the likes of C.L. Maddon? He gave me continuous encouragement and support and helped with the spelling of the Spanish words that I am prone to use from time to time. He was also quick to point out the times when I was not being politically correct and encouraged me to leave my personal opinions to myself when writing this novel. C.L. is a man who loves to read and devours volumes of literature. This is just one of the reasons why I consider him an expert and value his opinion: Thanks again, C.L. for being a good friend.

Preface

The idea of writing this book came to me slowly. It began when many of those who had read *Reflections* and the Freddie Steele story began telling me that this story was way too short. Although it was the longest story in the book, everyone seemed to want more. Many times I heard the comment, "This story would make a good book," when referring to the Freddie Steele story. The problem was that the story was a true account of the summer of '59 and anything more would only be gilding the lily as far as I was concerned. It was then that I began toying with the idea of producing a work of fiction. I had never done this before, and I wasn't sure if I would be capable of it. Dialogue was completely new to me; and although I am an avid reader, I was forced to look through other works of fiction to find out roughly how it is done (I never paid attention to this before).

Finally, I sat down one evening and began the story. I found out quickly that I had created a character that I didn't like, and I would be stuck with him for the entire book. This needed to be changed. I began from the beginning once again, and finally there emerged characters I could live with and the story began to take shape. I then discovered that I was not creating enough background information to allow the reader to "be there" when reading the story. I remember mentioning to someone that I would be working on this book for at least a year, and I believed it.

After the third or maybe the fourth chapter (I'm not sure), the story began to take on a life of its own. I found that I couldn't wait to get back to the computer to find out what would happen next. On those few occasions when I was searching for a way to continue the story, a simple walk normally worked wonders for me. Then I had to learn how to integrate the actions of groups of characters into a single purpose. In no time at all, it got to be a lot of fun, and I ended up completing the novel in 45 days—the rough draft, that is. I then spent another 45 days editing and enriching the story. My goal was always to write a book that would be hard to put down, and those few critics who have read the final draft have universally stated exactly that: "The book is hard to put down." (I hope they were not just trying to save my feelings.) I was surprised when I discovered that a publisher was actually interested in my novel, and I still feel surprise about that from time to time. It has inspired me to begin another fictional story, for which I have nine chapters completed, using the same characters.

The reader will find this book good entertainment for the entire family. Those of you who enjoy graphically explicit sex will be disappointed here. It may help to sell books, but it diminishes the value of the story, as does the use of bad language. The most satisfying part of writing such a book are the comments people make about how much they enjoyed it. This, above all else, is the fuel that drives the train; and I thank you all in advance for reading this book.

Chapter One:
JACK MORGAN

Jack Morgan sat quietly on the uneven boulders that formed the breakwater for the Santa Barbara yacht harbor. He had been to this location many times before, and the effect was always the same. It was a place that few knew of and even fewer would risk the incoming tides to reach. Jack had never seen another soul at this small hidden pocket of seclusion, nor had he detected the presence of anyone ever having been here. The misty outlines of the Channel Islands faded in and out with the waning afternoon sunlight. This visual effect was further heightened by the increased humidity brought in with the prevailing westerlies. *Just what was so compelling about those lonely uninhabited islands that stimulated his imagination and hovered like a forgotten lover just beyond his conscious mind? For that matter,* Jack wondered, *why did he seem to visit this chilly pile of rocks so often?* Too many afternoons to count were spent here scanning the horizon, hearing the harsh scream of the seabirds and the crashing of the surf on the breakwater.

These islands were just far enough away to appear simply as outlines jutting up from the Pacific Ocean at the point of the horizon. Why were these islands calling to him after all those intervening years? Was it just the restless soul of Jack Morgan beckoning him once again to explore new places? Maybe it was all of these things and more. And then, what was drawing him here to the breakwater and why did he continue to come time and again to this hidden rocky promontory?

Jack was a self-educated man with a formal education scarcely worth mentioning; but he had always been an avid reader who consumed volumes of literature on a regular basis. One could say that Jack Morgan was well endowed with good old country common sense, a trait that he inherited from his mother's side of the family. Another name for this common sense thing was wisdom. Wisdom is an elusive thing that many profess to have, but with which few are actually blessed. Jack was one of the blessed ones.

Jack Morgan could also be characterized as a jack-of-all-trades and master of many, with his current employment as a fry cook at an unpretentious coffee shop that catered to the working class. Jack could also repair your car, start your diesel engine, set a sail or weld a bead with equal skill, as well as many other skills that had accumulated in his personal bag of tricks during his 25 years of traveling about in North and South America.

Jack had first set foot on those distant islands some 20 years past, when in the employ of that crusty old pirate Freddy Steele. Freddy had disappeared from this part of the California coast some years earlier, but the impact that Freddy had on young Jack Morgan's life was as clear today as though Freddy had never left. It was not so much that Freddy had influenced his life, which he had, but more that Freddy's influence brought to life the total Channel Island experience, although Freddy Steele actually played only a minor part. Jack would never admit it, but he was becoming in some ways like Freddy Steele as he grew older. To Jack's credit, he had adopted Freddy's good traits, while discarding the bad ones. For reasons only God knew, Jack was once again called to these forgotten isles, as though his original experience there had merely whetted his appetite, with the main course still waiting to be served. For whatever reasons,

Jack Morgan could be found here woolgathering each afternoon when time and his job permitted.

Try as he might, he only rarely saw the island of San Miguel, the westernmost of the Channel Islands and also the most intriguing. Jack had been on this island several times before, and each visit could be likened to visiting a holy shrine or a place of spiritual power. There was a presence of peace and serenity there that seemed to affect all who ventured upon its' rocky shores. One found oneself speaking in whispers as if normal sounds would be a sacrilege to some island god. The other islands did not have the powerful effect of San Miguel. Jack wondered sometimes if it was just the imagination of his youth or if this phenomenon was real. This was just one of the many questions Jack would like to find answers to someday.

After several hours of sitting in a cramped position, Jack slowly stood up and stretched his lanky 45-year-old body. All too soon a rush of pain flowed into his cramped extremities as blood began circulating there once more. He stretched his limbs several times, then began gathering up his simple belongings for his hasty retreat from the incoming tide. It was nearing time for his shift to begin at the Harbor Coffee Shop; and as much as he disliked this job, he needed to make haste if he wanted to keep it, as unrewarding as it was. The obnoxious butthead who owned this greasy spoon had made it glaringly clear what would happen to Jack if he were to be late again. With that thought in mind, Jack left the harbor breakwater at a brisk pace. This job was one that he needed badly right now; jobs in general were becoming harder to find, even bad ones like this.

As Jack hurried up the trail through the eucalyptus grove that partially hid the modest bluffs overlooking the yacht harbor, he noticed the BMW convertible again parked at its usual location. He tarried for a moment to check that the keys were in the ignition as usual. *Whoever owned this very expensive automobile should be a little more careful,* he thought. After all, not everyone would be as honest as Jack, should an opportunity such as this present itself. As he stood there next to the car while casually admiring its sleek lines, Jack thought he detected movement from the corner of his eye. As he quickly turned to get a better view, there was nothing visible that he could discern.

"I must be getting paranoid," he mumbled to himself as he continued on his way. Out of reflex, Jack felt for his knife and was quickly assured of its presence. Without giving the keys another thought, Jack hurried to the top of the hill, then on through the downed fencing and onto the paving of Date Street. Winter had arrived in Santa Barbara and the barren trees lining the street seemed to further emphasize the dilapidated state of the neighborhood. He continued on, past the random piles of human discard and the many boarded-up structures, to the two-bedroom apartment he shared with his girlfriend Susan French and her 12-year-old son, Josh.

This was a side of beautiful Santa Barbara that few ever saw or even knew existed, although there are places like this all across America. It was a place that those who toiled at semi-skilled occupations or lived off the public dole called home. If there were a menial task that paid minimum wage, one could be certain that here or someplace just like this would be where the worker lived. It was now more of a barrio than a slum. The strong Hispanic presence had a calming influence on the neighborhood. Family values were the norm here, regardless of the level of poverty. Jack was always amazed at the strong work habits of these people, who sometimes worked three jobs just to make ends meet.

It was nearing time for his shift to begin, and Jack needed to hurry as he entered the apartment. He grabbed a clean uniform from the hall closet, while glancing at the note left for him by Susan. She and Josh had gone shopping and would be home later. It sometimes amazed him how thoughtful she always was about the little things that seemed to matter the most. Susan was a simple person who accepted life on its own terms while always playing the cards she was dealt. She was also an amazingly happy woman who seldom complained about her lot in life. The hold she had over Jack was that she had no hold and never tried for one. The knowledge that he could leave at any time had kept him here in Santa Barbara for nearing a year now—somewhat of a record for staying in one place for Jack Morgan. Much like the words from the Glen Campbell song, *Gentle on My Mind,* "It was knowing that the door was always open and the path was free to walk."

Susan was the only child of a missionary family and had spent much of her early years in Ecuador. It wasn't until Susan was ready to enter high school that the family finally returned from Central America. Because of this, Susan was bilingual and equally at home here in the barrio and in American suburbia. Susan was a comely woman who projected a powerful presence wherever she happened to be. When Miss Susan walked into a room, many conversations ceased and eyes turned to her regal carriage. She was no beauty queen, but Susan radiated an inner beauty that many, including Jack, found irresistible. Susan was neither a clinging vine nor one who allowed herself to be dominated by others. She was simply a kind and gentle woman who had never lost sight of the basic goodness of the human spirit. She understood her responsibilities to Josh and to Jack, as well, and always did more than her share to energize their relationship. Susan also found Jack Morgan irresistible, as did Josh. Jack was always considerate and thoughtful, and as an added bonus, was not bad to look at. Susan was always conscious of the envying looks thrown her way by unhappy females when the two were out together in public. Jack had been a good companion for her, and the only father Josh had ever known. It was getting hard for Susan to imagine a life without Jack, although he had been here for less than a year. This was as close to a happy family as Jack had ever had; it was the major reason that he had stuck to his poor excuse for a job. It was not the work that Jack minded but the lack of respect shown him by his employer. This was the main reason he resented going to work so much.

Jack donned his cooking whites on the run as he hurried the six blocks to the Harbor Coffee Shop. He arrived with three full minutes to spare. Georgie was waiting for him at the punch-in clock, not speaking but merely glairing at Jack as he reached for his time card and punched in. Georgie couldn't hide the disappointment on his face because Jack had actually made it to work on time. He had been looking forward to giving Jack a major tongue lashing; now it would have to wait for another time.

What was he thinking? Jack wondered. *Were he to fire me, someone would have to pull a double shift, or worse, Georgie would have to cook; a job he hates even more than he dislikes me.*

"Lucky for you, mister, that you finally got to work on time," Georgie commented as he smiled through his nicotine-stained teeth.

"I'm just naturally lucky, I guess," Jack replied while moving quickly into the kitchen, more to avoid Georgie's acid tongue than to begin his shift. *Georgie is a man who was truly twice-cursed; he is both overweight and obnoxious. What a cross to bear,* Jack thought with a private chuckle as he turned to his task of cooking for those fearless souls who would try to cheat death once more by eating the food served at the Harbor Coffee Shop.

Chapter Two:
CARL WEBB

Carl Webb slowly climbed into his BMW convertible and started the engine, then engaged the mechanism that closed the convertible top. He sat there patiently while German engineering smoothly did its part once again. He then closed the windows and turned the heater on to its low cycle. The book was now closed on Jack Morgan. He had passed all of those simple tests that Carl had set up for him, including the tests of his basic honesty and lack of greed, both critical elements for what Carl had in mind. Jack had been highly recommended by Freeman Barnes, one of Carl's trusted former associates, for the project Carl had been putting together for better than a year. It had taken five full months just to find Jack, following a trail that began in Manitoba, Canada and finally ended here in Santa Barbara, California. Carl was thankful for Susan French and her compelling female persuasions, for without her there was no telling whether Jack would ever have been found. Carl made a quick mental note to do something really nice for Susan when it was appropriate. This man Jack Morgan was a gypsy, for sure.

Carl had been in Santa Barbara for the past two months, observing Jack and leaving bait occasionally to test his character. It was time to move on now, with the next step being a meeting with Jack to introduce himself and then soon after, when the time was right, to present the project to him.

All in good time, Carl thought, *all in good time.*

Carl Webb had been one of the original members of the salvage crew who discovered the Spanish ship *Atocha* off the Florida coast. Since that time he had engaged in three other successful salvage operations in the Gulf of Mexico and increased his personal wealth each time. The problem with Gulf salvaging now was that too many of the European countries were filing lawsuits at each discovery. These countries were unwilling to participate in the expense of locating these wrecks, but were quick to stand in line for any share of treasure recovered, once one was located. Carl was tired of the unending legal hassles connected with treasure salvaging in the Gulf of Mexico and wanted to do something under the radar and unnoticed by those carrion birds from Europe. This was the reason he was here in California, and the reason he was interested in the talents of Jack Morgan.

Carl was a young 55-year-old who had always kept himself in good physical condition. He was an expert diver and an underwater salvage expert, and had a Bachelor of Science degree in mechanical engineering. Carl was also a deadly fighter and a student of the martial arts, more of a hobby now than a passion. Carl used this training to keep himself fit, rather than to hone his already considerable skills.

The years had taught him to select carefully those with whom he cast his lot. This was why he had spent a considerable amount of time tracking down and getting to know Jack Morgan and the person he truly was. It was now time for them to get better acquainted, and for Carl to make an offer he hoped Jack would accept. Carl knew that it should not be hard to do, considering the unrewarding job that Jack was managing to hang onto. *Time to go to the Harbor Coffee Shop and order up a bad meal,* he thought. Choosing a bad meal would be the easy part, because the odds were that everything on the menu was bad. On a personal note, it said much about the character of Jack that he could find and hold a job in the face of rising unemployment and the accompanying recession brought about by détente. If Jack could stomach such a job, then Carl could surely stomach a bad meal.

Without further ceremony, Carl headed for the Harbor Coffee Shop and parked near the front, where Jack would see the BMW when taking an order. This seemed to be as good a strategy as any to break the ice with Jack, and then hopefully set up a meeting at a neutral location—somewhere other than the Harbor Coffee Shop. Carl entered the restaurant and noticed that the sign said, "Seat yourself." With that in mind, he moved to one of the rear tables with no other customers close by. Before long Carl was visited by a dumpy and under-motivated waitress, who spent more time straightening her hair than paying attention to the customers. Jack could tell that this woman would be a real porker before too long; she was already succumbing to waitress spread, that affliction caused by working too many hours around fattening food. Her dismal appearance was further degraded by the t-shirt she was wearing that said, *I'd like to help you but I can't fix stupid.*

"What'll ya' have to drink?" she finally quipped.

"Water with lemon, please," he answered as he turned his attention to the menu thrust in front of him. The waitress disappeared to get his drink, allowing Carl time to look around. The waitress's name was Jane, he discerned from the number of verbal references voiced by customers in various stages of consuming their dinners. *I can't go wrong with a cheeseburger*, Carl thought as he closed the menu. Jane finally returned with his water, minus the lemon and the ice. The water was lukewarm tap water. This was starting off badly already.

"Ya know whatcha want?" Jane inquired. "We're out of lemon and ice," she stated flatly, as though he should have known beforehand.

"Sure, I'll have a cheeseburger with fries, please."

"OK, whatcha want on it?"

"Whatever comes with it will be fine," Carl said while privately vowing not to touch any of the food served here. "And I'll have a cup of coffee if you don't mind. Forget the lemon."

"I don't mind; that's my job," Jane finished brightly, trying to be pleasant enough perhaps to get a nice tip when Carl's meal was finished.

In the meantime, Carl was beginning to wonder if he would survive this meal. *Lucky for me, I'm not very hungry,* he thought to himself.

As Jane went to the kitchen to order the meal, Jack finally noticed the BMW in the parking lot.

"Jane, who's driving that BMW?" Jack inquired.

"Some guy at the back table. Never seen him before, but this is his order," she replied as she placed the cheeseburger order on the order rack.

Jack needed to get a better look at the BMW; if it was the same one, he had already decided to ask why the owner had the bad habit of continually leaving his keys in the ignition. Perhaps more to kill some time during his shift, Jack left the kitchen to inspect the car. He still had three more hours to go on this shift, so he might as well solve this mystery regarding the BMW.

It might make time go by faster, who knows? Jack thought as he turned toward the back door. A quick trip outside confirmed that this was indeed the same vehicle. Soon this minor mystery would be solved and Jack would have his curiosity satisfied once again. Jack came out of the kitchen and headed directly for the back table. He noted that the man sitting there looked both prosperous and intelligent.

Neither of these personal traits would cause one to be so forgetful or careless as to risk losing such a fine vehicle, Jack thought. He walked up to the table without hesitation.

"Hi, my name's Jack Morgan and I couldn't help but notice your car outside. I've seen it many times before, parked on the bluff overlooking the yacht harbor."

"It is my pleasure to meet you, Jack. My name is Carl Webb."

"Well, Carl, I also couldn't help but notice that you have a bad habit of leaving your keys in the ignition of that beautiful car; sooner or later, someone is going to liberate it, if you get my meaning. There're a lot of desperate people out there and more losing their jobs every day. It's just not a good idea to tempt fate, especially around here," Jack said.

"Thanks for the advice, Jack, but things aren't always what they seem. For example, I've wanted to meet with you for some time, and I was wondering if you could be available some time tomorrow at your convenience. I'd like to talk over a very serious and rewarding business proposition."

Jack was speechless. *This guy seemed to know him, but what did he really want? He didn't look perverted or anything kinky like that. Why not take a chance?* Jack thought. *Surely, there was no threat here that he could detect. Better to remain cautious, but anything legal would be better than this menial job,* he reasoned.

"Sure, Carl," Jack responded. "How about 10:00 a.m., at the fishing pier? I'll spring for a real cup of coffee."

"Done," Carl said as he stood up and dropped $20 on the table, then extended his hand to Jack. "Until tomorrow."

Carl left the restaurant without looking back and left the parking lot with the same finality. The job was done, for now.

We will see how things develop tomorrow, but I have a good feeling about the outcome, Carl thought as he headed for his hotel suite.

Jack was stunned by the events now swirling around him. *Who was this man Carl Webb and what would he be offering tomorrow?* Jack disliked the way he was being treated at his job, but it was too much to hope for anything better. If it didn't work out tomorrow, Jack needed to keep his cool and not say or do anything that would jeopardize his employment here. Still, Jack strolled back into the kitchen with a new bounce in his step. *Maybe, just maybe, but who knows?* Tomorrow would tell. Jack realized that he had forgotten to get the answer to his query about the car keys. He made a mental note to himself to find the answer to that question in the morning, for sure.

Georgie was waiting by the time clock when Jack approached to punch out that evening. Georgie was up to his usual bad habit of glaring at his employees as if his eye contact could cause bodily harm.

Time to get out of here before some real insults start flying, Jack thought, as he left the restaurant and headed down the darkened street to his and Susan's apartment. As hard as he tried, this job was beginning to get the better of him.

Chapter Three:
THE YUBA RIVER

It had been almost ten years earlier when a much younger and eager Jack Morgan accepted a job on an eight-inch suction dredge. He had answered an ad in the San Francisco Chronicle regarding the need for an experienced diver. When the person interviewing him named Freeman Barnes discovered that his experience had been in the Pacific Ocean at depths of up to 120 feet, he suddenly became much more interested in Jack Morgan. An appointment was soon set for a personal interview. Jack had agreed to meet him at the No Name bar in Sausalito, California that very afternoon. Jack knew from experience that there was real interest in his talents, but he also knew that as much as he needed a job, he needed to be cautious. *But what the hey,* he thought; it was a beautiful spring day and there were no jumpers visible on the Golden Gate Bridge as he made the crossing in his 1955 Willys Jeep. The winds were brisk and there were many yachts on the bay with full spinnakers set. Jack briefly wondered if an event was in progress to explain the large number of sail-boats all with a similar sail in place. All too soon, the drive across the bridge came to an abrupt end and a tunnel reared its head in front of him. After that the Sausalito exit came quickly into view. Before Jack was ready, he found himself looking for a parking spot in a very congested and busy business district.

From previous experience, Jack knew that Sausalito had a limited number of parking spaces, and the fines for illegal parking were $250 for the first offence. He got lucky that morning and found a parking space less than three blocks from the No Name bar. After parking, Jack hurriedly entered the dimly lighted tavern. He was early and the bar was empty with the exception of the bartender. Jack slid onto a stool where he could see the door and ordered a beer. It wasn't long until Freeman Barnes came through the door with a big smile on his face while heading straight for Jack.

"You must be Jack Morgan."

"That's me, and you must be Freeman Barnes?"

"That's correct. And I'm surprised you got here so soon."

"The traffic was light and there were no jumpers on the bridge today," Jack replied.

Jack and Freeman warmed to each other and it was soon apparent that there was good medicine between them. It would be less than half an hour later when a deal was completed, and it went like this:

Jack was to receive a draw against profit shares with either a weekly or monthly payday. Expenses such as transportation and camping supplies and equipment were to be borne by the mining company. Jack was to perform the duties of head diver for this dredging operation. Jack had never worked on a gold dredge before and had much to learn, but then none of the crew had been submerged in over 20 feet of water before, so everyone had much to learn. The object of this mining operation was to dredge out a glory hole, which could be over 100 feet deep. No one could know just how deep it would be until they actually reached the bottom.

The location of this mining operation was a remote area of the High Sierras on the north fork of the Yuba River. The land was owned by Southern Pacific Railroad and the mining contract was between Southern Pacific Railroad and Freeman Barnes. The location was so remote that it had to be supplied by

Southern Pacific Railroad helicopters. *What an amazing adventure,* Jack thought.

There were 12 members of the dredging crew, and eight were divers who worked in pairs and rotated with one-hour shifts beneath the surface of the water. There was also a 13th member of the crew based in Grass Valley, California, and it was his job to purchase supplies and handle all things connected with the operation and make them available in a timely manner.

A typical day on the Yuba River would begin with a wake-up call at 6 a.m. with breakfast promptly at 6:30. Generators were fired up at 7 a.m., and then the dual air compressors were drained of condensate water and started, with the compressors alternating for each day's work and the other serving as a backup. Then finally the dual Volkswagen engines were fired up on the dredge and the Venturi pumps were put in operation as the day's work began. Venturi pumps were booster pumps that entered the main eight-inch dredging hose at 20-foot intervals as the hole pressed downward. Their purpose was to increase the lifting power of the suction dredge by adding pressure-driven water from each pump.

The divers were all equipped with coldwater wetsuits and heavy rubber boots because the winter snows were still feeding the river runoff. Each diver had both a depth gauge and an underwater watch. They were required to commit to memory how long decompression would be required and at what depth, depending upon the time of submersion at the working depth. Jack had organized this part of the operation so that it worked like a well-oiled machine. His previous experiences with Freddy Steele at the Channel Islands were more lessons of what not to do, and he had learned those lessons well.

The divers worked as a team, with one running the suction nozzle while the other would be moving and loading rocks into the rope basket. They would rotate in half-hour increments. The larger boulders were set aside and would not be removed until the last shift of the day. The divers would stay at their tasks until relieved by the next shift, or until an hour's time had been reached. Rotating in one-hour shifts allowed minimum decompression time and allowed those relieved to go topside and warm up from the chill of the spring runoff. Once topside, the divers would take a 15-minute break and then begin working with the concentrates.

The other four crew members ran and serviced the equipment, cooked for the crew, and maintained the camp. All in all, Freeman Barnes and Jack Morgan ran a tight ship. The dredging operation ran non-stop for 12 hours each day, with both Jack and Freeman taking a diving shift in rotation with the other six members of the diving team.

As the glory hole moved ever downward, the need to clean the riffles on the dredge became a daily chore due to the increasing richness. The rule was that when visible gold could be seen on the last riffle, it was time to clean the concentrates from the dredge: this became a daily event.

When the dredge was finally shut down for the day, it was time for the cleaning to begin. First the visible gold was removed by hand and stored separately. After this, the black sand concentrates were removed and placed in 50-gallon drums. The black sand was then screened by hand to 1/4 inch with any visible gold also removed during this process. The quarter-inch concentrates were hand screened once again at 80 mesh to remove the fine gold. This 80-mesh material was then run though a Blue Bowl in an operation that never stopped, with six Blue Bowls running continuously. The quarter-inch concentrates were then run through a Gold Screw to capture the free gold, then reset for black sand and run through the Gold Screw once more. Lastly, the black sands were reunited and shipped to a refiner who extracted the remaining micron gold, other precious metals, and rare earths from the material. This dredging operation was shipping 4,000 pounds of black sand each week via helicopter to the nearest ground shipping point. This single phase of the mining operation alone paid for all the overhead expenses as well as the draws of the crew.

The profit split of this operation was quite generous as well, with the equipment and the claim receiving one share each. Then Freeman Barnes claimed three shares for himself and Jack Morgan claimed two shares; one for diving and one for supervising the diving operation. The remaining 11 crew members were each in for one share apiece. There were a total of 18 equally divided shares which would be distributed once the operation was concluded, less expenses and the 15 percent due to Southern Pacific Railroad. With the richness of the glory hole becoming more evident to the crew members every day, there was much anticipation as to what the final outcome would be. It was an exciting time each evening when the day's production was announced. No crew member had a truly realistic idea of just how rewarding this operation would be by the end of the summer, when the bottom of the hole suddenly turned bright yellow.

Promptly at 7:00 a.m. the dredge was shut down for the evening with any maintenance needed taking place after the shutdown. Dinner was served at 8:00 p.m. and lights were out by 10:00. By 9:00 p.m. most of the crew were already asleep, as the exhaustion of the day had taken its toll. And so it went that summer, seven days a week every week, as the days drifted into weeks, which in turn drifted into months.

Once the dredging operation was understood by Jack, he commenced with a training program and safety procedures. The first thing he did was to lose the swim fins and put the divers in tough boots. The divers would then pull themselves upward when surfacing on safety ropes installed at four locations in the hole and descend using the same method. The individual air hoses were coiled above in such a manner that they self-fed to the diver as required. There was also a fifth and sixth unused air hose, each with a facemask, air regulator, and a weight belt. This was to be used in an emergency if a diver or divers had to bail out (drop the weight belts and shed the masks and air hose) to reach the surface quickly. The need to re-enter the water and submerge to the decompression depth quickly was satisfied by this extra precaution. Jack saw to it that all divers practiced this skill each week. When an emergency actually occurred, and there were several, the diving crew was up to the task of escaping a possible life-threatening situation.

The decompression was to eliminate nitrogen narcosis, (the buildup of nitrogen in the blood), also known as the bends. The

27

bailing-out drill was to train the divers to exhale all the way to the surface. Holding one's breath with compressed air in the lungs on the way up to the surface ruptured the lungs and was almost always fatal. This condition was known as air embolism, and it was eliminated by remembering to scream all the way to the surface. The wetsuits were extremely buoyant and would actually throw the diver out of the water at the surface, once the weight belts were removed.

When the rope basket was filled with rocks, the two submerged divers would escort it to the surface and remain there until the rocks were safely in a position where they could not fall back into the hole. This was a simple procedure and it eliminated the possibility of having the basket of rocks fall onto the unsuspecting divers. The diver not working the suction nozzle was required to remain a minimum of five feet clear of the nozzle at all times to eliminate the possibility of being sucked into the hose.

It was a demanding job and it drained much energy from the crew by day's end. Jack, who was an avid reader, always had a large quantity of books on hand, which he shared liberally with anyone looking for something to read. There was little else to do as the dredge took a great physical toll on those who toiled on it. It was a tedious job, as well, but all could see where the end result would eventually take them and they all knew that there had to be a bottom somewhere down below.

The glory hole was actually the chimney of an extinct volcano with vertical cliffs nearing 600 feet in height on both sides. There were enormous ponderosa pine trees flanked by lush ferns, and wildflowers everywhere that never stopped blooming from early spring until late fall. The river was loaded with 12-inch trout that seemed to jump for flies constantly. Then there were the continuous visits of wild animals that had little fear of those men working there. The water became much warmer, as well as the air, as summer unfolded across the high Sierras. This place was incredibly beautiful and pristine. It would take Jack's breath away sometimes when the afternoon shadows danced across the river gorge. All the crew enjoyed the simple pleasures of sitting by a campfire and seeing the moon rise over the mountain cliffs, or watching the sun come up on those early summer mornings when the air was crisp and clean and smelled of a thousand things. These were precious memories to the entire crew and something that all would greatly miss later.

The crew became leaner and meaner as the summer progressed, with many members losing 35 to 55 pounds during this experience. There was beer served after dinner each evening, but most of the crew members either declined or drank only one or two occasionally. The mornings came early and all knew the value of a good night's sleep. Jack was a natural storyteller and was always in demand to tell his tales of diving in the Pacific Ocean with that outlaw Freddy Steele, or commercial salmon fishing in Alaska, or just recanting some of his more memorable experiences while traveling around in North and South America.

Freeman and Jack became very good friends as the summer progressed. The two gained respect for each other's abilities and leadership skills, and Freeman allowed Jack to handle the gold during the cleanup and weighing. Freeman could be assured that Jack would represent Freeman's best interests during this very delicate period of handling and storing the day's gold take when he could not be present. The glory hole continued to progress ever downward and there were some members of the crew who were beginning to think that it might never end.

Finally, at 92 feet the floor of the hole turned bright yellow. It was late September and the Yuba River was running at its low point. The dredge was delicately used to remove the lighter material from the top of the gold, and then shut off. From this point on it would be strictly a bucket operation. The winch which was used previously to remove rocks and boulders was now the principle workhorse for the operation. If one can imagine, the floor of the hole was approximately 20 feet in diameter. The gold averaged between eight and 12 inches deep and it took five days to remove. The dredge was then fired up once again and the floor vacuumed for the last time.

The operation was now over and the crew waited patiently for the results of their summer's work. When it was finally announced what the value of a share would be worth, many of the crew thought this was surely a mistake; it just couldn't possibly be that much. Once the sticker shock was finally over, the crew was in a dream world. The value of each share was the incredible amount of $578,000. This was more money that most of the crew had ever seen before or ever even imagined.

Freeman and Jack said goodbye to one another shortly after the shares were distributed. Freeman wanted Jack to come back for the next season if he could be persuaded; but for Jack it was never money that motivated him.

Freeman finally broached the subject with Jack as the two were en route to Grass Valley.

"You know, Jack, I could use a man like you next season. Did I mention that we will be working a similar hole, and it could be as big or bigger than this one?"

Jack took a thoughtful moment before answering. "Freeman, I truly appreciate your generous offer, but I must decline. This summer was eventful and was magic for me; I will never forget this time, nor will I forget your friendship, which I value very much. However, I have had my eye on a hunting lodge in British Columbia and now I can afford to buy it with my two shares, thanks to you."

"Jack, I understand, but you will be missed by me and all of the returning crew," Freeman stated. He could tell from the tone of Jack's reply that there was no negotiation possible, as Jack's mind was set.

With that, the two shook hands and Jack moved on to what was next on life's table. The two corresponded for a number of years, and then finally lost touch with each other. For Freeman, this dredging experience was merely a business operation, while for Jack it was an amazing happening that he would never forget; but it was time to travel down the road, as his restless nature required of him. The two friends never met again, and Jack eventually received word that Freeman had died while salvaging a sunken ship in the Gulf of Mexico.

Jack tried his hand at running the hunting lodge and it worked well for a time, but the restlessness in Jack's soul kept calling to him. The day came when Jack signed the operation over to the employees and took his leave. There were few dry eyes as those grateful men and women who benefited from Jack's generosity said their final goodbyes to their benefactor. Jack never returned and eventually lost touch with everyone connected with the lodge, more because this represented a life-style that he had spurned and that was best forgotten.

It should be noted that the lodge was renamed the Jack Morgan Hunting Lodge a year after his departure. A painting of Jack taken from a photograph adorned the great room of the lodge with the inscription, *"Our benefactor and founder Jack Morgan: wherever he may be, we all wish him Godspeed."*

Chapter Four:
MISS SUSAN

Susan French had earned a Master's Degree in marine biology while attending the University of California Santa Barbara. It was a profession that she was never able to pursue due to her responsibilities to her son Joshua. Susan and Josh's father, Randy Butler, were planning a spring wedding after their graduate work was completed.

It was both a rare and tragic event that cost Randy his life twelve years past. For Susan it was as if her world had come to an end when she received word of Randy's death. The finality of the event left her drained and morose. She never had the chance to tell him of the life growing inside of her but she knew that somewhere, somehow, Randy knew that they had conceived a son together.

Randy had been fatally attacked by an enraged moray eel when he inadvertently approached too close to the eel's lair. These were dangerous sea animals if aroused but normally if one stayed out of their territory they were docile. This particular eel ripped its razor sharp teeth into the inside of Randy's upper thigh and severed a major artery. Randy bled to death before he reached the safety of the diving boat. The attack was so quick and so severe that it would be some time later before it was noticed that Randy was missing and then several hours more before the body was located. This group of graduate students was doing marine research on the leeward side of Santa Cruz Island when the attack occurred. It was just a twist of fate that Susan was not present when this fatality took place. Susan had never taken to the ocean since that time, although she was a highly skilled and disciplined scuba diver. It was not that she harbored any ill feelings about scuba diving due to Randy's demise, but the burden of caring for a young child had left her with little time to pursue this activity.

It had been 12 years since the tragedy and Susan's and Randy's son, Josh was growing like a weed. Susan had devoted her energy to providing for her son and had acquired a teaching credential to that end. Susan had taught third grade at the John F. Kennedy Grammar School in Goleta, California, for the past ten years. Her dream of being a marine biologist was now a thing of the past, as the reality of raising a child had forced her to make some difficult decisions. It would have been nice to pursue her dream career but what was wrong with this one? When she thought about it, having Josh and helping him grow and expand his horizons was equally rewarding.

Susan had met Jack Morgan in the Borders bookstore near the UCSB Campus and the attraction had been intense and immediate for both. It would be safe to say that each was smitten and within a short time both Susan and Jack had their first date. From this point on the two would be inseparable. Within a week, Jack had moved into the French apartment after the whirlwind affair of getting to know one another. The two fitted well together and before long a deep and profound love for each other developed. It was an affair based completely upon the respect and admiration the two had for one another and neither of the two took it for granted. Both Jack and Susan energized their relationship continuously by their acts and deeds toward one another. It was a new thing for both of them. Jack had experienced many casual relationships in the past but never had he met anyone until Susan to whom he was so single-mindedly devoted. The same could be said of Susan.

Then there was Josh who had found a friend, a father, and a mentor who was always patient with him and never tired of answering his many questions about things important to 12-year-olds. Jack always had time for Josh regardless of his schedule and never hesitated to assist him with all things Josh required.

Jack Morgan was born in San Diego, California, the seventh of seven children to a father who was a dentist and a mother who was a pediatrician. Of his six siblings, all had Masters Degrees or better except Jack. Jack had always heard the calling of the migratory birds and the lonely train whistles late at night much more clearly than the call for an education. When the family went to Mammoth Lakes for a ski outing, more times than not, Jack would be found lying in the snow and watching the flakes falling gently to the earth around him. He was like the wind over the prairie or the ocean at sunset; beautiful to experience, then gone in the wink of an eye.

He was a restless child who saw little need for a formal education and one who truly heard the calling of faraway places. Jack finished high school but his grades were so poor that his parents enrolled him in a junior college with the hope that he would take stock of himself and get accepted at a major university. This lifestyle was not for Jack and before the first semester was completed, Jack had accepted a crew position on a tuna boat that would be at sea from four to six months at a time. What would soon become typical for Jack's behavior was that although the money he made on the tuna boat was good, the experience was the true event. After the cruise was completed, Jack moved on to other endeavors while never having a desire to return to the tuna boat again. Jack rarely saw his family after that cruise. Although he missed them sometimes, and they always missed him, he seldom found time to return to the family from which he had come. As he grew older he seemed to be further and further detached, and then when his parents passed away he lost touch with his siblings entirely.

Now he found himself working at a job that would be all right if not for the lack of respect shown him by the owner. At another time, Jack would have walked out at the first display of disrespect but he knew that jobs were hard to find right now and he had an obligation to Susan and Josh to help support the family. Jack was one who always took his obligations seriously, a personal trait that had always served him well and defined Jack Morgan, the man.

Jack stood six feet three inches tall and weighed 220 pounds. He had the body of a swimmer; long and lean with well-proportioned arms and legs. His reddish brown hair was still thick and unmanageable and he always appeared as if he needed to be groomed. He was an extraordinarily handsome man who turned the heads of wistful females wherever he went. Jack's deep blue eyes radiated strength and wisdom, and combined with his friendly smile, had the ability to make people like him instantly. Jack was a man among men who stood out in any crowd as being someone special. He was also a humble man who accepted the scraps that life left on his dinner plate without complaining. *After all,* he reasoned, *this was the lifestyle he had willingly chosen.* He was truly a man who marched to the beat of a different drummer and was much like the flowers in spring-time; there for a while for all to enjoy, then gone without cere-mony with the season's passing to other life challenges.

Jack could see that Susan and Josh were home as he reached the gate leading to the front door. Josh heard him coming and went to the front door to meet him. Jack smiled and raised his hand in a friendly salute as he stepped through the door and into the waiting arms of Susan. Susan had earlier made dinner just for herself and Josh, knowing that Jack would not be hungry af-ter working a shift at the restaurant. Later on when the two were alone, Jack began to tell Susan of the strange encounter with the man named Carl Webb, and the even stranger mystery concern-ing Carl's BMW.

"The thing that puzzles me the most is that he seems to know me and has spent a great deal of time looking for me. For the life of me, I have no clue why this is so."

"Well, Jack, tomorrow the mystery will be solved for certain. No need to stress over it tonight," Susan said.

With that, the two drifted off to other concerns and before too long were sleeping the sleep of the innocent.

Chapter Five:
FREDDY STEELE

It had been over 20 years past when a younger and more innocent Jack Morgan inquired around the fisherman's pier at Morro Bay, California, if anyone was in need of a deckhand on a fishing boat. He was told that Freddy Steele might be in the market for help as his boat was newly out of dry dock. It was also mentioned that he would be leaving for the Channel Islands soon. Jack was encouraged by this information although he had no idea where these Channel Islands were located. He eventually spoke to Freddy at the local watering hole, the Mariners Safe Harbor Pub. A meeting was hastily set up with a wave of Freddy's hand, and this was the reason Jack was sitting in the waning sun this afternoon.

"This is a job that I know something about," he thought, as he sat patiently waiting for Freddy Steele to show up. His attention was briefly diverted by the sound of harbor seals squabbling near him somewhere beneath the pier. Freddy was already one hour late and Jack was just beginning to gather up his belongings in preparation to leave when Freddy finally appeared.

Freddy's eyes were glassy and his cheeks were flushed, and Jack could instantly tell that Freddy was drunk. Freddy was all smiles and compliments to Jack, and before he knew it he had agreed to work for Freddy on his newly-refurbished boat. Jack found himself on a whirlwind tour of Freddy's boat the *Betty Lou*, as Freddy swept him along while quizzing him on his knowledge of diesel engines and bilge pumps, as well as a myriad of other things that Jack was mostly familiar with. Toward the end of the tour, Freddy was showing Jack his diving gear and asking if he would like to learn how to deep sea dive? For Jack, this represented another new life experience so of course, his answer was yes. Little did Jack know then how much this knowledge would cost him in terms of life-threatening experiences, but with the optimism of youth he agreed to all of Freddy's proposals.

Freddy left him as quickly as he appeared after asking Jack to report the following morning with his gear in hand to move aboard the boat. The balance of that coming day would be taken with gathering supplies for the run south, which was scheduled to take place the day following. Jack was happy with the arrangements, but it would be much later when the true nature of Freddy Steele, although not altogether bad, would be clearly evident to him. Right now Jack was just happy for employment but it was never clear what he would be earning with Freddy. This was something that would need to be discussed before they left the dock on the coast run. As it turned out, it would be several weeks later when he finally cornered Freddy and got the commission arrangements spelled out. It was fair and generous and Jack was happy with his share of the operation.

Freddy was a short but powerful man who was built like a weightlifter with massive legs and arms. He stood five feet ten inches tall but seemed much taller at first impression. He was a charmer who knew how to get his way, which he did with most things. Freddy had a meticulous mustache, which he trimmed daily, and piercing green eyes, as well as a generous smile that affected all around him. Freddy was a genuine character and he knew it. He laughingly liked to say that God had made whiskey to keep the Irish from ruling the world. Who knows? Maybe he was right. Freddy was on the wrong side of 40, with his hair turning gray, but it was always well trimmed and never out of place. He knew the value of first impressions and dressed impeccably when the occasion called for it. Freddy was one who projected a presence wherever he went and was a damned efficient man with everything he turned his hand to unless his brains were scrambled with Irish whiskey. The ladies flocked to him continuously and Jack would later laughingly refer to him as the gray-haired chick magnet.

Freddy Steele's boat was large and well appointed by fishing boat standards. It measured 45 feet from bow to stern with an 18-foot center beam. The boat drew eight feet of water at the keel and was equipped with a 500-horsepower Cummins Marine diesel engine. There was also a 500 CFM air compressor on board powered from the main engine with multiple air taps from bow to stern. The dual fuel tanks held 500 gallons each and there was a 50 KW generator used for internal boat power, which also could be used to run the refrigeration if needed. The refrigeration was in turn able to make ice in abundance if required but that would be rare as Jack would find out. Freddy did not like to freeze any of his harvest because he said that it lost much of its goodness after being frozen. Jack came to agree with him as he got to know Freddy's operation better. Freddy had much additional storage space in the hold that could be converted to cold storage if needed, simply by making ice and covering the catch for the trip home. This was rare because Freddy dealt in quality rather than quantity, but sometimes the fishing was just too good. The boat was both comfortable and roomy and Jack felt at home there immediately.

Then there was the other crew member Roland Hawke, who was a simple man but likeable as Jack quickly discovered. Roland was not the brightest crayon in the box but he knew his job well. He was that age when all he thought about was girls, and when he wasn't thinking about them he was talking about them. *After all,* Jack reasoned, *at least one knows where one stands with him."* To Jack's knowledge, Roland did not have a girlfriend. He guessed that Roland was either shy or the demands of this lifestyle prevented him from hooking up with someone. Either way, listening to him continually expounding on the virtues of the opposite sex got to be tiring after a while. Roland was not a bad-looking man and was in the flower of his youth. He was just over six feet tall and weighed 190 pounds. The only thing that bothered Jack about Roland was his excessive drinking. Roland had a knack for bad timing when throwing a drinking binge, or so it seemed to Jack.

Roland had been working for Freddy for four years and by now he was able to anticipate most of Freddy's needs. Roland was not much of a mechanic but he was a whiz with electronics and was charged with maintaining and tuning the gadgets Freddy had installed on the *Betty Lou*. Jack inquired out of curiosity as to just how the boat had come by that name, and nobody knew including Freddy. When Jack thought about it, *Who cared, really?*

The *Betty Lou* had an elongated bow sprint similar to a swordfishing boat with a 50-caliber harpoon gun resting in its holding clamps. Jack was to find out later that Freddy harpooned blue sharks and harvested them as part of his payload. These sharks were plentiful in the channel between Santa Barbara and the Channel Islands. There was no need to hunt them because they would come hunting for you when you approached their habitat. The blue sharks averaged 12 feet in length and weighed between 200 and 350 pounds each. They were aggressive fish and accustomed to feeding on the garbage that the city of Santa Barbara dumped into the channel regularly. These fish were actually quite tasty and the fish and chips restaurants took all that Freddy could harvest. Freddy usually harpooned between six and eight of these foul-tempered fish both coming and going, which he claimed paid for the expenses on the boat.

The sharks were brought aboard on a block-and-tackle boom one at a time. The fins were harvested first, and then the fish were filleted with a two-handed stainless-steel saw. The head and skeleton were placed in the bait storage tank if the *Betty Lou* was on the way out or dumped back into the channel if they were on the way in. The filleted shark meat was cut into steak-sized strips by hand and packaged in five-pound boxes more or less marked blue shark fillet with the current date and the actual weight placed on it. Once the box was weighed and marked, it was placed on a small conveyor that took it below to the refrigeration facilities. Once there, it was stacked and stored in such a manner that it could not shift in heavy seas. This was all done while the *Betty Lou* was in transit. It was a time when all the crew members worked together as Freddy placed the *Betty Lou* on auto pilot.

The fins were skinned, and then cut into two-inch circles with a device that looked very similar to a large cookie cutter. Once this was done the circles were struck with a wooden mallet on each side then rinsed, packaged, weighed, and marked "scallops." The odd pieces of shark fin were marked shark fin chowder stock and were also weighed and packaged. All the processing was done above deck and as quickly as the fish were brought in. The dead sharks were towed behind the boat on separate ropes, and then reeled in one at a time for processing. Occasionally, the accompanying blue sharks would go into a feeding frenzy and begin tearing chunks out of the sharks being towed behind. When that happened, the damaged sharks were released and the *Betty Lou* continued on. All in all, each operation was done with a typical Freddy Steele efficiency, as was all seafood that crossed his deck.

The *Betty Lou* was equipped with state of the art radar, sonar, and a coastal Loran navigation system with which Freddy could return with pinpoint accuracy to any location previously visited. There was a 300-gallon freshwater supply tank with a capacity to distill fresh water from seawater at the rate of ten gallons per hour if needed. Seawater was heated by the engine then used for washing and bathing. Freshwater was only used to rinse the saltwater off, and Jack appreciated this luxury of having a bath each day. This represented quite a lifestyle improvement for Jack when considering that the tuna boat Jack had crewed on in the past had primitive facilities for bathing. Then there was also a pressure saltwater pump for use when washing down the decks and holds once the seafood processing was completed.

Once underway, the autopilot was engaged and set for the conditions of the seas. This one item alone made standing watch during those all-night runs much simpler, and simplified fish processing as well. Jack had to admit that Freddy had quite a boat here and looked forward to the experience of working with him. Then there were those mystery Channel Islands looming in the background that Freddy and Roland continually referred to.

Earlier, when Jack was just beginning to work for Freddy, he cornered him and asked him to explain the commission structure and what he could expect to receive and it went like this: There were nine shares to be divided and the shares were distributed with three shares going for the boat and all the accompanying overhead. The diver claimed three shares for his work under the ocean. The remaining three shares were split with the crew (one and one-half each), with Jack and Freddy changing hats each day as they rotated with the diving duties, then worked as part of the crew. The same split applied to the harpoon gun, with the one manning the harpoon getting three shares. This was a good arrangement that all were comfortable with.

Freddy Steele could be characterized as a hunter and gatherer of the sea and also an opportunist. Anything that would generate revenue was fair game for Freddy, with no regard for seasons or regulations. Freddy operated under the radar for the entire time that Jack worked for him, with most of his cargo taken out of season or from restricted areas. Freddy set and routinely worked 55 lobster traps which he kept safely hidden under the cover of the Pacific Ocean. With the help of his coastal Loran he could relocate his lobster traps with ease, even though there was never a surface buoy to announce the presence of each trap.

Freddy would drop anchor in the general area of the lobster trap and then drop to the ocean floor to visually inspect the trap. On the way to the trap Freddy was always equipped with a spear gun with a 12-gauge charge on the tip. He would kill any fish that neared him with either the 12-gauge charge or the standard spear for smaller fish.

These fish were sent to the surface on nylon lines and were filleted and processed immediately while Freddy continued to hunt the area looking for any fish, abalone, rock crab or scallop, which he gathered on his way to the lobster trap. Once the trap was inspected, Freddy usually called for a line from the surface, which was attached to the trap. As the trap was raised to the deck of the boat, so then did Freddy ascend to the surface and come aboard. Any lobsters in the trap were removed and harvested immediately. New bait was then placed back into the empty trap, which was the discard from the fish cleaning operation, and the trap would finally be lowered back to the bottom of the sea. No divers were allowed to go down with the fresh bait in the water, and the *Betty Lou*'s anchor was raised to move on to the next location. With Freddy doing all the diving there was only time for eight to ten location visits a day; but after Jack began to dive, that number was increased to 18 to 20 locations. All the traps could then be visited in a three-day run which left more time for other endeavors.

Abalone was treated much differently than the fish and lobsters harvested by the crew of the *Betty Lou*. Once on deck, they were immediately removed from their shells and trimmed, then placed in a deli-saw and cut into one-half-inch thick steaks. With that part completed, each steak was then struck on both sides with a large wooden mallet. Next the steak was rinsed and separated from the other abalone steaks with a thin onionskin paper to aid in removing the abalone during final preparation. Once this was completed, the abalone was weighed, boxed, marked and on its' way to cold storage. The only other seafood that resembled the abalone was the shark fins pretending to be scallops. Freddy got the idea from watching fish processors cutting up skate wings in like manner to sell as scallops. The shark fins were actually tastier and more in demand than the skate wing variety of scallops.

Jack didn't mind the diving after some hard lessons were learned of the many dangers, which Freddy had neglected to tell him about. The boat production climbed dramatically as Jack became more adept and everyone profited by this. Jack inquired

43

of Roland as to why he never opted to dive and therefore have a claim for more money. Roland said flat out that diving terrified him, and even the thought of going underwater caused him to have nightmares. He was a deadly shot with the harpoon gun however, and that made up some for his lack of diving.

It must be the fear of drowning, Jack thought later when he learned that Roland could not swim a stroke. *This is an odd job for one like Roland to have, given his shortcoming; but then many sailors could not swim a stroke during the Second World War. Oh well, to each his own,* Jack thought.

He mentioned to Roland once that it was just not wise to walk around above deck in rough seas without a life jacket on. Roland shrugged his shoulders and said that he was much too careful to allow anything to happen to himself. *This Roland can be a very foolish man sometimes*, thought Jack.

Freddie had quite a black market network set up along the California coast. It was a plan that was both well conceived and well executed. North of Goleta, California is a large cattle ranch that owned nearly 50 miles of California shoreline. It was one of the many holdings of that well-known newspaper magnate from San Francisco and it was administered by a career ranch man-ager named Laurence Bodine, known as "Lefty" Bodine to his friends, among whom Freddy Steele could be counted as one. Freddy saw to it that Lefty and his family were never short of fresh seafood and Lefty never short of Irish whiskey. For that small gratuity, Freddy was given the combination to one of the locked ranch gates. This unpaved dirt road that entered the prop-erty off the old Highway 101 was also the road to Freddy's Cove.

Soon after Jack joined the crew, Roland developed a crush on Lefty's oldest daughter whose name was Evelyn. She would come out to Freddy's Cove soon after the *Betty Lou*'s arrival and remain there until her parents came looking for her. Jack was happy for Roland because he now had a girlfriend, and as an added bonus, Roland now occasionally talked of things other than girls and stayed sober all the while when in Freddy's Cove.

Freddy's Cove was a small sheltered harbor along the coast-line with a sandy beach. It could not be observed from the sea, nor could it be observed from any location at all except from the air or the beach itself; a perfect place if you will, for the pirate Freddy Steele to off load his cargo. It could not be navigated into by using standard maritime techniques due to the many uncharted hazards. Freddy had charted the way through the shore reef by using both his sonar and personal observation from below the surface of the ocean. These coordinates were a well-kept secret until the time when Freddy was too drunk to function; then they were given to Jack, who flawlessly guided the *Betty Lou* into the sheltered harbor. As usual, Freddy had no memory of giving Jack this information. Freddy also maintained a refrigerated vehicle in the cove with which to transport his seafood. It was marked Ace Plumbing, but to Jack it didn't look anything like a plumbing truck. Nobody else seemed to notice.

In the harbor Freddy had a permanent mooring on a float to which he attached his stern line. Then the bow line was attached to an exposed rock with a steel ring, also installed by Freddy. Once the *Betty Lou* was secured, the boat was put on generator power and the inflatable raft was launched. There was always more cargo than the truck could haul, and it was also a time for shore leave and relaxation by the crew. There was still much to do the first day in port with the restocking of the *Betty Lou* for the next cruise, with everything but fuel taken on here in this hidden cove. The delivery truck had no trouble disposing of its valuable cargo, as the fresh seafood was in great demand by the restaurants in the area. Those who knew Freddy would wait for his products because of the freshness and the out-of-season seafood he always provided. It took more time to load the truck and drive to the restaurants that it took to sell the products. Within two or three days, the holds would be empty and the *Betty Lou* would be re-supplied. Then Freddy would be planning the next trip out.

Freddy had a jungle telegraph or something like it for finding out what was running within the cruising range of the *Betty Lou*. What the crew would be harvesting was always a surprise, as each trip began. Freddy seemed to know where the albacore were running, or the bonita, or the salmon and was quick to change direction for a run for fresh fish. Jack always enjoyed the blue-water cruising beyond the continental shelf, and if fish were caught, so much the better.

The Achilles heel of this operation was the drinking habits of both Freddy and Roland. The two would begin drinking soon after dinner was completed and would continue until one or the other passed out from the alcohol. There was a definite code-pendency here that Jack worked around whenever he could, but occasionally disaster would strike. One such narrowly-averted disaster occurred when Jack had been a member of the crew less than three months.

Jack had just awakened Roland for his shift on the bridge, and to Jack he seemed relatively sober and coherent. Soon after Jack retired, Roland, in an alcohol fog, curled up and went to sleep on the bridge deck with the boat running under full power. Jack had just settled in to bed when the *Betty Lou* went aground. There was a low-pitched whine as the boat buried itself in the soft sand then the Cummins diesel engine began an unhealthy growling noise. Jack was up and running for the bridge but he could tell that a serious problem was unfolding around the *Betty Lou*.

There is a sandbar to the northwest of San Miguel Island that was created by two converging currents. It is known as the Sand Spit due to the plumes of salt water and sand cast skyward by the crashing of opposing surfs. This phenomenon stretched for over a mile out to sea. Good old Roland had allowed the boat to run directly onto the Sand Spit where the *Betty Lou* was stuck fast atop the sandbar. With the fierce surf converging from two directions it was much like being in a pan of boiling water. Freddy was up immediately and furious with everyone in general, especially Roland, while taking the helm. After several minutes of rocking back and forth it was clear that the boat was stuck and there was nothing Freddy could do at this time to free it. Meanwhile, Jack had consulted the almanac and knew that the tide was just changing from low tide and it would be another six hours until high tide. This would add almost three feet of water under the craft, but there would be additional help needed if they were to escape this sand bar. Freddy and Roland were useless just then, but when the high tide arrived, Jack would need the help and cooperation of both men.

Jack had been diving with Freddy for over a month now and was becoming fairly competent. The *Betty Lou* had 400 feet of anchor chain and a mechanical winch with which to extract it from the ocean. It was Jack's plan to dress in his dry diving suit with weights, mask, and air hose from the boat. Once he was so equipped and standing in front of the *Betty Lou*, Freddy was to release the 40-pound Danforth anchor and feed out the chain as required by Jack. It was Jack's plan to walk out in the churning surf and drag the chain as far as he could then find something under water to secure it to. The real trick here was to secure it in such a way that it could be retrieved by the boat once the boat escaped the sandbar. It all sounded simple, until one imagines the physical strain of dragging that much chain and carrying an anchor while searching for deeper water in which to attach it. All this activity would be taking place while carrying a full-weight belt weighing 50 pounds with the remaining gear adding another 25 pounds to Jack's load. Then, as an added impediment, he would be churned around as though he were inside a washing machine. How Jack did it was in itself a major feat of human strength and determination.

Jack needed to wait until sunrise to begin this task in order to be able to see what he was doing under water. Once he began this plan he soon realized that the weight of the anchor chain was such that he would have move it in 100-foot increments, a herculean chore that took him the best part of three hours to complete. Jack eventually got the anchor safely into deeper water with the chain laid out in front of the boat. When coming back to the boat, Jack noticed that sand was building up at the bow and if allowed to continue, the boat would never move into deeper water no matter what they did. Jack went to work at the bow of the boat like a dog digging for a bone until he could finally see that there was now a fighting chance of freeing the *Betty Lou* if Freddy acted quickly.

When Jack finally climbed aboard the boat he collapsed on the deck from sheer exhaustion. He was spent completely and now it was up to Freddy and Roland. He dropped his weights and face mask, then secured his air hose and climbed up onto the bridge, too tired to do anything but sit and watch the show. Freddy manned the helm while Roland slowly took up the slack in the anchor chain. When all was ready, Freddy gunned the engine while Roland engaged the anchor chain winch. Slowly at first the *Betty Lou* began to move inch by inch as she gained momentum. With the prop cavitating uncontrollably and the sand boiling up around the vessel, the boat moved forward steadily with the keel scraping upon the sandy bottom for almost 150 knuckle-biting feet. Then suddenly the *Betty Lou* was off of the Sand Spit and floating in deeper water. Jack's plan had worked flawlessly and before long the *Betty Lou* was once again on its way to its original destination. Jack was too tired to care, but both Freddy and Roland now looked upon him with a new respect. Both knew that but for Jack, they would still be resting on the Sand Spit.

There are four principal islands in the Channel Island group beginning with the closest to the mainland, Anacapa. This island was not much more than a large rock with grass growing on it, but there was a natural harbor there that would accommodate a tour boat should a tour boat ever want to stop there. Anacapa is better known in the history books as the home of a nest of pirates who preyed upon California costal shipping until the United States Navy finally put a permanent stop to them. The waters around Anacapa Island abounded with a vast array of sea life that attracted the *Betty Lou* on a regular basis. The ocean floor fell off quickly there, and it was easy to stay too long submerged in 100-feet or more depths. These depths required the diver to have a lengthy decompression time later. As Jack became ever more proficient in diving, Freddy would drop anchor, then Jack would descend from the bow and Freddy from the stern. Freddy would always choose the dry suit, boots, and full face mask, while Jack would many times opt for the wetsuit and fins for increased maneuverability. This gave him much more freedom and increased his production when gathering abalone, but it also made him more attractive to the larger predators who could easily mistake him for a seal. Jack needed to be ever vigilant and also carry the 12-gauge short spear gun on his thigh for close-in protection. He never actually had to use it but there were some tense moments with orcas and great whites. At Anacapa, the wet suit was always his first choice. From the boat he could swim down to the point where the island fell off into the deep abyss, and from there he would take short forays into deeper water to harvest the larger abalone from the near vertical cliffs.

The most scenic of the islands was Santa Cruz Island, the next one in line. The northeastern tip of this island was lush with trees and with many protected coves and natural harbors. To the southeast, as the island fell away, the land above the ocean changed to an arid climate with cactus and other desert-type plants. But, not so beneath the sea which abounded with a vast array of sea creatures. Freddy liked this place for the lobsters as well as the leopard sharks, which brought almost double the price paid for those hateful blue sharks. One must remember however, that Freddy Steele was the ultimate hunter gatherer, and if he could only harvest blue sharks that was all right because they paid for the trip with a little left over for Irish Whiskey. Freddy's needs were always simple.

The third island was Santa Rosa Island, which had a good reef on the leeward side where the *Betty Lou* visited many times to harvest sheep's head fish, a colorful rainbow-colored fish with short protruding fangs. This fish was a glutton and was easy to harvest, not to mention that it filleted well and provided large cuts of steak that were in great demand on the mainland. It was easier to fish for these critters than dive for them. Typically Freddy would chop up an abalone then throw much of it into the water. Soon the area would be churning with sheep's head and the crew would be pulling them in as fast as they could bait a hook and toss it back into the water. This was a reef that teemed with an amazing variety of sea life and one of Jack's favorites for just watching the sea creatures going about their business.

There were always the antics of the harbor seals or the grace of the elephant seals under water to provide diversion for Jack from the tedium of gathering shellfish. The island itself appeared more as a grassy hillside viewed from all sides. If there was anything more to Santa Rosa Island it was lost in the uninviting posture of the island itself. This was the only island that Jack had little interest in visiting, but the waters surrounding it were bountiful.

The fourth and the farthest from the mainland was San Miguel Island; it was also the most diverse both above and below the surface of the ocean. This was Jack's favorite from the beginning. The landscape was stunning and sometimes as mysterious as the reefs to the west of the island. Everything was better here: the fish and the shelled sea creatures were far more abundant here and larger in size. Any trip to this farthest of islands always resulted in a good harvest and a good-paying trip for everyone. There was also danger here, not just the usual danger of diving underwater but there were currents here that flowed sometimes like a raging river, and shame on the uninformed diver who happened to be in the water when those terrible currents came up. Always, near low tide and for an hour after, it was best advised to be working further away from the submerged reef to the west. Freddy was the only commercial fisherman who worked this Forbidden Reef and more than likely the only one ever. It was risky here but the rewards were great. Freddy knew the safe passageways in and out of the reef and had carefully plotted the routes with the help of his coastal Loran and his personal observation while submerged. It would be nearly six months before Freddy shared this information with Jack. It was a time when he desperately needed Jack to take the *Betty Lou* out of danger, when he had just lost a drinking bout with Old Bushmill's Irish whiskey. Luckily for Freddy, he was able to give Jack the correct coordinates before he passed out on the floor of the bridge. Of course Roland was just as drunk as Freddy and of no use, as usual. Although Freddy never remembered giving this information to Jack, Jack never forgot those headings for the passageway into and out of the Forbidden Reef and Freddy's Cove. To this day he could see them in his mind's eye at will.

The Forbidden Reef was simply marked on the map as uncharted hazards, a gross understatement at the very least. It was a happy fishing ground for Freddy Steele, a never-before picked over or fished place, and he always left this area with his holds bulging with seafood. Luckily for Freddy he had Jack aboard that fateful day, or he would have become just another statistic added to the list of wrecked ships on this most hazardous of all maritime perils on the pacific coast.

Occasionally Freddy would get an order for fresh clams and this always meant a trip to San Miguel Island to a place where giant clams grew in abundance. This was a well-paying cargo that took three days to harvest and safely store below deck. Typically, the *Betty Lou* would drop anchor within 200 feet of the sandy beach to the windward side of the island. The raft was inflated and 30 plastic half-barrels were transported to the shore along with five-gallon bottles of fresh water. Once the gear was in place, the crew began digging up clams and placing them in the half-barrels, a chore that took less than 30 minutes with all three working, due to the abundance of these enormous clams. With this completed, the barrels of clams were filled to the top with fresh water. Freddy explained that this was done to cause the clams to spit out all the sand they were packing within the shells, a process that would take about five hours. It was during this time, with the clams soaking in fresh water, that Jack took his leave to explore San Miguel Island.

Neither Roland nor Freddy had an interest in seeing the island but they both greatly enjoyed the fire Jack built for them before leaving for the summit. Jack left the two relaxing on the warm sand and sharing a bottle of Irish whiskey as he made his way up the slopes to the crest of the island. As Jack reached the summit he experienced an overwhelming peace and serenity that stayed with him and followed him everywhere as he wandered around on the upper reaches of the island. All of his senses seemed to be heightened during this experience. His hearing was sharpened to the point where he could hear the individual pebbles crunch underfoot or the call of a seabird from across the island. His sight was also heightened as well, with even the smallest details of all he surveyed becoming clear to his enhanced vision. As Jack walked steadily westward, these heightened senses seemed to increase as if there was something up ahead beckoning him onward. Later, when describing this experience Jack would characterize it as a spiritual event rather than a religious one.

All too soon it was time to return, and as Jack looked as his watch he realized that he had been up here for over four hours. *What an amazing place,* he thought. *Where did the time go?* Jack could not imagine how he could have been here so long, but it was time to begin his return trip to the clam camp. As much as he regretted leaving this remarkable place, his sense of duty would not allow him to shirk his obligations to Freddy and Roland. One thing for sure, Jack would be back here again and he intended to bring Roland next time. Jack wanted to see if he was imagining those astonishing feelings of peace and serenity and if Roland would be affected in the same way. *Time to get back to reality,* Jack thought as he hurried down the steep slopes to the sandy beach below. He would need to make haste or risk being caught out here after dark without a flashlight, something he would be prepared for next time.

As Jack approached the camp he could see the heightened activity as Freddy and Roland were preparing to clean the clams. A table was set up with portable lights and a small generator from the boat. The clams were placed on the table with the muscle hinge cut and ready for extraction. The clams were quickly removed from the shells, cleaned, and then placed in plastic bags of approximately ten pounds each. There would be no weighing and marking done here on the shore. Once the barrels were empty, new clams were quickly dug up from the beach and placed in the barrels, with the cycle beginning anew. Within two hours all the clams were cleaned and the new ones were soaking in fresh water. Jack had to admit that Freddy ran a tight ship when he was not falling down drunk. The clamshells were placed in the raft and then dumped in the bay beyond the shore line; Freddy left no visible trace of his activities.

Both Freddy and Roland wanted to head back to the boat for the night, but Jack elected to stay on the beach, something he really enjoyed. This proved a perfect opportunity for him. Jack built up the fire and unrolled his sleeping bag in the soft sand. He had much to think about that night as the constellations reeled across the heavens. The only sound was the soft rumble of the generator aboard the *Betty Lou* and the occasional scream of a seabird passing overhead. The air was warm and comforting as it drifted downward from the island heights. It would be much later in the night when Jack finally drifted off to a deep and satisfying sleep.

All too soon morning arrived and Freddy was ashore firing orders to the crew. Jack was up and prepared for this because he knew that when it came to gathering seafood, Freddy was damned efficient. The cycle was repeated again and the shells disposed of as before. Jack had asked Roland to accompany him to the interior of the island during their break and surprisingly, Roland was willing to explore this day. This was unusual for Roland, whose recreation normally consisted of getting drunk. Once more, Jack crested the summit with Roland on his heels, and once again the feeling of peace and serenity surrounded him. He stood back to see if Roland would be experiencing the same effect and he could quickly see that Roland was equally affected.

"This is amazing," Roland mumbled softly. "What kind of a place is this?"

"I'm not really sure," Jack said, "but I wanted someone else to come here and feel the energy of this place so I would know that I was not imagining things. It's like walking into a church or a sacred burial site, as best as I can describe it."

"Yeah, it sure is," Roland replied.

They wandered for a while on the island crest while being pulled to the west ever so gently as Jack had been pulled the day before. What was it here that was calling each of them with such a gentle persuasion? Jack knew that whatever was calling to them was not harmful. This he was certain of. All too soon the foray came to a close with the demands of their employer taking the forefront. On the way back to the clam camp, the two agreed not to share this experience with Freddy. Freddy had an acid tongue for anything he did not understand, and neither of the two wanted this experience to be ridiculed by his ignorance. The clam camp was broken that same afternoon and the *Betty Lou* was off to other fishing adventures. Jack and Roland would return here three other times and they likened it to visiting a place of spiritual power, but neither knew why this was so.

Diving on the Forbidden Reef was both dangerous and immensely rewarding to the crew of the *Betty Lou.* There were six hours out of every 24 when the currents raged across these shallow rocks like a tidal wave. One and one-half hours before and the same time after low tide, which occurred twice each day, were the times to avoid this reef at all costs. A diver could not hold against the force of this oncoming water and would be swept before it, then down into deep water and certain death. Even a surface vessel needed to be clear of the north side of the reef during these periods or risk being swept onto those deadly protruding rocks. Jack was fascinated by this phenomena and asked Freddy why this was so. Freddy knew more about the Forbidden Reef than anyone alive and had a pretty good idea of what was going on here.

Freddy pulled out a chart of the California coast which showed both San Miguel Island and Point Arguello to the north, then began a detailed explanation of what he believed to be the reason for this daily occurrence.

"Point Arguello is the westernmost point of the continental United States, with the lands bearing both northeast and southeast from either side of this point," He said. "As you can see, Jack, Point Arguello and San Miguel Island line up with one another with the Forbidden Reef in the direct line of the Japanese current as it clears Point Arguello. Imagine the force generated by that massive amount of water moving from the Gulf of Alaska to the equator. First it is hampered by the land mass of Point Arguello then by the shallows of the Forbidden Reef during the twice-a-day low tides. These currents are caused as much by the pushing of the water mass behind the reef when finally passing Point Arguello. Then the reef drops off quickly to the continental shelf. This is what I think causes those deadly currents across the reef. It just makes sense to me," Freddy stated, then allowed Jack some time to let his explanation sink in.

"Freddy, it makes sense to me, too," Jack said abstractly as he concentrated on the chart laid out before him.

Jack worked for Freddy for almost a year doing all things asked of him, and sometimes a lot more, before the call to wander became a tune too persuasive to ignore. Jack liked and enjoyed working for Freddy, and aside from his drinking binges, he was always a fair man to work for. Jack had learned much from Freddy Steele and was grateful for the opportunity to work with him. But all things have a beginning and an end and so it was with Freddy Steele. It was just another chapter in Jack's life, and a good one too.

Chapter Six:
THE FISHING PIER

Carl was out early enjoying a brisk walk along the deserted beach north of the fishing pier. It promised to be a marvelous morning. The ocean was calm, as is normal between winter storms, and the winter sun was bright and sparkling on the surf. It was a cool 50 degrees this day with not a cloud in the sky. It felt good to Carl as he stood watching two seagulls fighting over the remains of a rock crab. He could also see some seals out well beyond the shore break. They appeared to be feeding on the sea creatures hiding in the kelp beds, and they provided Carl with some quiet entertainment for several minutes. *It's at times like these that I realize just how much I miss the ocean,* he thought as he glanced at his watch. He realized then that he needed to hurry to make his appointment with Jack. This was one meeting he did not want to miss; too much was riding on the outcome.

Carl Webb was originally from Minneapolis, Minnesota and had grown up on the Webb family farm raising soy beans and corn. He never really disliked farming, but it was just not what he wanted to spend his life doing. After graduating from MIT with a Bachelor of Science degree in mechanical engineering, Carl spent four years working for a well-known engineering contractor. He eventually decided that this construction thing was just not for him. He hated deadlines and felt that this current work environment was stifling his creative talents. One morning he walked into the construction office and turned in his keys. This was the last time Carl worked for anyone else in his life. The following year he was working side by side with Mel Fisher in the Gulf of Mexico, treasure hunting.

Carl had never been married but he had a special person in his life. Shirley Porter was his high school sweetheart and the two had never stopped caring for each other. Both had careers or callings to pursue, which they both did separately. Shirley resided in New York City and worked as a Wall Street executive. Carl resided wherever he happened to be when the sun went down. They corresponded and spoke to one another several times a week, and took vacations together when they could both get away. They owned a condo together in Aspen, Colorado, always their favorite destination.

It was Saturday morning and Jack had arrived early with Susan and Josh. He had enjoyed a leisurely breakfast with them, but now it was time for the mother and son to take a walk on the beach while Jack met with Carl. As Susan and Josh hurried away, Jack took a seat on one of the benches lining the pier. He was still a little early but he had a feeling that Carl would be right on time, and he wasn't disappointed. There were not many people out and about this morning and he spotted Carl walking down the beach toward the pier. Jack had just a touch of the jitters in anticipation of what this morning would bring. Carl had left him the night before with a lot more questions than answers. As Carl approached into hailing distance, Jack leaned over the pier and called out to Carl.

"Good morning Carl, wha'do you take in your coffee?"

"Good morning, Jack, black is fine long as it's fresh."

"Done," Jack replied with the same mannerisms that Carl had used the night before. This drew a chuckle from Carl as he left the beach and climbed the stairs to the pier entrance.

When Jack arrived with the coffees, Carl was seated on the bench and little was said at first as the two quietly sipped their coffee and sized one another up. It was Carl who finally broke the silence by asking, "Do you know a person named Freeman Barnes?"

"Freeman and I worked a glory hole together on the Yuba River about ten years ago," Jack replied. "But I have since received word of his death in a diving accident in Florida," he added.

Carl thoughtfully set his coffee down and looked Jack in the eye. "Freeman was working with me when he died, and I would not be sitting here today having this conversation with you if not for him. He saved my life at the expense of his own," Carl finished quietly. "Maybe at a later time I will tell you how it happened, but the memories are still too fresh right now. He was a friend of mine and one of the best diving partners I ever worked with."

"Freeman was also a friend of mine," Jack quietly stated.

For a while the two sat there in silence while each remembered Freeman Barnes in his own way.

"Freeman said that it was you who taught him everything he knew about safe diving practices and he was always your friend, as well," Carl said.

"That's good to know," Jack replied.

"Freeman also told me some stories about your experiences on the Channel Islands and a place you called the Forbidden Reef." Jack nodded silently as Carl continued, "It is this Forbidden Reef that I have an interest in, and that's also the reason that I've been searching for you for so long."

The two sat talking through the morning hours about the Reef and the hazards that were there, and by lunchtime a deal was struck. Jack liked Carl immediately and the two could see that a new friendship was in the making. The conversation finally ended with the arrival of Susan and Josh, and by then Jack had a new job. The money that Carl had offered him that morning was staggering and Carl could not be persuaded to lower that amount. He only stated that he knew of Jack's worth and intended to compensate him well for his time, as well as offering a healthy percentage should the expedition prove successful. Carl promised a full explanation of what they would be searching for, on the trip to San Diego. *After all,* Carl reasoned, *he already had a lot of money invested in Jack just with the expenses of tracking him down.*

Jack needed a day to end his affairs at the Harbor Coffee Shop, but the following day, the two were scheduled to take a trip south and inspect Carl's boat. Jack privately wondered why Carl did not have his boat moored here at the Santa Barbara yacht harbor, a question that would be answered sooner than he thought. There would also be a diving job for Susan during summer break or fulltime if she could take a leave of absence from her teaching job. Then Carl offered to allow Josh to come along and help sail the boat when his studies permitted. From that point on, Carl could do no wrong in Josh's eyes. Jack was so enthusiastic about what they were about to do that he forgot to inquire about the BMW keys once again.

As for Carl, he thought that Freeman was right; Jack Morgan was a likable and capable man and perfect for the job he had in mind. Things were progressing quickly now and come Monday, both he and Jack would be on the way to San Diego to inspect Carl's very special custom-made sailboat. According to Carl, it looked for all intents and purposes like a recreational cruising yacht, but there was much, much more to it, as Jack would be finding out soon.

Chapter Seven:
THE KONA KAI YACHT CLUB

It was close to 9:00 a.m. when Carl pulled up in front of Jack's and Susan's apartment. There was little need for an early start with the Monday traffic in Los Angeles County in full bloom. Both knew that timing was everything when dealing with the traffic congestion in this part of California. With any luck they would miss the ugliest portion of the commuter's blues this day by timing their arrival in LA County for around 10:30 a.m. At least this was Carl's hope. At any rate, he and Jack had much to discuss and this drive would give them an opportunity to do so.

It was overcast in Santa Barbara and threatening to rain. The surf was up with eight-foot combers crashing ashore, and the winds were blowing at a steady 25 knots. This was not a good day to be at sea but rather a good day to talk about being at sea.

"Jack, have you ever heard about the steamboat *Winfield Scott?*" Carl asked as they entered the 101 freeway southbound.

"I'm sorry, but I haven't," Jack replied.

"Well, the opinion of most historians is that the *Winfield Scott* went down near Anacapa Island in 1853. It was loaded with 49er gold and returning 49ers. There were few survivors and much confusion over where the ship actually floundered. I

60

wondered, did Freddy ever mention this steamboat to you when you worked for him?"

"Not really, Carl. I would have remembered if he did. He was an articulate man when he wasn't brain-fried from all that Irish whiskey he loved so well."

"I have reason to believe that the *Winfield Scott* actually went aground and floundered to the west of San Miguel Island in the place you call the Forbidden Reef."

"That would not surprise me," Jack said. "That is one dangerous place to be, and the only person who ever had it figured out was Freddy Steele when he worked it years ago."

"There are also strong gold hits using satellite technology in the same reef area, which do not occur near Anacapa Island," Carl added. "Did you ever mention to Freeman Barnes that you also knew the coordinates and compass headings for entering and leaving this reef?"

"I must have if you are mentioning it now. I was prone to telling sea stories to pass the time while working on the Yuba River. The men working there seemed to enjoy them, so I would have to say yes, I did mention it," Jack finished.

"Now for the 64,000-dollar question, Jack. Do you still remember those directions?"

"It's funny, but those coordinates were burned into my memory as if I were branded with them," Jack replied. "It is just one of those things you never forget, like your birthday. Maybe it was the life-and-death importance of knowing this information that never allowed me to forget. Freddy stumbled onto the bridge too drunk to stand up and gave them to me just before he passed out. We had scarcely 20 minutes before the currents would be roaring across the reef. As it was, the *Betty Lou* just made it out of there that day," Jack stated quietly. "I don't think Freddy remembered ever giving them to me," he finished. "How about telling me about your boat, or at least the name of it," Jack asked.

"It's better to see the boat first, and then I'll give you a detailed briefing," Carl replied. "Since you asked, the name of the boat is the *Freeman Barnes.*"

"A good choice," Jack replied, after allowing the impact of the name to sink in.

And so it went as the two journeyed southward toward San Diego and the Kona Kai Yacht Club. As Jack would find out, this mystery boat was actually a four-million-dollar motor-sailer disguised as a ketch-rigged recreational sailboat. Carl had the boat built to his specifications by the Porter Corporation of Bridgeport, Connecticut. He was disappointed that he could not be on the *Freeman Barnes* when it made its maiden voyage, but he was searching for bigger game just then—Jack Morgan. His crew of five had sailed the craft to Panama and through the canal, then northwest to Hawaii, and finally catching the prevailing winds to San Diego, where the boat was now berthed. The *Freeman Barnes* was in the yachts-in-transit section, where visiting dignitaries normally berthed. Money always has its privileges.

On a lighter note, Carl inquired about Jack's former employer Georgie and how the transition went.

"You know, Carl, I sincerely tried to do the right thing with Georgie, but he is the most selfish man I have worked for in a long time."

"How's that?"

"Well, he really didn't care that I was leaving, but only that he had no replacement for me and would have to work the shift himself. That made him completely unreasonable and very angry at me. He couldn't understand why I was leaving him in such a predicament. I haven't been so glad to leave a job in a long time," Jack said.

Carl and Jack stopped for lunch in San Juan Capistrano, as this represented the southern end of the commuter traffic, and by 2:00 p.m. were entering the Kona Kai valet parking area. As the attendant took Carl's BMW and began driving it toward the valet parking lot, Carl pulled out a device similar to a compact two-way radio and pushed the disable button. The BMW stopped in its tracks and the attendant could not restart it. Carl then pushed an enable button and the car started once again for the attendant.

"Does this answer your question about the keys?" Carl asked.

"It certainly does," Jack said with a big smile on his face.

Before long a golf-cart shuttle arrived to take them to their berth. When Carl gave the instructions to the driver to take them to the *Freeman Barnes*, he looked at Carl with new respect.

"Is the *Freeman Barnes* your yacht?" he inquired.

"Yes, it is," Carl stated matter-of-factly.

"Man, that is one gorgeous sailboat," he offered as a compliment.

"Thank you," Carl stated in a tone that indicated that the conversation was over. He was not being snobbish with the driver, just being cautious about all the questions he knew were circulating around.

Jack was impressed. This was the most amazing sailing craft that he had ever seen close up. Carl was patient and thorough as he conducted the tour for Jack. This motor-sailor was 110 feet from bow to stern with a 32-foot center beam. The craft, fully loaded, drew 24 feet at the keel. The electronic array in the pilot house was all state-of-the-art equipment and came with a full-time electronics technician named Leonard Smith, a soft-spoken black man with eyes that radiated intelligence. He had originally installed the equipment on the *Freeman Barnes* and had signed on in the beginning to make the maiden voyage to San Diego. Carl had later persuaded him to stay with the crew during the upcoming treasure hunt.

Leonard was originally from Detroit, Michigan, a place where most of his family still resided. He joined the Navy after graduating from high school, and his intention was to make a career out of this branch of the service. He was a first-class electronic technician and had a bright future ahead of him with the Navy until he was injured on the flight deck of an aircraft carrier. Leonard was in the wrong place at the wrong time while testing a piece of equipment he had recently repaired. A visiting helicopter made an improper landing on the deck, and the rotor blades of the chopper hit the conning tower on final approach. The helicopter took a nosedive into the deck and ignited upon impact. Leonard was hit with several pieces of the rotor blade and sustained multiple injuries to his legs and knees. He was later discharged from the Navy for medical reasons. After a long recovery, Leonard took stock of his life and began attending college on the GI bill. He eventually graduated from Syracuse University and received a Bachelor of Science degree in electronic engineering. Leonard had never looked back after receiving his degree. He was installing state-of-the-art equipment in top-end sailing vessels in Bridgeport, Connecticut when Carl found him.

Leonard had always loved the sea, and it didn't take much persuading by Carl to recruit him for the cruise. Leonard had recently split up with his current girlfriend, so his ties to Bridgeport, Connecticut were minimal. He enjoyed the reputation of being on the cutting edge of the new technologies and equipment; and because of this, he was seldom out of work. Carl was lucky to have him aboard. Carl also had a fulltime gourmet cook and a housekeeper. All the crew members including Leonard helped with sailing duties when needed. There were staterooms here, not bunks, and the boat always smelled fresh and clean from stem to stern, no matter where Jack went.

On the practical side, the mizzen mast was in reality a structurally-reinforced member that could serve as a functional crane once a special yardarm was attached. There was a full compliment of winches and cables available on deck to this end. The ship was powered by twin 1,000-horsepower Hemi Marine diesel engines that could be used together or one at a time depending upon the need. All the sails were mechanically self-furling, with the option of manually raising and lowering any sail by hand should the need ever arise. There were four air compressors on board, two for filling scuba diving equipment, and two 1,000 CFM compressors with 4,000 feet of air hose in 200-foot rolls for servicing submerged divers. There were two underwater self-powered sleds stored discreetly above deck, and a room dedicated only to the storing and servicing of scuba equipment. Then there was a reverse-osmosis water system that provided all the fresh water the crew could use. Also, there was a portable assembly to install over the props when needed to generate prop wash. This focused the propeller turbulence downward and blew away sand particles to expose treasure or any heavy metal lying there. And on and on and on, with too many amenities to mention, but all with one common denominator: all were functional items either actually or possibly needed for the treasure hunt about to begin.

"I can see now why you didn't bring this vessel to the Santa Barbara Yacht Harbor," Jack said while the two were inspecting the galley and the main assembly room.

"Yes, that remains a problem for which I have no solution at this time," Carl said. "We will need to return to the Kona Kai Yacht Club every two weeks for resupply as it stands now."

"Carl, did Freeman ever mention Freddy's Cove to you?" Jack asked.

"Not that I remember, but what about this Freddy's Cove?"

"As I remember, you said that the *Freeman Barnes* drew 24 feet at the keel. Is that accurate?" Jack asked.

"It is," Carl said.

"Well, Freddy's Cove and the entrance through the shore reefs at low tide have a depth of 36 feet or more. Like the coordinates into the Forbidden Reef, Freddy also gave these to me under similar circumstances, but I don't remember telling Freeman about this," Jack finished. "There are four precise positions that when reached, the ship must change direction rapidly or risk running aground. The channel was carved by an ancient water course from the time when the Pacific Ocean was 300 feet lower than today. Some places in the channel are less than 50 feet wide, so precision is everything," Jack added.

Jack then explained what Freddy's Cove was and where it was located. It would be perfect for their plans if Lefty Bodine was still the ranch manager and things were still the same there. It was definitely worth checking out. The *Freeman Barnes* could be moored and resupplied there, and then fuel could be purchased at the commercial fishing pier in Santa Barbara, saving both time and money, but mostly time. The two decided to make a personal visit to the ranch upon returning to Santa Barbara.

Chapter Eight:
THE RANCH

It was overcast and chilly that morning when Carl and Jack headed north on highway 101 to the ranch headquarters near Goleta, California. It had been years since Jack had been there, but the land had changed little with the passage of time. Just before the town limits of Goleta, Jack pointed out the ranch road that would ultimately take them to Freddy's Cove, provided that this day's trip was successful. Many things could have changed as the years marched by, but both Jack and Carl felt that there was little to lose and much to gain by coming here. The ranch headquarters road was another 30 miles north from Freddy's Cove Road, as they had begun calling it.

The countryside was lush and green with winter grasses, but it was too early for the profusion of wildflowers that would soon be gracing the hills. Before long they had reached the main ranch road turnoff, and without further ceremony they began the ten-mile drive on the gravel road to the headquarters. Both Carl and Jack were becoming apprehensive because so much was riding on this visit.

Some things never change and the main compound was one of them. The houses, corrals, and barns looked much as they had 20 years ago as Jack stepped out of the BMW and looked around.

"Well, I'll be. Could it actually be Jack Morgan after all these years, coming back for a visit?" The voice was coming from the office and had a vaguely familiar ring that Jack couldn't quite place.

"You have me at a disadvantage," Jack said. "You seem to know me, but do I know you?"

"You should, after all the times you saved Freddy Steele's and my asses at the Channel Islands."

"This could only be Roland Hawke," Jack said with a smile.

Out of the office door came Roland, bigger and more mature than Jack remembered. He walked up to Jack and gave him a tremendous bear hug, lifting him off the ground in the process.

"That was for all those times you saved the *Betty Lou* when Freddy and I were too drunk to stand up," Roland stated. "I always wanted to thank you, but when I turned around twice you were gone to God knows where," Roland continued.

"Roland, I'm just as surprised to see you here, surrounded by a successful career; and I'm just as pleased to see you again after so many years," Jack replied. The two visited for a time, then Jack asked where Lefty Bodine was, as he and Carl had some business to discuss with him.

"I'm afraid you have to settle for me," Roland said. "Lefty retired eight years ago and moved to Montana. I've been running the ranch since then. Marrying Evelyn may have had something to do with my getting the job, but we've been happy here and have a great family to show for it. It just proves what a good woman can do for a man, despite the man's former drinking habits," Roland finished.

"So you gave up drinking that Irish whiskey, did you?" Jack asked.

"It was either the whiskey or Evelyn; the choice was made clear to me."

"I know you made the right decision. There was a time when I gave you and Freddy no hope for survival. It demonstrates just how wrong a man can be," Jack said. "And speaking of Freddy, whatever happened to him?"

"I really don't know. He left the cove in the *Betty Lou* almost ten years ago and nobody has seen him since. Personally, I think he was working on the Forbidden Reef and his luck ran out," Roland said. "I know that he was headed for San Miguel Island when he left here. What happened after that is anyone's guess. His only crew member at the time had the same taste for whiskey and drank as much or more than Freddy ever did. I think Freddy chose a good drinking companion rather than a good deckhand," Roland finished.

"Maybe Freddy died the way he wanted to: not many of us get the chance to choose," said Jack. "I can't imagine Freddy actually being dead, though. I always thought he was too tough a hombre to kill."

Roland nodded agreement.

"Roland, Carl and I came here today to discuss the possibility of using Freddy's Cove for a covert treasure hunt at the Channel Islands. We aren't fishermen like Freddy, but we are prepared to offer you some serious cash money upfront, as well as a percentage of anything recovered for the use of the Cove," Jack said.

"Jack, you're hurting my feelings. I owe you so much that I could never repay. How could I accept any money from you and your friend Carl after all the times you saved Freddy and me?" Roland said.

"Just call it a business arrangement, Roland," Carl said. "Think of how much better your family will live because of it; and besides, I can afford it."

Carl and Jack left the ranch that morning with a new combination lock to be placed on the access-road gate. Only they and Roland would have the combination, a safety issue to keep other ranch hands from the area. Roland had no cattle on that section of the ranch and would not use it for grazing until Carl's and Jack's business was completed. Carl and Jack headed for Freddy's Cove before returning to Santa Barbara, so plans could be made for bringing the *Freeman Barnes* up the coast from San Diego.

Jack had been giving the cove some serious thought about how the 110-foot *Freeman Barnes* could fit there and what modifications to the moorings would be needed to make it safe.

The road in was rough and in disrepair. It was obvious nobody had been here for a long while and that was good. As the BMW finally made its' grand entrance into the sheltered cove, Carl was speechless. *What a magnificent place,* he said to himself as he pulled to a stop at the edge of the beach. Jack was all business just then as the reality of navigating a 110-foot boat through the shore reef was bearing down on his shoulders, and he was having doubts about whether it could be done with such a large craft. When such variables as wind direction and speed, tides, and currents were considered, Jack doubted that the *Freeman Barnes* could respond quickly enough to stay in the center of the channel.

"That's because you don't know the equipment in use aboard the *Freeman Barnes*. Jack, this boat can turn on a dime in gale-force winds. The computer will accelerate, change directions, reverse engines, and do anything else necessary to keep the craft exactly on the preprogrammed course. I also didn't mention the 18-inch bow thrusters on variable-speed drive units. These devices can vary the revolutions of the bow propellers from 0 rpm to 3,600 rpm in less than five seconds," Carl explained.

"OK, I'll give you that, but we'll need to make some changes on how the boat is moored here. Freddy always attached his bow line to the rock and his stern line to the placed mooring. That will have to change because this cove is very small, and the only chance of turning around will occur near the entrance into the cove. The *Freeman Barnes* must execute a 180-degree water rotation in place, and then back the stern toward the mooring rock. Once the stern is secured, the bow line can easily be retrieved and secured as well. The placed mooring will need to be reinforced and extended to accommodate the *Freeman Barnes*," Jack finished.

"I agree with everything you said, Jack, and we'll need to do the modifications on the bow mooring before the *Freeman Barnes* comes here," Carl said.

The two lingered for several hours on this secluded beach and Jack built a fire, as was his custom. The two new friends took some time to enjoy all the new sights and sounds of this exceedingly beautiful and private place. All too soon it was time to return to Santa Barbara, but the day had been fulfilling and rewarding beyond all expectations.

Carl could see clearly then that he had made the right decision when recruiting Jack Morgan. The two would need to make another trip to San Diego within the week to get the scuba equipment necessary for the mooring modification. Jack had suggested using 100 feet of chain, with one end attached securely to underwater rocks and the other end attached to a strong bow line on a surface buoy. This was a simple but effective solution to the mooring problem facing the *Freeman Barnes* while in port.

Chapter Nine:
PREPARATIONS

It was decided to leave for San Diego the following morning to pick up the needed equipment for the mooring modifications. The window of opportunity was opening quickly, as the winter months at the Channel Islands were drawing to a close. This was usually the most ideal time for working the Forbidden Reef, when the winter storms were finished for the season and the prevailing westerlies were being held at bay by the absence of pacific high pressure. It was a transition time when the waters were calm and visibility was at its best. Beginning in about 30 days and lasting for about the same period of time would be the best time to search the reef for wreckage. The crew of the *Freeman Barnes* intended to take full advantage of this opportunity, but there was much to be done in a short period of time.

It was 5:00 a.m. when Carl pulled up to Jack's and Susan's apartment. Jack had been ready for some time, and he hurriedly said a quick goodbye to Susan as he stepped out the front door. Frost had settled on the rose bushes and the walk was slippery as Jack hurried over to Carl's car. Traffic was light as Carl entered the 101 freeway heading south once again. The two were hoping to slip through the commuter traffic ahead of the morning gridlock, but that remained to be seen. One never knew how one would fare in the commuter rush until one was in it. Then it would be too late to turn back; this was an inescapable fact of life in Los Angeles County. That morning they got lucky, and were enjoying a leisurely breakfast in San Juan Capistrano by 7:30 a.m.

It was always Carl's policy never to announce his arrival before the fact, and this day was no exception. The *Freeman Barnes* was surprisingly shipshape and polished up, as if the crew knew that he was coming this morning. Carl was thinking that he would need to check on the jungle telegraph concerning his whereabouts, but that could wait. This morning they had much on their plates and needed to get on with what had brought them to this beautiful city in the first place.

Jack and Carl hurried aboard the boat without ceremony, and within the hour a meeting of all hands was called by Carl. When all were assembled, Carl began the introductions.

"Gentlemen, I would like to introduce you to your new first mate, Jack Morgan. Jack knows more about the Forbidden Reef than anyone alive and also knows how to enter and leave this reef unscathed. You will find him a knowledgeable diver and a first-class sailor, and it goes without saying that I expect all of you to give him your full cooperation. He speaks for me in my absence, and I know that you will soon come to respect him when you get to know him better. Jack, would you say a few words to the crew?" Carl requested.

"Thank you, Carl. Soon we will be embarking on a dangerous but also possibly rewarding treasure salvaging operation. Timing is everything where we are going. The passage of 15 minutes at the wrong time will turn the placid waters of the reef into a raging river from which there is no escape. To make matters even more dangerous, we must both enter and leave from the north, and even a short delay will make departure impossible. There is only one known way in and one way out, and that is coupled with limited mobility once on the reef itself. If we are ever caught in the current we will be swept into the upper protrusions of the reef, then the remains of the ship will be swept downward into the abyss as if we were never there." Jack paused for a moment to let his statement sink in. "I understand that there are two divers other than Carl and myself here. We will soon be establishing rules of procedure that must be never deviated from for many good reasons, but all of this will be explained later in detail. Right now I would like to thank Carl Webb for the confidence he has in me; I will try to live up to the billing he has given me. In the meantime, it will be my sincere pleasure to get to know all of you better. Thank you."

The first to introduce himself to Jack was Scott Shepherd, the acting first mate and the one who had taken the *Freeman Barnes* from Bridgeport, Connecticut to San Diego, California. He was also a diver and Jack liked him instantly.

"Glad to meet you, Jack. I've heard many good things about you. Welcome aboard." Scott spoke sincerely.

"Thank you, Scott, I'm looking forward to working with you."

Then there was the cook, Rena Schroeder, a striking woman with a German accent and a big smile. "Good to have you aboard, Jack. Sometime we will have to talk about your favorite foods and how you like them prepared."

"Thank you, Rena. Maybe later we can talk about that, but it is good to meet you just the same." He smiled back at her.

He had already met Leonard Smith, the electronics technician. They shook hands and smiled at one another. "We will need to get together soon to program some coordinates and headings into the ship's computer, but it can wait for now," Jack said.

"Any time is a good time for me," Leonard said.

Ramon Jaramillo was next in line and his main job was doing all of the ship's minor maintenance; he was also in charge of the housekeeping. Carl knew very little about him, but he had needed someone with Ramon's background when he hired him. Ramon mumbled greetings and shook hands much like a dead fish, while not looking Jack in the eye. Jack felt a little uneasy about Ramon, but soon dismissed it as nervousness on Ramon's part. *After all,* he thought, *Ramon made the maiden voyage with the rest of the crew and there were no complaints.*

73

Now it was Robert Harvey's turn to meet Jack. He stepped forward and shook hands.

"Welcome aboard the *Freeman Barnes*," he said.

"Thanks, Robert. I understand that you are a first-rate diesel mechanic and a dependable diver," Jack said.

"I hope never to disappoint you in either of those two vocations," Robert said.

"Thanks, Robert, I'm sure you won't," Jack replied.

There would be two additional crew members to be hired at a later date. Once the expedition began in earnest, there would be many more duties to perform, while the existing crew needed to concentrate on diving and searching the reef.

After the introductions were completed, Carl was quick to turn to the task at hand, which was moving some diving equipment onto a rental truck for the trip up the coast. Scott Shepherd was in charge of all the diving equipment aboard the *Freeman Barnes*, so Carl called him aside when the opportunity presented itself.

"Scott, would you be kind enough to help Jack and me load some equipment into a rental truck we just picked up?" Carl asked.

"Would that be the list of equipment we received last night?" Scott asked.

"You have me at a disadvantage, Scott; what list?"

Scott pulled out an equipment list received by fax and handed it to Carl. When Carl read it, he broke into a grin.

"Jack, you don't waste any time, do you?" Carl queried amusedly.

"I thought it would help expedite things if the *Freeman Barnes* knew ahead of time that we would be here this morning to pick up this equipment," Jack said. "I hope I was in line by doing it," Jack finished.

"No problem here, Jack, I'm just not used to this much efficiency from you so quickly. I need a little time to get used to it, that's all. This also explains why the *Freeman Barnes* was in such a state of readiness when we arrived; they knew we were coming."

"I'll try to be more subtle next time, Carl," Jack said with a grin.

The equipment was already on the dock and waiting. Within minutes the crew had it loaded onto the rental truck. It consisted of six sets of double air tanks, filled and ready. Then there were four air regulators, four weight belts with extra weights, four coldwater wetsuits complete, and four sets of swim fins and facemasks. This took care of the diving equipment. Then there was 150 feet of galvanized chain with two removable locking clevises and a buoy with 75 feet of two-inch braided rope. Then finally, there was a self-inflating rubber raft for use when installing the chain on the ocean floor and setting the buoy.

Jack intended to use Susan for this small operation for two reasons. Firstly, because he knew she was an experienced and competent diver. His second reason was that he wanted to showcase her talents to the other divers so there would be no questions raised when she became part of the diving crew.

Before long they were back on the road to Santa Barbara with Jack driving the rental truck and Robert Harvey his passenger. Ahead of them in the BMW was Carl with Scott Shepherd. They arrived at their destination early that afternoon and set the following day for modifying the mooring at Freddy's Cove. Carl did not let grass grow under his feet when it came to something as important as this. He also wanted to monitor Jack's mooring layout, just to see if Jack was as good as everyone thought he was. Carl was not disappointed. As it turned out, Jack's layout and subsequent execution were flawless. Susan was there with her own equipment and proved herself to be all Jack had said she was. The mooring was in place before noon, and the group enjoyed some quality time together, stretching out on the sand while eating hotdogs roasted over Jack's campfire. All the men were captivated by Miss Susan's grace and charm and awed by her extensive knowledge of the Pacific Ocean.

This expedition is starting out right, Carl thought as he ate his second hotdog. *I could get used to this place in a hurry.*

The next thing on Carl's agenda would be the shakedown cruise to the Channel Islands, and then a trial run into Freddy's

Cove. If all went according to plan they would be embarking within the week from San Diego, and they would not be returning there. They would be inspecting the Forbidden Reef from a distance and taking some satellite readings, but there would be no entry into this reef until all the other wrinkles were smoothed out. Carl was a cautious man, which explained why he had been so successful in the past.

Next to Jack, Scott Shepherd was the most diversely-qualified member of the crew. His extensive maritime background on both fishing vessels and commercial shipping gave him a wealth of experience to draw on. Then Scott also loved to sail and scuba dive, and had an equal amount of experience in these two endeavors. Scott had never been married but managed to have a girl in every port, like the song says. He was friendly and cheerful most of the time, and it was plain to see that he enjoyed what he did. Scott originally hailed from Beaverton, Oregon and came from a family that was proud to work in the woods lumberjacking, a calling that Scott had never felt. It was always the call of the sea and those faraway ports that Scott responded to. He loved and missed his family, and they him, but neither understood the other's calling. Scott Shepherd was a standup guy who demanded respect wherever he went, and Carl was lucky to have him on his crew.

Chapter Ten:
THE SHAKEDOWN CRUISE

It was raining steadily in Santa Barbara that morning when Susan, Jack, and Carl began their final trip to San Diego. The *Freeman Barnes* would be having a new homeport within the next two weeks.

Susan was doing the driving while Carl and Jack sat engrossed in an intense conversation. Was it possible to tie off the *Freeman Barnes* on the Forbidden Reef and ride out the low tide inrush current? It was something Jack had never considered. His experiences with Freddy Steele said absolutely not, but then, Freddy had an unhealthy fear of the Forbidden Reef; or maybe it was a healthy fear, who knows. The three were en route to San Diego to take the *Freeman Barnes* out for its first real shakedown cruise. Carl had never assumed the command of his ship until now and had no feel for the nuances of his brain child. He had put every conceivable device and type of gear aboard that he thought might aid him in treasure recovery; but until he was at the helm and had taken his boat through its paces, there was much he didn't know. He had off handedly posed the reef question to Jack and was surprised by Jack's reaction. Jack's response was not to be confused with fear but Jack was a man who always took his responsibilities seriously. He was unwilling to risk the *Freeman Barnes* to that additional hazard without absolute certainty that the ship would survive. Carl could see the wisdom in Jack's words and respected him for that.

Susan had been sitting quietly while being lulled by the hypnotic effect of the windshield wipers and concentrating on her driving responsibilities. It was her job to drive back to Santa Barbara once she had dropped off the men. She had not been invited into the conversation, but she had some facts about the reef that neither of the two knew because of her marine biology studies.

"May I intrude upon your conversation for a moment?" Susan asked quietly. Both men were stopped in their tracks and completely disarmed by the politeness of the request.

"Susan, of course you may. I only hope that you didn't feel left out of the conversation," Carl said.

"Maybe I did, just a little. There are some facts you may not be aware of."

Susan began to tell of a study done by the university that went like this: "The Channel Islands represent a transition zone for warmer tropical water meeting with cooler currents coming down from the north. The warmer water rises to the surface, while the colder currents fall off the continental shelf creating a siphon effect. This only occurs during low tide when the shallowness of the reef accelerates the flow of water into the depths. The forces are incredible there during this period and each 100-feet of water depth is equal to 600 feet of actual depth in terms of water pressure. Standard scuba gear doesn't work much past 40 feet when the currents are running because the air demand quickly depletes the tanks. This is a very dangerous place you have chosen to conduct a treasure hunt," she finished.

Both Jack and Carl sat quietly digesting what Susan had just told them. They both knew of the dangers present there but this information added a completely new wrinkle, a siphon effect that changed all the rules of diving.

"Thank you for that information, Susan," Carl finally said.

The rest of the trip was uneventful as both Carl and Jack were immersed deep in thought while considering what Susan had said.

Freddy Steele was pretty close in his assumptions about why the reef was so deadly, but this siphon thing creates a whole new set of variables, Jack thought. *I'm sure there's a way to work around this; and, after all, we are talking about just six hours a day with the rest of the time being safe for diving.*

"Jack, this really doesn't change anything about our exploration other than to more rigidly enforce our safety regulations, don't you think?" Carl said.

"I do, but I also think that we should keep this information to ourselves for the time being," Jack answered. "No point getting the crew worked up over something we are avoiding anyway."

Little else was discussed for the remainder of the journey, as both had much to chew on.

All too soon they were in San Diego and Jack and Susan said a quick goodbye on the dock. She would be getting a real tour of the boat once it was safely moored at *Freddy's Cove*, but for now it was best for everyone if she made herself scarce. Jack and Carl hurried aboard and each was taken with the many things to be done before embarking from the harbor.

Jack noticed two additional crewmembers present and made it a point to introduce himself to them. The first was James Grey, a 20-year-old who claimed to have previous experience aboard cruise ships. He was just a little bit too cocky for Jack, and his experience didn't quite ring true when compared to his age. He was hired as a general laborer-deckhand and was under Ramon's supervision except for sailing duties.

Well, the expedition needed additional help, and as long as the new employee could do the job he was hired to do, it should be all right. But he deserves watching, for now at least, Jack thought.

The second new crewmember was a personal friend of Ramon's, and Jack had equal concerns about him as well. His name was Juan Nunez, and his English was terrible.

What was Ramon thinking, recommending someone who had such a communication problem? Jack thought. Jack's instincts told him again that all was not as it should be. This Juan Nunez also needed to be watched. Too much was riding on the efficiency of the crew, but Juan's main job was to be Rena's assistant in the scullery. Maybe he was getting a little paranoid, but it wasn't like either Jack or Carl to surround themselves with suspicious people. He would also talk to Rena about this new employee when time permitted. Juan was hired to fill nonessential positions and to free other crewmembers for the real work of locating and salvaging the sunken treasure. Because of this language barrier there would be way too many essential chores he would be unable to perform. He was also walking around in hard-soled work shoes, which was a major breech of yacht protocol. He would speak to Ramon about this when he saw him. Getting the *Freeman Barnes* under way was now his major priority.

All too quickly it was time to embark and Jack manned the bow line while Scott manned the stern line. Carl gave the signal to release the lines and both Jack and Scott dropped the lines free and climbed aboard the boat. Carl was at the helm with Leonard Smith close by taking readings on the instruments. Carl gave the *Freeman Barnes* hard right rudder at one-quarter throttle, while simultaneously energizing the port bow thruster to 1,800 RPMs. The *Freeman Barnes* moved sideways slowly from the dock and out into the center of the channel. Once there, Carl dropped the power to the main screw and shut the bow thruster down. He then engaged the main screw once again and began slowly edging the *Freeman Barnes* out past the moored yachts and toward the main channel and the open sea. Meanwhile, Robert Harvey and Scott Shepherd pulled the mooring lines up from the dock, then finally the fenders which they stowed immediately. Jack had to admit that Carl was a gifted pilot when it came to close-in maneuvers. *We're lucky to have him,* he thought.

This was to be a ten-day cruise, first out to blue water beyond the continental shelf, then northeast well to the north of the

Channel Islands. Once all tests and drills were performed satis-factorily they would approach San Miguel Island from the north. When they arrived at the Channel Islands they would be using directional precious-metal detection using satellite technology. There was much to do, and this would be an eventful cruise for all hands. Many duties needed to be assigned to all members of the crew. No one was exempt from this duty except possibly Juan Nunez, but that might change quickly.

As Carl worked the boat past the moorings and toward the breakwater, he had Leonard Smith engage both the radar and the sonar. These instruments gave Carl a visual of above and below the ocean surface and aided him while leaving the harbor. The sonar alarm was set for 35 feet and went off constantly while the boat was exiting the confines of the yacht harbor. The plan was to cruise for several hours under power to test the twin diesel engines. After that, the sails would be set and various sailing drills would be executed by the crew members until Carl and Jack were confident in the crew's ability to sail the ship. Carl knew that most of this crew had taken the *Freeman Barnes* on its first shakedown cruise, but the stakes were higher now and the margins of error were radically diminished.

The horizon was cloudless and the wind was from the north northeast at a steady14 knots. The temperature was a mild 70 degrees and a five-foot sea was running, with no shipping in the vicinity.

What could be better than this? Jack wondered.

Carl started the second diesel engine and increased both throttles to 50 percent. The *Freeman Barnes* leapt forward once the second screw was engaged. They were soon cruising at a comfortable 20 knots with much more throttle left, and Carl kept the engines there for the first hour, letting the crew get used to the movement of the boat.

While this was going on, Jack had called James Grey and asked him to secure the mooring lines. James had presented himself as an experienced deckhand and Jack wanted to know if this was true. He could see instantly that James knew little or nothing of the position he had applied for. *This will be a long ten days*, Jack said to himself as he began to show James how to properly coil and stow the mooring lines. When this task was accomplished Jack began to show him some basic knot-tying such as the bowline, the quick-release bowline, the square knot, the quick-release half hitch, etc. James claimed that he already knew how to tie these knots, but he had forgotten them.

"James, we will be unfurling the sails before too long. Do you have any experience with that?" Jack asked.

"Not really, Jack."

"OK then, just stay close to me when the time comes. This boat is mostly self sufficient and the sails can either be unfurled by hand or mechanically; however, the sails must always be set by hand with a quick-release tie should an emergency occur. The sails will automatically release if one of the side rails dips into the water, but in some cases it could be too late to avoid a disaster," Jack explained. He was now certain that James had lied about his experience, but this was Carl's call to make right now, not his. There were just too many demands on Jack right then and he didn't have the time to work with James.

Maybe Scott or Robert could help instruct James," he thought. He would ask them when he saw them again.

Personally, Jack would have preferred another choice for a deckhand. His feeling about James was getting stronger by the minute.

In the meantime, Carl was immersed in the joy of running his own ship and was preparing to engage maximum cruising speed. The only thing he did not know yet was how fast the boat would move through the water, but when this test was over he would know.

"Stand by to increase speed to full cruising power." Carl spoke through the ships intercom. With that warning issued, he changed the throttles to lead and slave configuration, then turned up the lead throttle to 80 percent of power and the *Freeman Barnes* responded once more. The ship leapt through the water while raising itself upward over eight feet by the thrust of the engines. A 110-foot yacht would normally not plane over the water surface; but by raising, it reduced the water friction on the hull and increased the speed to a steady 50 knots. With five-foot seas Carl could do this, but with any higher swells it would be foolhardy and dangerous. Carl was no fool, he was just finding out what his boat would do. The remaining 20 percent reserve power would be used only in an emergency.

While this was going on, Jack and Scott began inspecting the holds and all equipment storage areas for gear that was not properly secured. Running at this speed would give them an overview of the boat's weaknesses as well as its' strengths. This would continue for over an hour before Jack and Scott made their rounds and reported to Carl. Now it was time to do some sailing.

Carl reduced speed to idle and energized one of the two 65 KW generators while letting the craft drift through the water. Once the generator was up to speed and the ship's power was switched from the main engines to the generator, Carl shut down the motors.

Carl energized the ship's intercom and gave the order to stand by to unfurl the mainsail. Jack had rounded up James, but Juan was nowhere to be seen. Scott and Robert uncovered the mainsail while Jack and James manned the hand cranks. All sails were to be raised and lowered by hand during this cruise, although the *Freeman Barnes* could do this automatically. Once the mainsail was free, Jack and James began the lengthy task of raising the sail. Scott and Robert waited until the sail was completely up, then began setting the sail to the wind. Once the mainsail was filled and the ship began to move silently through the water, all hands stopped and cheered. It just felt good to be in control of the elements and to be propelled through the water by the wind. All were moved by the experience, as if this was their first time sailing.

Next the jib sail was cranked out of its holding tube and was promptly set in like manner to the mainsail. The wind had increased to 18 knots and the seas were building. The jib was set with three-quarters of its canvas to the wind, with the remaining canvas in the holding tube. Carl decided not to set the mizzen sail just then, with the rising seas and the wind picking up. Once the sun set the wind should drop, and that would be the time to put on more sail. As it was, the side rail had scarcely three feet of freeboard. The *Freeman Barnes* cut through the water like a racing sailboat at a steady 14 knots, an amazing speed for a motor-sailor this large.

As the sun dropped below the western horizon, Jack stood on the bow sprint taking in the sights and smells of the Pacific Ocean. *One really doesn't know how much these simple pleasures are missed until they are finally restored,* Jack thought.

What he didn't miss, however, was what he called the flat light on the water just before dark and just before dawn—the light that gave no light. It always made him feel as if he were alone and cast away, but then the feeling didn't last long. Jack had once been told that the flat light affected many people in like manner. Maybe it was just his genetic memories surfacing from a time when the world was younger and his ancestors crossed the oceans on flimsy boats.

Then it was the call to dinner and to reviewing the watch assignments. Jack was a very busy man that first sailing afternoon and had little time to express his concerns.

The rules of the *Freeman Barnes* while under way were simple, but strict when it came to standing watch. Everyone above deck and outside the confines of the bridge was required to be in a life jacket and a safety harness. In the event of a man overboard (MOB) the safety harness would sound the alarm and automatically cause the release of the sails or shut down the engines, while recording the position of the man overboard. There would be several drills regarding such an emergency during this cruise. Although the boat was equipped with an autopilot, those on watch were required to steer the boat manually while using the compass and additionally monitoring the radar and the sonar. In the event of an emergency, the one on watch could sound an alarm similar to general quarters on a naval vessel. For training purposes, each watch was supervised. Jack had the second four-hour watch with Ramon. Maybe he was wrong about him, so Jack specifically requested that he and Ramon stand watch together.

Their watch was uneventful. Ramon did all things asked of him and did them exceedingly well. Although Jack was watching him intently, his knowledge and skill were both superb. What troubled Jack the most was that Ramon knew a lot more about navigation and sailing than his application had indicated. *Is he a natural sailor, or is he more experienced than he is letting on? He definitely knows more than he should, but where did he come by this knowledge?"* Jack thought. Ramon continuously evaded Jack's probing questions about his previous experience and continued to avoid eye contact.

There is something definitely wrong here, but just what it is, I don't know yet, Jack thought.

"Ramon, why did you recommend someone who could barely speak English and because of this, can't stand watch or perform other duties the rest of us must do?"

"I was just trying to help Juan, and I will be willing to stand his watch with him until he can do it on his own," Ramon replied.

"That will work for now, but Carl will have the last say about this. While you are coaching Juan, get him into a pair of soft-soled shoes before Carl sees him. If you have nothing in his size let me know and I'll try to find a pair for him."

"Yes, sir, I will," Ramon said.

All in all, the sailing drills went very well and eight days later the *Freeman Barnes* could be found approaching San Miguel Island from the north. Jack had given the Loran coordinates and compass headings to Leonard who converted those coordinates to minutes and seconds. Before Jack was willing to commit the boat to the reef, he and Leonard would launch an inflatable raft to test Jack's memory. They would be taking a magnetic compass, a GPS with pre-set waypoints, and finally, a portable fish-finder sonar to visually inspect the bottom on the route into the reef. Carl had requested that Jack and Leonard not reveal the actual coordinates and headings to the crew members, and both could see the wisdom in this request. Jack's memory had served him well and the two entered the reef at exactly the same point that Freddy had used many years before. Jack and

Leonard maneuvered flawlessly out into the central lagoon. With this chore completed, it was time to set some moorings for the *Freeman Barnes* to use when in the Forbidden Reef confines.

While Jack and Leonard were laying out the passage into the Forbidden Reef, Carl and Scott were busy working with the directional metal detector. This device was set up on the craft to instantaneously record the exact coordinates of the *Freeman Barnes* with the use of satellites and the magnetic direction of the target, corrected for magnetic declination. Once a second hit on the same target from a different location occurred, the computer would instantly triangulate the hit and give exact coordinates of its location. Carl had developed this equipment for use in Florida and there was nothing like it on the market. It was perfect for maritime exploration due to its speed and accuracy. For the purposes of this hunt the molecular frequency of *all* gold was being used here, which included both refined gold and natural nuggets; but it easily could have been rubies or anything else were the frequency to be changed. While Carl was looking for the wreck of the *Winfield Scott* he was surprised to get not one but seven separate major hits on various parts of the Forbidden Reef. Whatever was here was huge, and the multiple hits indicated that there may have been other shipwrecks strewn across this reef since the coming of the Europeans. Carl had learned not to jump to conclusions but he had to admit that this treasure hunt was becoming very promising.

With the *Freeman Barnes* safely moored to the east of the Forbidden Reef it would be Carl, Jack, Scott, and Robert who would complete the mooring chores. Both the mooring lines were laid out with150 feet of chain attached to rocks and then to a 75-foot two-inch braided line, then finally to a floating buoy. This chore would take a full day of diving for all four, but would be well worth the effort to protect the boat. This location was close to the center of the reef and was a pool of deeper water that was now being called The Lagoon. This lagoon could only be reached using the route Jack and Leonard had laid out. The Lagoon would serve as the focal point of the exploration that was to follow.

The sea life in the lagoon was an amazing visual treat for the divers. In addition to shellfish such as abalone and scallops there were huge lobsters and rock crabs foraging on the bottom and moray eels lurking from cracks in the rocks awaiting unwary sea creatures. Two varieties of shark could be observed swimming casually in the lagoon. The leopard sharks and sand sharks seemed to be well-represented here. Then there were both elephant seals and harbor seals feeding on the abundant sea life and skate wings (a smaller variety of sea life that resembled the larger manta ray) hanging out on the sandy bottom. It was much like visiting an aquarium where the fish were closely packed together for viewing, except that this was real and so were the predators. The diving crew was always alert for an occasional blue or tiger shark cruising through the area. These sharks were unpredictable and vicious and would be better known by the public as a predator were they to feed in the surf where people swim.

As Jack entered the waters of the Forbidden Reef, it seemed as though he had never left this place. The jagged edges of the tilted limestone still reached for the surface with their deadly appendages just a little too short to break the surface. This reef had been above water during the last ice age, and because of this the softer materials were eroded away, leaving only the jagged rock formations. These underwater rock protrusions appeared like skeletal aberrations with many missing teeth, where nothing would grow on the upper reaches but spiny sea urchins.

Regardless of the abundance of sea life on the reef, there was an ominous presence here that made everyone ill at ease once entering the water. One could call it an overactive imagination on the divers' part or just a case of the willies, but all who entered the water felt it. The Forbidden Reef was a place of death. Once the moorings were secured, the *Freeman Barnes* retreated to safer waters and dropped anchor for the evening.

The following morning, and in spite of all the negative feelings from the day before, Carl felt comfortable enough to bring the *Freeman Barnes* into the Forbidden Reef for a trial run. He always said that a coward died a thousand deaths but a brave man only one. Leonard had programmed the route into the ship's computer so it was an effortless trip into the reef. Once at The Lagoon destination, the *Freeman Barnes* executed a 180-degree turn in place, and within minutes the bow and stern moorings were secured and the boat went onto generator power.

Carl wanted to test the crane-mizzen mast and launch the custom-made diving bell. The crane-mizzen mast was actually constructed of a titanium alloy that was both hardened and strengthened far more than a standard sail mast needed to be. The cables used were stainless steel aircraft cable of the best quality.

The yardarm was made of the same alloy as the mizzen mast and was used strictly for the purpose of using the 10,000-pound winch to launch and retrieve equipment. It could rotate 180 degrees from front to back and the load could be extended to the end of its length using a small stationary motor-and-cable assembly on the yardarm itself. Double-strength aircraft cable was tightened from the leading end of the yardarm, then to the top of the mast itself onto a swivel fitting, then on to the opposing-side yardarm brace that rotated with the main yardarm, and then finally down to the mainframe structure of the *Freeman Barnes* to an assembly of curved stainless steel that allowed movement of 180 degrees. There were also two additional support cables in place and outside the turning radius to strengthen the mizzen mast during the rotation of the yardarm. This equipment was used to launch and retrieve both the diving bell and the two underwater sleds, and would also serve as a bucket winch for retrieving or delivering items to the bottom of the lagoon. It was one tough piece of equipment, as was all equipment Carl had installed on the *Freeman Barnes*. Once in place the cables were torqued down to the point where one could almost play a tune on the cable itself. The entire assembly could be installed, adjusted, and ready to go within two hours. Once the *Freeman Barnes* began working here, this assembly would remain in place until the run back to Freddy's Cove.

Once the yardarm was set in place on the mizzen mast and all cables secured, the cable was threaded through the pulleys and the winch was activated. The aft hold was opened and the cable was attached to the lifting ring of the diving bell. Once above deck, the three air lines were attached: incoming, exhaust, and high pressure air for the scuba tanks. Next went the power cables, the fresh-water line, and the communication line.

With the electrical limit switches hooked up and all the power cables in place and working, it was show time. Jack and Robert entered the diving bell, and the door was secured and sealed. There was a 30-inch round open hole in the bottom for access by the divers. Jack had two filled scuba tanks with regulators and weight belts placed on the side brackets of the diving bell for emergencies. When all preparations were completed, the bell was lifted above the side rail and moved horizontally out above the water surface. Once Carl had confirmed that the two were good-to-go, he gave the order to lower the diving bell. This diving bell was to be the command headquarters during the search. Once in the water Jack began filling the ballast tanks and the diving bell began to slowly submerge.

This diving bell, as it was called, was another brainchild of Carl Webb. Originally Carl was searching for a method to make a comfortable haven where divers could come and go without fear of nitrogen narcosis and take a break from the diving regimen. The original design was for a pressurized command center with easy access by divers from below. New technology was needed here and the result was the variable-depth pressure-relief valve, a ten-dollar word for a device that adjusted itself to both the inside air pressure and the outside water pressure. The simplicity of the design was its greatest virtue. Pressurized air was released into the cabin of the diving bell. When the pressure rose to the point where air would soon bubble out of the bottom hole, the relief valve would open and stabilize the pressure. This value would vary depending upon the depth, but the diving bell had been tested successfully at 120 feet; this was thought to be the maximum depth for salvaging while using standard scuba gear. The diver could return to the diving bell, leave his tanks on the side for refilling, then come into the bell for a visit or break, or simply grab a filled tank and be off again to the depths. These were the systems that were originally planned for the diving bell.

Then the additional equipment began to accumulate on the diving bell. First were the communications between divers and the bell, and then the bell and the boat; then floodlights, directional homing signals for the divers to follow, and rechargers for the batteries used in the underwater sleds. All in all, the diving bell, as well as the sleds, was much like the *Freeman Barnes*; there was much more here than appeared on the surface.

"What a view," Robert said as the two were nearing 40 feet in depth. "What an amazing array of sea life." Robert was briefly mesmerized by the purple, violet, and red colors of the sea lettuce gently swaying with the ocean surge. All too soon it was back to business again.

Jack also had to admit that the view was stunning from inside the diving bell. The two turned to the testing of the various systems, and before long their chores were completed. With this done, the diving bell would be extracted and the *Freeman Barnes* would be headed home to Freddy's Cove. It had been a successful shakedown cruise, but now it was time to return to the mainland. The weather reports said that another winter storm was on the way, and it would be a good time to return and stock up on supplies.

There were still unresolved questions about James Grey and Juan Nunez, and for that matter, Ramon was an anomaly, a man who claimed to know little but actually had a great deal of maritime skill. Once back in Freddy's Cove Jack intended to bring his concerns to Carl.

Jack also had the occasion to speak with Rena about her new helper, Juan.

"Rena, what kind of a worker is Juan?" Jack asked.

"Truthfully, I'm not sure. He does what I ask him to do, but I sense some hostility in him. It's as if the tasks I give him are demeaning; he always does the work adequately but slowly," Rena said.

"Rena, please do me a favor and report anything out of the ordinary concerning his behavior," Jack asked. He wasn't ready to make any accusations; he just had a feeling that he was missing something here. Better to be safe than sorry. He had assigned standing watch shifts to both Ramon and Juan together, but now it seemed as if this could have been a mistake. Juan's English was just as bad as ever.

The *Freeman Barnes* left the Forbidden Reef as effortlessly as it was entered and was on its' way back to the mainland under full sail when Carl called Jack to the bridge.

"Hi, Carl, I haven't seen much of you these past nine days. This must be important," Jack said with a smile.

"Jack, what do you make of this radar image?" Carl asked without ceremony.

Jack looked closely at the image and said, "Carl, if I didn't know better, I would say that it matches the radar image I got two nights ago."

"That's what I thought: at five miles it's not a clear image but there are similarities to the image I picked up last night. Truthfully, I would say that we are being shadowed," Carl said. "But the real question here is by whom, and a far better question is why?"

"Leonard, do you have the directional radio receiver operational?" Carl asked.

"I do, and the mystery ship is transmitting right now," Leonard said as he read off the coordinates of the ship's position. "It seems to be hovering just on the fringes of our radar range and it is now matching our direction and speed. It looks as though we will be having some company before too long. However, I don't think that ship knows yet that we are aware of its presence," Leonard finished.

"Leonard, can we get some satellite imagery of this ship before the sun sets?" Carl asked.

"I think so. Give me a half hour and I may have a picture for you to look at."

"One more thing, Leonard. Can you extend the radar range without tipping him off?"

"Unfortunately, I can't. If I were to increase it, he would know immediately that we were on to him; it's better to leave it as is for now."

"Good enough. Thank you for the information, Leonard," Carl said.

"Jack, what is your take on this?" Carl questioned.

"It is too early for me to have an opinion, but this can't be good. I think we should ditch this boat before we set a course for Freddy's Cove. That should give us some breathing room."

"How would you ditch this mystery ship?" Carl asked.

"One of Freddy's tricks when he thought he was being followed was to head for Santa Cruz Island to a place he called the yacht cove. Once in the cove you can't be picked up on radar because you are completely surrounded by the promontories. If we were to furl the sails and cruise at 70- or 75-percent throttle we can be there well before dark. Once there, we can drop anchor for the night. One more thing, under no circumstances can we transmit a radio of any kind or this mystery ship will be on us again. I think that's how he's keeping tabs on us now. I also think he will hold back and wait for us to transmit again and that should give us enough time to reach the cove unnoticed," Jack finally finished.

Carl nodded his head in agreement, then turned to the intercom and issued the orders. This was becoming far too interesting for his tastes in adventure, but at least he had the benefit of Jack's knowledge. That knowledge could mean the difference in the skirmish that was likely to occur.

"One more thing, keep this conversation confidential," Carl said.

Jack and Leonard both nodded agreement.

"There is one additional thing we should do, Carl. Ramon and Juan have the midnight-to-four a.m. watch tonight. I would like to relieve them and stand that watch myself,"
Jack said.

"Is there something you aren't telling me?" Carl asked.

"Nothing concrete yet, just a hunch of mine," Jack answered. "We can talk about it when we get back to the mainland. All I know right now is that they are both being deceptive about their experience."

"You will inform me if anything changes?" Carl asked.

"As soon as I know something, you will know it, too." Jack said. When he got back to Santa Barbara, he intended to run all three names and socials through his friend with the FBI. There was no reason to tell Carl about it unless there was something wrong after the reports came in.

Chapter Eleven:
THE YACHT COVE

Once the sails were safely furled, Carl fired up the engines and then allowed them to warm up, while continuing in the same direction as before at basically the same speed. Before long Leonard had a good satellite image of the mystery ship printed out and in Carl's hands. Now they would have an idea of what and who was shadowing them.

"What do you make of this, Jack?" Carl asked.

"I don't have that much experience with commercial shipping, but this looks like an older transport built before the days of containerized shipping," Jack answered.

"I've seen way too many boats like this while working in the Gulf of Mexico. If I didn't know better I would say that it is a classic Columbian mother ship, but what is it doing here? These ships normally stay well out in international waters. The maximum cruising speed of these boats is around 12 knots, if my memory serves me," Carl said.

"Leonard, once we begin cruising, increase our radar range in one-mile increments every 20 minutes up to 20 miles. That should cause this boat to think he is matching our speed until we disappear around the leeward side of Santa Cruz Island," Carl directed.

"Consider it done," Leonard replied.

The leading elements of the new winter storm were beginning to unfold around the *Freeman Barnes*. The wind was picking up and the seas were rising. It was now time to show this mystery boat their heels without tipping it off, and head for the yacht cove. The wind was coming from the west northwest at 25 knots and the seas were at seven feet and building. Jack pulled out the chart for Santa Cruz Island and laid a course for the northeast corner of the island.

The announcement was given to stand by to get underway, and then Carl turned the throttle to 60 percent. Before long they were traveling at a brisk 30 knots. With a quartering tailwind and rising seas, the *Freeman Barnes* was just able to keep the storm's effects at bay with the use of speed and the autopilot. However, if the wind and the seas increased much more they would be forced to slow down to a more manageable level. Their luck was still holding as they turned the ship south around the northern tip of Santa Cruz Island. A quick check of the mystery ship revealed that the deception with the radar had done its' job, and that ship was still traveling at the same speed and direction. As they set a new course for the entrance to the yacht cove, all exterior devices such as radar, strobe, and running lights were shut down to prevent the mystery ship from homing in on them visually.

The yacht cove was a deep natural harbor that was almost impossible to see from the sea. The channel into the cove extended from southeast to northwest, with the island hillsides covered with greenery and blending in with each other in the waning light. Jack had been here many times before in the *Betty Lou* with Freddy Steele. It was one of his favorite places to be at the Channel Islands, and it looked as if it had not changed since his last visit years before. The harbor was deep with the water depth dropping sharply to 50 feet or deeper within 30 feet of the rocky shoreline. The harbor was also roomy without underwater rock hazards and was shielded from most of the wind. The

Freeman Barnes was taken to a comfortable location, and then Carl let out the anchor for the evening. Leonard took another satellite image of the mystery boat and noted that it was on a course that would take it around Santa Cruz Island to points south, while missing the yacht cove by several miles. Everyone could breathe a sigh of relief knowing that they had eluded this strange ship, at least for the time being.

When Jack had an unpleasant task to perform it was his policy to take care of it as quickly as possible. With that thought in mind, he located Ramon coming out of his room.

"Ramon, you and Juan will not be standing watch tonight. I'll be testing some new equipment this evening so you both got lucky tonight," Jack said.

"But Jack, I don't mind standing watch. Maybe I can help you with the equipment testing tonight," Ramon stammered.

"No, get some sleep," Jack said in a tone that allowed no further discussion.

Ramon acted as if he wanted to speak, and then thought better of it and moved on to his business.

He sure was reluctant to give up his watch, thought Jack. *That is a strange reaction.*

The following morning the crew of the *Freeman Barnes* awoke to dark gray skies and the sound of rain beating on the decks. The wind was coming in gusts of up to 30 knots and the normally placid harbor was being churned by the constant wind chop.

"Jack, what do you think of our chances of making a run to *Freddy's Cove* this morning?" Carl asked.

"The *Freeman Barnes* could make it there easily, but we've never tested my coordinates for entering the harbor. If we have a choice, let's wait out this storm for another day, then head on in to *Freddy's Cove*. This will give Leonard and me an opportunity to prove the coordinates before committing the *Freeman Barnes* into the channel," Jack said.

"On a lighter note, this cove used to be loaded with lobster," Jack continued "It was a place where Freddy came to relax and he never commercially fished here; he saved it for times like these. Why don't we take a day off and let the storm move through before we leave? The remains of a gambling casino can be visited just up the bank near where the iron ring is imbedded in the rock. Not much is left of it now but the foundation and a few walls, but it's interesting to look at," Jack finished.

"Thanks," Carl said. "We could get lucky and ditch this mystery ship permanently by waiting a day, but I doubt it."

"Leonard, what do you have on the mystery ship this morning?" Carl asked.

"It's gone but I don't know where, except maybe so close to the mainland that the satellite could be missing it," Leonard replied. "There is nothing in the vicinity within 20 miles as of five minutes ago," Leonard finished.

"OK, then we'll all take a day off, but keep me informed about the ship if it shows up," Carl said.

Chapter Twelve:
BACK TO FREDDY'S COVE

That stormy morning was filled with underwater exploration by all who subscribed to this pastime. The Santa Cruz Island seascape was unique in many respects. The pea kelp appeared like a surreal underwater forest whose shadows blended in and out with the intermittent sunlight. It was a visual cornucopia for those fortunate enough to experience it. It reminded Jack of the first time he had visited the Carlsbad Caverns of New Mexico; it was the beauty and the majesty of nature at one of its most superb monuments. This panorama of visual delight was brought on in part by the changing sunlight in the crystal clear waters of the cove. This was an unforeseen bonus given to the crew while waiting out the winter storm moving through the islands. Those few divers fortunate enough to be there during this remarkable presentation were truly blessed that day. Before long the ship's larders were filled with fresh lobster, pink abalone, and scallops. Then, all too soon, those privileged visitors from the world above retreated back to the *Freeman Barnes* for the feast that had already begun beneath the water of the yacht cove.

The afternoon drifted by uneventfully while the crew relaxed in comfort and dined on fresh seafood. By nightfall the skies were clearing and the seas were falling. With the coming of morning they would be on their way to Freddy's Cove. Jack was still unwilling to allow Ramon or Juan unsupervised access to the bridge until he had some better information about their background. The three in question, which included James Grey, had little intercourse with the rest of the crew during that afternoon and had even less to do with the fresh seafood. Jack had to search for Ramon, and when he was found he was in his room with James and Juan. Jack informed Ramon that once again there would be no need for his or Juan's services that night. He could see the disappointment and suspicion in Ramon's eyes, but this time he didn't dismiss it as imagination. In a different time, Jack would have had these three locked up to keep them out of mischief until these issues were resolved. He decided then to inform all the watches that night to do a bed check on these guys. Something was definitely wrong, and now he knew it.

Just what is this Ramon up to? To be resentful of being relieved of a tiresome duty is just too strange to be dismissed as loyalty to his job, thought Jack. *It's all the more reason to keep these three under close supervision for the time being.*

The night passed without incident and the following morning Carl had Leonard do one more satellite scan before leaving the cove. This time the mystery ship was picked up again almost 30miles distant and well to the west of the Channel Islands. The anchor was raised and the *Freeman Barnes* was soon on its way eastward towards the entrance into Freddy's Cove. Carl decided to continue to run with radar and sonar off, and observe radio silence until reaching the cove. Jack had earlier given the coordinates and the headings into *Freddy's Cove* to Leonard, and this information was safely in the ship's computer. The two planned to prove the channel entering the cove with the inflatable raft and instruments, as had been done before at the Forbidden Reef.

Upon arrival at the entrance to Freddy's Cove, the raft was launched as the *Freeman Barnes* stood off the coast while waiting for the signal from Jack and Leonard. Once more Jack's memory had served him well, and the way into the cove was still in the same place that Freddy Steele had left it years before. Jack and Leonard went on into the cove in the raft, while Carl had the *Freeman Barnes* enter the cove under complete control by the ship's computer.

"He sure trusts your programming, Leonard," Jack casually observed.

"Yeah, Jack, almost as much as he trusts your judgment," Leonard returned politely.

They both smiled at that remark.

After the *Freeman Barnes* entered the cove, Carl took control of the ship then executed a 180-degree turn in place. Once that was accomplished, the ship was slowly reversed until the stern line was retrieved. Once it was secured, the ship moved forward with the starboard bow thruster engaged at 800 RPMs to counter the effects of the wind. It was another picture-perfect mooring by Carl, who made maneuvers like this look simple.

Within the hour all crew members disembarking the ship for some badly-needed shore leave were assembled on the beach. Leonard Smith and Scott Shepherd would remain onboard and were due to be relieved by Jack and Susan in two days. The shakedown cruise had been a complete success, and now the heady task of treasure hunting would soon begin in earnest. It was the time Carl liked the most about treasure hunting. This was when the amateurs went home and the professionals took their place. This was the reason Carl Webb had come to California and spent so much time finding Jack—to find treasure. The pieces of the puzzle were all falling quickly into place.

"Jack, Is it all right for Juan and I to remain onboard while we are in port?" asked Ramon.

"Not this time, Ramon. We will need both you and Juan to help re-supply the ship. Maybe a later time would work, but not now," Jack answered.

Ramon and Juan nodded their heads and moved back onto the beach near their bags. The two waited quietly without expression, as if resigned to their fate.

Within the hour Susan arrived with the new GMC Suburban Carl had purchased before leaving for San Diego. With the enthusiasm only sailors a long time away from home could have, all the departing crew members were quite cheerful and just a little giddy as they loaded up in the Suburban for the trip back to Santa Barbara. Carl had seen to everyone's accommodations in town, and all had the night off with the re-supply chores to begin tomorrow. Carl, Jack, and Susan had agreed to meet the following morning early, but tonight was definitely family time for Jack and Susan. There would be much to discuss tomorrow morn, but it seemed a long way off right then. Robert and Rena had taken charge of re-supply and were already placing orders where possible and making lists of things needed to be picked up the following day.

Before reaching their apartment, Jack and Susan stopped at Norm Bennett's home. Norm was an energetic man who shared Jack's love for sailing. Jack had met Norm during one of his many sojourns to the yacht harbor where Norm kept his 30-foot ketch-rigged *Islander*. Jack had noticed the amount of time Norm spent working on his boat, and he had complimented him one day about the mint condition of the vessel. A friendship soon blossomed and Norm invited Jack, Susan, and Josh on many sailing excursions in the waters near Santa Barbara. Norm was a widower who had never done much socializing since his wife died several years before. The four had become good friends; and because of this, Jack and Susan turned to Norm for help in solving the mystery of Ramon and friends.

This new information caught Norm's attention because it fitted the profile of some fugitives for whom the Bureau was searching. Norm worked for the Federal Bureau of Investigation (Special Task Force/Illegal Drug Trafficking) and considered this information from Jack a hot tip. Maybe it would be a dead end but then maybe not. His instincts told him that Jack was on to something. He was given permission by his superiors to disclose any fraudulent information to Jack, but only if the names and socials proved to be bogus. This was the situation that evening when Jack stopped by with the information on Ramon, Juan, and James.

Carl approved of this action taken by Jack, although he did not know the details and had not observed Ramon's behavior as

Jack had. However, Carl trusted Jack's instincts. They would have an answer in the morning about these questionable employees. Right now Jack and Susan were off to pick up Josh and have a quiet family dinner of their own, something Jack had greatly missed during the cruise.

Early the following morning Jack got a call from Norm Bennett.

"Yes, this is Jack. Don't you ever sleep?"

"Not when I get a hot tip on someone the entire department has been seeking for over four months," Norm said.

"Can you and Susan meet me for breakfast?"

"Only if Josh is invited, too," Jack replied.

"Of course, of course he's invited. I don't want to seem pushy; but can you meet in half an hour? This is important," Norm finished.

"Sure, we'll see you there," Jack answered.

When they entered the restaurant, Norm was already seated at a large table with papers stacked neatly to one side. They could tell that Norm was excited about something. As soon as beverages were ordered, Norm began talking.

"Does this person ring a bell with you?" Norm asked Jack as he passed him a mug shot of the person of interest.

"It sure does, that is Ramon Jaramillo," Jack answered quickly.

"And do you recognize these two birds?" Norm said as he handed two more mug shots to Jack.

"Yes again, they are James Grey and Juan Nunez," Jack answered.

"To summarize, these three are fugitives from justice. They were arrested while on a Columbian speed boat after dumping their cargo into the Gulf of Mexico. The Coast Guard was very casual about detaining them and allowed them the run of the ship. "Juan killed a seaman on night watch, and then Ramon lowered a speedboat into the water while the Coast Guard cutter was running at cruising speed. It took some real expertise to do this, but he got it done. Our people think he was in either the American Navy or the Coast Guard at one time, and this is where he acquired his knowledge of seamanship. The murder and theft went unnoticed for almost four hours: They must have made a run to the coast of the United States; there wasn't enough fuel to go anywhere else. They made a clean getaway, and we have been looking for them ever since. We know they have stateside connections, which is how Ramon got to Connecticut and why Juan and James showed up in San Diego. It was four months' ago when the escape took place," Norm finished. I do have one more question for you, Jack. How did these lowlifes get hooked up with Carl in the first place? He has a reputation for carefully screening all his employees.

"I asked the same question. Ramon was hired through an employment agency and he had impeccable references. Juan and Jack were taken on as temporary help when recommended by Ramon. That's all I know about it," Jack said. "What caused you to match these names up with the fugitives from Florida?" Jack inquired.

"When you described Ramon's seamanship qualities it struck a nerve, and from that point on it was a no-brainer to ID these crumbs," Norm said.

"Are they dangerous?" Jack inquired.

"Damn right they are, especially the one you call Juan Nunez. He enjoys his work far more than he should," Norm emphasized. "He is a *very* dangerous man. One of his tricks is to pretend not to understand or speak English very well. This is just a ruse to put his victims off guard."

"I always suspected that. Now what should we do?" Jack asked.

"Where are they now?" Norm asked.

"At the Santa Barbara Inn, but I don't know which rooms," Jack replied. "Let me call Carl and find out," Jack said as he headed for the pay phone.

It would be several minutes before he returned to the table.

"I'm afraid I have some bad news for you, Norm. Those three never slept in their rooms. They have been gone since yesterday afternoon. Carl was just coming here to tell me this when

I called him. They must have suspected that I was going to check up on them." Jack said.

"Jack, Susan, Josh, I hate to be such a poor host, but I need to go and secure the crime scene, such as it is, at least until our lab people get there to try to get some prints," Norm said as he stood up and prepared to leave.

"Norm, isn't the *Freeman Barnes* also part of the crime scene as far as fingerprints are concerned? I don't think you'll find anything at the hotel, but they may not have been so careful on the boat. I'll call Leonard and ask him to close their living quarters up and not touch anything," Jack said.

"Good point. We'll need to go there as well. I'll be in touch soon; gotta go now," Norm said.

"We understand; thanks for your help, Norm," Jack said as they shook hands. Then Norm turned and hurried out the door.

"Carl is on his way over," Jack said to Susan and Josh. "We may as well relax and enjoy the morning."

"What are you going to do about crew members now?" Susan asked.

"I'm going to go see Kevin Mitchell down at the yacht harbor office. He has a nephew who has some real diving and sailing experience. He will know other people with similar experience, I'm sure," Jack said as he continued with his breakfast. There would be plenty of time later to find and recruit some good crewmembers.

After hearing what Norm Bennett had to say, Carl was in full agreement and left the personnel matters in Jack's capable hands. He was troubled by the violent nature of those three he had let into his personal world. But Carl was an optimist of the best kind. Like the little boy who walked into a room full of horseshit, Carl was always looking for the pony.

Chapter Thirteen:
BACK TO THE REEF

Spring was just around the corner, and the countryside near Santa Barbara, California, was blessed with a profusion of wildflowers. These remarkable flower arrangements blended contentedly with the green winter grass that covered the surrounding hills. It was one of those days when it was impossible for anyone to remain in an unpleasant mood, with temperatures in the 70's and gentle breezes drifting off the Pacific Ocean.

In terms of human comfort, what could be better than this remarkable day? thought Jack as he, Susan, and Josh headed for the yacht harbor to see their friend Kevin Mitchell. Kevin was the harbor master and was on duty this fine day. He was always glad to see his good friends stop by because it gave him a welcome break from the humdrum of his daily toils. After social amenities were exchanged, they jumped right into the main reason for the visit. Jack could never be accused of having patience when something was on his mind.

"Kevin, do you remember telling me that your nephew was an experienced diver and had some sailing experience, as well?" Jack asked.

"I do, and I also think he's still available if you need him. His name is Richard Mitchell and I know that he's just doing odd jobs right now. Would you like me to call him for you?" Kevin asked.

"I sure would, Kevin, and while you're at it, ask him if he has a friend with like experience in need of work. We're looking for two hands to fill some unforeseen vacancies," Jack answered. "It's only a temporary job but it pays extremely well."

Without further prompting, Kevin began dialing the phone. Richard was home and also had several friends needing work. Within 15 minutes of making the call, Richard appeared in the parking lot of the yacht harbor with three of his friends in the car.

Richard was a huge man who stood six foot four inches tall and weighed close to 300 pounds. His easy manner and engaging smile charmed both Jack and Susan immediately. Then there was his friend Michael Munson, who was almost as large as Richard and just as friendly. Jack and Susan liked them both immediately. These two men had ten years of diving experience between them, as well as approximately the same amount of time sailing. Both were students at the university and their major was marine biology—perfect for the jobs now available on the *Freeman Barnes*. Jack hired them on the spot, subject to Carl's approval. The third spot on the roster would be filled by Susan in two weeks, so it wasn't available any longer. Richard's other friends were almost equally qualified, and Jack got their names and phone numbers for any future openings. All four were good, wholesome California boys and would have been an asset to anyone's work force. It was a sign of the times when people of this caliber were without work, but that would change eventually; it always did.

Richard would be assuming Ramon's duties, and Michael would be taking over Juan's job. In addition to this, the two would be in the diving rotation once exploration began. Both young men were excited about the prospects and looked forward to the coming cruise.

Richard and Michael had been friends for most of their lives. They had grown up in the same neighborhood, attended the same schools, and they shared the same interests. Both learned to sail and scuba dive while participating in family outings. Both sets of parents owned sailboats and loved all things connected with the Pacific Ocean. They were avid fishermen, scuba divers, and sailors. Unlike many people who purchase sailboats that never leave the dock, these two families were rarely in port when vacation time arrived. It was only natural that Richard and Michael would choose careers in marine biology. It meant a commitment of both time and money, not only for the two families, but also for the boys. Sometimes there was little money for tuition and the two were forced to take menial jobs to make ends meet. This was the situation when Kevin Mitchell called the two with a lead on a temporary job. These were two middleclass young men from good families, without much life experience but plenty of heart. Jack could ask for no more from anyone and was glad to have them aboard.

With this chore completed, Jack, Susan, and Josh, together with their two new crewmembers, headed for Goleta, California and Freddy's Cove. They hurried along that afternoon at the request of Norm Bennett, to get the FBI people onto the boat. When they arrived at the ranch gate, the FBI group stared at them impatiently, as if it were their responsibility that the crew had to work this faultless afternoon. Like a billboard sign saying the "Feds have arrived and everyone is now in deep shit," two of its black four-door sedans were sitting near the gate entrance. Norm was there to run interference for Jack and Susan, so all went reasonably well; but Jack knew that a call to Roland Hawke later was definitely in order, if for no other reason than to clear the air about those damned black cars. Before long, Jack's group was heading out across the ranch on the road to Freddy's Cove and the *Freeman Barnes* anchored there.

It was Jack's and Susan's plan to not relieve Leonard and Scott until their shift was completed. Both Richard and Michael were with them this afternoon for some orientation time on the *Freeman Barnes*, but they would be returning to Santa Barbara the next day with Leonard and Scott. They still needed Carl's approval before all would be official; that would be just a formality.

Jack had already had them sign an all-inclusive non-disclosure agreement, which all members of the crew were required to sign. However, it was Jack's policy to keep Carl involved in all decisions of this nature, and Carl really did have the last say.

This was the first tour Susan and Josh had of the *Freeman Barnes,* and Jack spared nothing in presenting this amazing ship to them and the two new hands. There was a fully-equipped four-person decompression chamber in the storage hold that would be activated once the diving started. It was everyone's wish that this would be one piece of equipment that would never be used, but it was comforting to know that it was there if needed.

The FBI lab people were closed-faced but efficient and found a multitude of prints in the living quarters of the three former crew members. In less than two hours they were finished and loading up in the raft for the trip back to the beach.

"Can we use the vacated cabins now?" Jack inquired.

"Yeah, we're finished," One of the faceless FBI gnomes mumbled.

"I'll call you later, Jack," Norm Bennett mentioned while debarking on the raft.

"We'll be here for three days before we're relieved, but you can call us here on the ship's satellite phone," Jack said as he wrote down the number for Norm.

Jack had some later thoughts about these three outlaws and they weren't good. *It seemed as if skipping town was a split-second decision on their part and it saved them. These homeboys have good instincts, and that makes them even more dangerous,* Jack thought.

He couldn't shake the feeling that he would be seeing more of these three hombres whether he liked it or not, and he was not looking forward to it.

Within four days the *Freeman Barnes* was resupplied with everything but diesel fuel, a commodity that would be loaded on the way out to sea. Carl and Robert showed up to relieve Jack and Susan; they would have two days before the *Freeman Barnes* would be at sea, this time for two weeks.

Jack wanted to talk to Norm Bennett before they departed in case there was anything they needed to know about the fugitives. Forewarned was forearmed as far as Jack was concerned. He couldn't help but think that the crew was lucky that the *Freeman Barnes* wasn't hijacked and the crew disposed of in the depths of the sea. The best decision he had made so far was not allowing Ramon and Juan (if those were their real names) to stand watch unsupervised. It was time to be even more vigilant, because he felt very strongly that there were still cards left to be played by Ramon and company before this affair would finally be over.

Richard and Michael fell into the work regimen of the ship like ducks take to water. Carl also liked them immediately and approved of their hiring. Jack liked the fact that he had to tell them what was needed only one time, and it was done quickly with skill and acumen. Ropes were coiled and stowed properly and knots were tied properly, and most important, all equipment and supplies under their care was secured in a manner that would prevent it from slipping its bonds in rough seas.

Chapter Fourteen:
FINAL PREPARATIONS FOR DIVING

Jack had two days before he needed to report to the *Freeman Barnes,* and there was much to do in Santa Barbara during this period. All supplies were safely stowed on board, and the two new crewmembers were doing a superb job. So Jack asked himself why he was becoming so apprehensive and tense, when things were going so well: the answer came quickly, it had to do with those three renegades who came within an ace of hijacking the *Freeman Barnes* and then skipped town like thieves in the night.

Jack turned his car onto the driveway of Norm's house and cut the engine. He stopped for a moment to enjoy the immaculate landscaping. Norm did the gardening himself now that his wife was gone, and Jack knew that he still really missed her. He wondered if Norm had been this particular about gardening when Mary was alive. This was a question he would never ask, but he couldn't help but wonder. Norm had asked him to come here personally because there was much to discuss. This wasn't like the normally light-hearted and carefree Norm Bennett with whom Jack, Susan, and Josh had spent many happy hours sailing in the past. Jack could hear it in his voice, and knew that whatever was going on was serious.

When Jack entered the house Norm began immediately with the issues both he and Jack shared.

"Jack, tell me more about Ramon, anything you may have just remembered or observed or never mentioned before when you were working with him," Norm asked.

"I didn't care for him from the beginning. There was always a veil of deceit about him, a hidden contempt for orders given him by the chain-of-command, which reflected indirectly upon Carl Webb and me. I could see it in his eyes, the lack of regard he had for everyone. Rena summed it up best when she said of Juan that there was resentment of the demeaning nature of the tasks assigned him. That would apply to all three of these knuckleheads, although with Ramon there was more: he was cunning, like a predator, and much smarter than he appeared. They made a real effort to hide their resentment from the rest of the crew, but it showed if one noticed the small things," Jack finished.

"Sounds like they had some mischief up their sleeves," Norm said.

"That is truly an understatement," Jack emphasized. "I believe that these three intended to hijack the *Freeman Barnes* and only luck prevented it from happening. Let me also say that I believe that I've not seen the last of these outlaws, and that is bothering me much more than it should."

"What causes you to think that, Jack?" Norm asked, his interest now growing.

Jack began telling the story of the mystery ship that had been shadowing them out near the reef and their subsequent escape from it by running away at a high speed, then not allowing Ramon access to the radios later. Jack then began telling Norm of the special amenities of the *Freeman Barnes,* and why it could be considered a prize.

"What's the cruising speed of this boat?" Norm asked.

"Fifty knots at 80 percent of throttle," Jack answered.

"And at 100 percent of throttle?" Norm continued.

"I'm only guessing, but I think the *Freeman Barnes* would begin to plane over the water and kick up the speed to 65, maybe 70 knots," Jack answered.

"What is the fuel capacity?" Norm inquired.

"Two 10,000-gallon fuel tanks," Jack said.

"Holy Shit, no wonder they are so interested in this ship. It could cruise nonstop from here to the Panama Canal and outrun all of the substantial warships of either the United States Navy or the Coast Guard. Quite a boat Carl Webb has," he noted "Just what your average drug smuggler needs to deliver the goods," Norm understated.

"Norm, I believe that these three are connected to this mystery ship in some way. I'm just not sure what their next move will be. Should I contact the Coast Guard; and if I do, what will I tell them? There's no proof of what I'm saying, but I know that it's likely to be proven true and maybe when it's too late," Jack said.

"You could be right. Incidentally, we have a positive ID on Ramon and Juan, but we're still working on James. Real names are Mano Herrera and Fernando Armijo. They were doing hard time in Mexico and escaped captivity four years ago—for drugs, as usual—James could be a newbie," Norm stated in his best FBI voice. Jack was impressed.

James Grey was off the FBI's radar mainly because it was not his real name. His real name was James Pickard and he was from Reno, Nevada. James had been a bad seed from the beginning. His parents had lost control of him at an early age, if in fact they ever had control; and before James turned 21, he had a rap sheet longer than his personal estimation of his self worth. His father was a lounge singer who eked out a living crooning to overweight middle-aged women. His mother called herself a housewife, which was just a layman's term for doing nothing to help support the family. The family was the embodiment of the phrase trailer trash; there is a special place reserved in hell for those of this persuasion.

James turned to a life of crime after dropping out of high school for the final time. Selling drugs was quite profitable, and an education was more of a hindrance than a help in this line of work. James was both cunning and street smart, two traits that allowed him to rise quickly in the Columbian drug cartel. He just happened to be on the same speedboat that was intercepted by the Coast Guard in Florida, and because of this had thrown in his lot with Ramon and Juan. James was no Einstein, but then he was not altogether stupid either.

"Jack, let me make the inquiries with the Coast Guard. This could account for the complete and sudden disappearance of these fugitives. The Coast Guard has a special interest here because of the death of that seaman in Florida, so we won't have much trouble getting them to cooperate. One other thing, Jack, this is a satellite phone that is self-charging when exposed to the sun for half an hour. This is a waterproof container that can be worn on your weight belt without anyone noticing. It is preprogrammed to my personal satellite phone, and you can use it 24/7 if the need ever arises," Norm said as he handed the phone to Jack. "One more thing: don't hesitate to leave a message if I don't answer immediately."

With that done, the two friends parted while promising to share any new information with one another.

Jack headed back to meet with Susan and Josh for lunch. All too soon he would be back to sea and diving at the Forbidden Reef, something he was looking forward to.

The days flew by and almost before he knew it, Jack was on his way back to Freddy's Cove. He and Carl would be taking the *Freeman Barnes* to the Santa Barbara commercial fishing pier for fueling and to pick up the remainder of the crew. Once that was completed the *Freeman Barnes* would be on its way back to San Miguel Island, and this time to do some serious searching for underwater treasure. Jack had to admit that the prospect was exciting.

Chapter Fifteen:
UNDERWATER EXPLORATION BEGINS

With the use of the starboard bow thruster and hard starboard rudder, the *Freeman Barnes* moved gently sideways until it came to a rest less than a foot from the fuel pier. Carl seemed to be getting better at this as time went on. Scott put out the fenders while Jack and Robert cast the mooring lines to the workers on the pier.

While the fuel tanks were being topped off, Richard and Michael boarded the ship and went below to store their gear in their respective rooms. They were both surprised when Jack informed them that none of their personal diving gear would be needed unless they had equipment they were reluctant to part with. All divers seem to be like this; they have lucky swim fins or whatever that they cannot be without while submerged. For example, Jack had an eight-inch stainless-steel stiletto, razor-sharpened on both sides, which he never failed to take with him on every dive. Richard and Michael were both again surprised when they found out that all the wetsuits were made in the diving room, custom fit to each diver. They were surprised yet again when they were fitted for urine bags. One of Jack's rules was no urinating in the water. The divers were to use the urine bags and bring them back to the diving bell for disposal. The reason was simple: urine attracts predators such as sharks and orcas. This was a mild discomfort compared with what could happen were they to attract a school of blue sharks or a pod of whales, and everyone understood this.

It was Carl's plan initially to set a course for the southern tip of Santa Cruz Island and hold that heading until the *Freeman Barnes* was well past the Forbidden Reef to the west of San Miguel Island. He would then sail back to the northwest to a point where the ship could make a leisurely approach to San Miguel Island and the entrance into the Forbidden Reef. There was a good reason for this. Carl wanted to search for the mystery ship or anything else lurking beyond the horizon, with enough advance warning to take whatever steps were necessary. His past experience with Ramon and the strange ship shadowing the *Freeman Barnes* earlier was still fresh in his mind. Carl didn't plan to be placed in that position again.

With the fuel tanks topped off and all the crew on board, Carl started the lead engine. He then turned full port rudder and 20 percent power, while engaging the port bow thruster to 1,200 RPMs. There were several minor adjustments made before the *Freeman Barnes* moved sideways away from the pier. Once the pier was safely cleared, Carl increased the port thruster to 3,600 RPMS while giving full starboard rudder to the ship. The result was a smooth transition as the *Freeman Barnes* rotated 180 degrees and then entered the channel leading to the open sea. Carl hadn't lost his touch.

Once the breakwater was cleared and the *Freeman Barnes* entered the tranquil waters of the southern California Pacific Ocean, Carl continued to cruise on 20 percent power while Leonard turned the radar up to maximum range. With this completed, Leonard began taking satellite images of the surrounding ocean. It was another of those amazing southern California days with the wind at a steady 12 knots from north northwest and three-foot seas, almost like a lake.

Once Leonard reported that there were no dangers within 30 miles of the *Freeman Barnes,* Carl passed the order to standby to unfurl the mainsail. The crew had improved dramatically since the shakedown cruise, and with the help of two additional experienced sailors, the mainsail was quickly raised and set. Once more a cheer went up by all hands when the sails filled and the ship began moving through the water. Next the jib was set with full canvas. The *Freeman Barnes* was then cruising at seven knots, and more sail would be needed. Carl passed the word to unfurl and set the mizzen sail which was also done with dispatch. With the addition of the mizzen sail, the *Freeman Barnes* increased its speed to a steady ten knots, a very respectable speed for such a large craft. The lead generator was engaged and the ship's power was transferred from the main engine, which was then shut down. There was no point to burning extra fuel when the wind could be used so efficiently.

It would be late morning of the following day when the *Freeman Barnes* gingerly approached the Forbidden Reef. The sails had been furled and the ship was back on main power. Both engines were in use at this time as an added insurance against the unknown. The Forbidden Reef seemed to be calling to them this day, or this is what many thought; but all could agree that just coming back here gave most of them the creeps. That is, all but the new crew members, who were just thrilled to be here and able to participate in this new diving adventure.

A check of the almanac called for a low tide in two hours, then another one 12 hours later. Carl elected to lay off the reef until the low tide had come and the currents had subsided, then move into the reef and work from three p.m. till seven, after which it would be too dark to work. There was not much time this day, but there was nothing anyone could do about it. It would be a good time for training the diving crew to use all the new gear that most had never seen before. The following week the tides would begin migrating to a more favorable time with respect to the sunshine. It would lengthen the diving time dramatically, with better sunlight. All the crew members knew that they could only play the hand that was dealt them. Although all were anxious to succeed, there was no point in stewing over the elements.

While the *Freeman Barnes* was lying off the reef, Jack and Robert began assembling the decompression chamber; and with help from Richard and Michael, it was soon up and functioning. There was still time to add two more of Carl's brainchildren to the already formidable arsenal. The first was two body heat restoring shirts. These were made on the same principle as an electric blanket but were waterproof with a soft rubbery surface. The chilled diver took off the top piece of his wetsuit, then put on the heating shirt. In less than five minutes the lost body heat would be restored and the diver would be ready to resume his underwater duties. Everyone liked the idea but it was yet to be tried. It would become standard equipment inside the diving bell provided it would work. All of Carl's inventions worked in principle, but some needed minor refinements.

The second brainchild was an air heater for the diving bell. This was constructed on the same principle as instant hot water and was set in line with the air hose that would provide compressed air to the diving bell. The compressed air was passed through heating coils which heated the air to 75 degrees during its journey to the diving bell. There was substantial moisture loss during this heating process, so warm freshwater taken from the ship's freshwater system was misted into the chamber concurrent with the warmed air. It was actually quite refreshing and comfortable to those in the diving bell. Carl had missed his calling. He should have been an inventor. So many things on the *Freeman Barnes* were like this heating arrangement. The genius was in the simplicity of the devices.

Much of the diving equipment to be used on the *Freeman Barnes* was either state-of-the art or beyond, if it was another of Carl's creations. The communication facemasks were somewhere in between, and needed some instruction in their use. The demand regulator mouthpiece was part of the facemask, and the proper method of communicating was to disengage the mouthpiece then speak as clearly as possible then put back the mouthpiece to draw a breath. The mask would move forward from the face without breaching the water seal, and required the use of one hand to remove and replace the regulator mouth piece. One can imagine that there was little idle conversation among the diving crew but the real prize here was verbal communication. This was something few of the divers on board the *Freeman Barnes* were fortunate enough to have experienced in the past. Then there were the special depth gauges that noted the depth and time at each depth which they in turn converted to cumulative decompression depth and time for the diver. The standard gear included timers, compasses, and homing devices that all needed to be mastered by the divers. There would be no forgiveness for the diver who failed to master and use the equipment issued him. The lives of their fellow divers could depend upon their ability to function in this hi-tech environment. On this rule, both Jack and Carl were inflexible.

Then finally Carl introduced his crowning achievement of invented diving equipment, the personal-defense weapon that all divers were issued that same afternoon. Up to this time there had been no mention of how the divers were to protect themselves if faced with an attack by one of the many predators who frequented the reef. Carl called it simply the "weapon of the future," and maybe it was from a diver's perspective. He got the idea from listening to Jack talk about Freddy Steele and the resources Freddy had used to defend himself while underwater. For lack of a better word, Carl came up with a handgun of sorts. The propellant was CO_2 taken from a three-inch cylinder and capable of ten charges before depleting itself. This was the greatest improvement from Freddy's design—CO_2 in place of stretched rubber. It increased the range of the weapon from 15 feet to 50 feet and eliminated the time needed to reset the rubber. Carl originally installed a small meter on the cylinder to indicate the charge remaining, based upon the weight of the cylinder underwater. This was completely unreliable and soon abandoned. The cylinders were normally changed after five shots were expended and every diver carried several extra cylinders. This handgun fired eight-inch spears with a shotgun charge on the tip, magnum-loaded with 4/0 buckshot. The spears were fletched with four-inch feathers for stability in flight, but this is where the similarity ended. One spear at a time would be loaded on the gun, then the shotgun charge was armed with a half-turn to the right once the spear was in place. There were sights of sorts on the weapon but it was more of a pointer than an aimer. When fired underwater the projectile would travel horizontally for 50 feet easily. It took only three ounces of pressure to detonate the charge. Carl demonstrated the weapon by firing it into an open area underwater, where it finally lost its impetus and drifted downward to the ocean floor. Upon contact with the seafloor, the charge detonated and fired the buckshot. Each diver was issued five rounds, four attached to the holster and one in the weapon unarmed. The weapons were carried on a thigh holster, which was out of the way but easy to reach. Carl had all weapons cached in the diving bell and the divers would pick up their assigned weapons at the beginning of each dive.

There were many sighs of relief among the diving crew knowing that they could now defend themselves from the minions of the deep. Like all weapons of self-defense, these weapons were seldom used. However, there were occasions under the ocean when the need for self-defense was vital, and this was the time when Carl's inventions were appreciated the most, when there was a real need for them.

It was a busy afternoon learning about all the new gadgets and getting comfortable with them; but then this was rapidly becoming an exceptional crew, and all were beginning to focus on the real reason for being here: treasure recovery.

All too soon it was time to leave the Forbidden Reef for the night. It took 20 minutes to raise the diving bell and as soon as it was on board, it was secured in place on the deck. The *Freeman Barnes* had its engines warmed up and left the area soon thereafter. With the computer in control, the ship was free of the reef in little time and headed for its night anchorage. There was a deep sheltered harbor near the reef that was large enough to accommodate a tour ship, and this was the destination of the *Freeman Barnes*. From this vantage point the radar could be used at its maximum range. The next morning, moorings would be set up in the harbor to speed up the nightly docking ritual. This was also the same harbor where Freddy Steele came for clams and where Jack went ashore and climbed the steep hills to the crest of San Miguel Island years ago. It was now generally referred to as Clam Harbor.

Jack gazed wistfully at the Island that night, wishing that he could spend some time there. He knew that the time would come when he could go ashore, and he was looking forward to it. Carl was no slave driver and insisted upon allowing the crew leisure time. Jack knew that as soon as the crew settled into routines and continued to improve their performance daily, this would translate to free time for him.

The next morning as the sun was signaling its pending arrival to the waters surrounding San Miguel Island, the diving crew was already preparing to install the moorings for the *Freeman Barnes*. This task had been duplicated at Freddy's Cove then once again at the Forbidden Reef. It was now becoming a routine procedure. The crew was diving without the use of the diving bell that morning, as they labored both fore and aft of the ship with chain, ropes, and buoys. While Jack was working with the chain he glimpsed the outline of a large fish moving in their direction. As it came nearer Jack could see that it was a blue shark, and it was a large one. Jack watched the shark change its direction and head for Carl, who was completely unaware of the danger. There was no time to fumble with the facemask to issue a verbal warning to Carl. Jack armed his hand weapon as he swam toward the shark on an intercept course. Blue sharks were unpredictable and anything was possible when one of these predators was hunting. They were always very dangerous creatures and needed to be avoided whenever possible. He could see that the shark would pass well in front of him, but something needed to be done quickly. From his days in the hunting lodge in British Columbia, Jack had learned how to lead birds in flight very effectively, but underwater was totally different. There was no time to think or calculate, so Jack did what he called a SWAG (scientific wild-ass guess), and fired the weapon. The shark leisurely swam into the path of the projectile, which exploded on impact, killing the predator instantly.

All the divers including Carl froze in their places at the sound of the explosion. There was a confusion of voices on the radios wondering what had happened. It was Carl who was the first to realize what had just transpired, as he noticed the body of the shark floating upside down near him, slowly descending to the ocean floor. He quickly gave a thumbnail account to the other divers of what had just happened. No one realized until then just how effective this new weapon really was. Jack had just killed a 300-pound blue shark with a single shot from the new weapon.

All the divers were giddy with excitement as they returned to the *Freeman Barnes* that morning. It was now proven beyond a doubt that this latest invention of Carl's was the cat's pajamas. Everyone now felt a higher level of security while submerged, with this new weapon in possession. There were many questions directed to Jack that morning about how much to lead a shark and so forth.

All Jack could say was, "Unlike a bird that flies through the air at a set speed, a fish in the water can move as fast or as slow as it wants to. On the bright side, the fish had no experience of the projectile being dangerous."

Although the shark saw the projectile coming, it did not register it as a threat. How long this would last was anybody's guess. The next diving window on the reef would be arriving in three hours, and this time the divers would be using the sleds.

Carl had laid out a search grid that would ultimately cover the entire reef, an area of almost ten square miles. Much of the preliminary work would be done with the sleds, and the crew would have yet another piece of high-tech equipment to master. On the positive side, the sled could cover one-third square mile in one day, provided that there were no killer tides to run from. In reality, the crew would be lucky to cover half that distance, but the potential was always there to do better. With the addition of the two new crew members, there were now six experienced divers to divide the workload up. Jack, Robert, and Michael became one crew and Carl, Scott, and Richard the second crew.

With the sled programmed to follow grid coordinates and the diving bell in place, the actual exploration began without fanfare that morning. Jack and Robert were on the sled while Michael was manning the diving bell. This was his first dive in the diving bell, and he was completely mesmerized by the abundance of sea life in the lagoon. There were several small schools of dolphins frolicking near the diving bell, and some of the younger ones would surface in the center hole to check out Michael. It was such a diversion that he had to force himself to concentrate on the tasks he was there to perform.

There was a 20-foot antenna on the sled that protruded above the surface of the ocean and continually monitored the course by the use of satellite technology. Jack and Robert were lying comfortably in a prone position on the sled with safety straps holding them in place. They were using the oxygen supply from the sled itself, with their filled but unused tanks safely attached nearby. Although the computer was guiding the sled, either Jack or Robert could override the controls instantly if needed. Occasionally it was needed when the sled neared one of the many underwater rock promontories that lurked, uncharted, just beneath the surface of the ocean. In addition to viewing ahead of the sled, there was a transparent bottom on the front third of the craft, allowing viewing of the ocean bottom as the sled passed overhead. All who used the sled agreed that it was always quite a show for the divers.

There is something vaguely familiar about all of this, Jack thought as the shed cruised over and around the jagged tendrils that had claimed so many ships in the past. *I just can't put my finger on it yet, but it will come to me eventually.*

Midway into the programmed route of the sled, Robert pointed to something out of place on the reef, and Jack took manual control of the sled to have a closer look. Michael was on the radio immediately, inquiring about the interruption of the program.

"We're stopping to have a look at something unusual and will be here for several minutes before we resume our course," Jack said. "Stand by for further information."

Whatever it was, it was bright red with a touch of green and was lodged in a crevice in 60 feet of water. Jack maneuvered the sled downward in a gentle spiral and came to rest on the ocean bottom within ten feet of the object. It was then that Jack recognized the object they had spotted from above. Here were the remains of the *Betty Lou,* such as they were: A single piece of the plywood stern planking with the letters ***BETTY L*** still visible in red letters with a green outline. The wood planking was jammed into a rock crevice that was holding it fast in place, but Jack could see that before long it would loosen and be swept to the ocean depths by the currents. Robert knew nothing of the *Betty Lou* and was puzzled by Jack's reaction to the sight of the wreckage. Jack realized that attempting to free the plywood would only destroy it. It was better just to take several good pictures and leave it where it was found. Jack picked up the portable sled camera and took four digital photographs at different angles, then transmitted the photos to Michael.

"How do the photos look for clarity?" Jack inquired.

"They're all pretty good, Jack," Michael returned.

"Send them to Carl immediately and ask him to print them; he'll know why," Jack said. "We'll be resuming our programmed route soon. How are the images and the data coming in?"

"The images are excellent, but I'll need to call Leonard about the data and let you know what he says," Michael answered.

"OK, please do that. If it is necessary to make adjustments, we'll need to know right away," Jack said.

The sled rose to within 16 feet of the surface and remained there until the surface antenna picked up an adequate number of satellites. Then it was off once again on its programmed route.

"What was that all about?" Robert inquired.

"That was the remains of the *Betty Lou,* and answers the question of its and Freddy Steele's disappearance several years ago," Jack answered. "You and I would not be doing this search right now without the pioneering work done by Freddy Steele. Rarely do any of us have the opportunity to choose the manner of our own deaths, but I think that Freddy did just that. May his soul rest in peace," Jack said reverently.

"Amen," Robert said as the two turned back to the day's assignment.

Robert Harvey was originally from Bridgeport, Connecticut and this was the farthest he had been away from home since his stint in the United States Navy. He had been a Navy Seal and had logged more hours underwater than the entire crew combined. Robert had participated in many covert combat missions during the Vietnam War and had spent 12 years in the Navy. Why he opted not to continue with this career was something he never talked about. Upon discharge, Robert enrolled in a trade school and became a first-class diesel mechanic. It was work that he enjoyed and he was very good at it, but he never lost his love of diving.

There was a time when Robert had a wife and family, but that was another thing he seldom talked about. He was always cheerful and thoughtful and was a favorite with the crew. Robert was fiercely loyal to Carl and performed many duties that were not covered in his job description. Robert was also a tireless worker and was forever up to the tasks assigned him. He was a valuable shipmate and venerated by all. Jack was also beginning to rely on Robert's can-do attitude and had begun to shift administrative duties into his capable hands.

The sled was continually transmitting data and photographs, taking precious metal readings, recording their locations, and completing a host of other chores as it went about its assigned tasks. The sled cruised over, through, and around the reef obstacles, sometimes on the preprogrammed course and sometimes on the manual override. It was taking Jack and Robert to places never before seen by humans, and it was all spectacular. This entire section of ocean had been dry land during the last ice age; and because of this, there were stunning vistas of sheer cliffs and ancient waterways to be observed by the two adventurers.

"Now I know what the Star Trekkers would feel like, if they were real," Robert commented.

"I agree," Jack said as they continued over the jagged and tortured underwater seascape displayed before them.

And so it went that first morning; then all too soon, the second crew arrived and the journey over the Forbidden Reef ended for the day for Jack and Robert. It was taken over by Carl and Scott, who continued on through the afternoon until the coming of the low tide forced them to conclude all operations for the day.

Jack and Robert arrived back at the diving bell and docked the sled where it would serve as a backup while charging its batteries and replenishing the air tanks. The two entered the diving bell, checked in their weapons, and then tried out the heating shirts. After several minutes both were comfortably warm.

"Score another one for Carl," Jack said with a smile.

All three divers vacated the diving bell and rose up to the decompression level required by the day's dive. Soon all were back on board the *Freeman Barnes* as another successful diving event had been completed.

The crew fell quickly into the duties and responsibilities assigned them as the daily diving regimen became routine. During this time the skill of all of the crew members continued to improve. They were becoming a team while working more closely together, and before long they were able to second-guess each other's needs. Because of the vigorous schedule while working within the limits of the changing tides and the available sunlight, Carl declared a day of rest for the crew. This was the first time Jack would be able to go ashore and explore San Miguel Island once again. It was something he had been looking forward to since he first arrived here.

The crew didn't waste any time setting up a barbecue/picnic on the beach near where the *Freeman Barnes* was moored. Robert and Rena teamed up to make sure the entire crew had everything they desired. Fresh clams were dug and placed in freshwater and lobsters were caught, as well as local fish. All the seafood was fresh from the surrounding waters, including some pink abalone. Jack demonstrated to the crew how to harvest these delicious treats from the ocean and how to prepare them for cooking. Before long, cooking fires were set and clam chowder was slow cooking, while the fish and lobster were grilled. The abalone were sliced, tenderized, lightly oiled, then seared in a hot frying pan for 15 seconds on each side. Everything was delicious and the entire crew let their hair down and enjoyed themselves. Nobody left hungry that day.

Jack could see that the party was doing well without him. Without further ceremony he let Carl know that he was going for a walk on the island and might not be back until dark.

Carl said that a raft would be left on the beach for him if the party ended; but if he chose to be gone all night, that would be all right as well.

With a bottle of water and some wheat crackers in a baggie, Jack set off on his solitary pilgrimage to the upper reaches of the island that had called to him. As before, Jack was surrounded by an amazing peace as he reached the summit of this small island. Spring was in full bloom there, with thick green grass sprinkled with a delightful variety of wildflowers. Everywhere one looked there was a profusion of colors, which added to the peace that Jack felt that day. He knew with certainty now that his experiences from 20 years before were not just his overactive imagination. Whatever was here was real, and it was all good. He was being drawn to the west as before, and this time he was not so reluctant to move in that direction. It was Jack's hope that he would discover the source of this profound peace and goodwill that surrounded him, but he wanted to do it in such a manner that the good vibrations would continue. As he thought about it, he wondered how such a positive and good thing like this could exist so near to such a diabolical place of death like the Forbidden Reef.

Jack continued westerly that afternoon, or rather, he strolled slowly while taking time to enjoy the moments along the way. The sun was hanging in the western sky and would soon be disappearing below the horizon as Jack stood before the vertical cliffs that marked the land's end, when he saw it. There before him on a prominent rock outcropping was a single carving displayed on its eastern face and directly in front of Jack. It was a cross around two feet tall on the vertical and one foot across on the horizontal. It appeared to have been here for a very long time. The rock carver actually cut material away from the outside edges of the cross, outlining it in native rock. Jack felt the edges of the cross and it was warm to his touch. He was beginning to feel that his journey was close to being completed. In the waning light Jack could see the remnants of a foot trail long in disuse. It was the late afternoon shadows that revealed that pathway to him; if it had been any earlier in the day, he would not have been able to see it.

Jack stood there tortured with indecision. He could see that the ancient footpath was near to vertical in some places and it was close to half a mile down to the rocky shoreline below. No telling how far down this cliff he would need to go to find what he was looking for. As much as he hated making the decision, he knew that it was the right one. He turned his back to the cross carving and began his reluctant journey back to the beach and the *Freeman Barnes*. Jack promised himself then that he would come back here once more and take that mysterious pathway to wherever it might lead. Jack couldn't have known then that he would be taking that pathway sooner than he expected, only under very different circumstances. Jack never spoke of what he had found and when asked, simply said that he had enjoyed an invigorating walk that day.

The *Freeman Barnes* continued the exploration phase for four more days, and then when the last day's diving activities were completed, the diving bell and the sleds were stored and secured for the trip back to Freddy's Cove. The *Freeman Barnes* arrived at the entrance to the cove at four a.m. the following morning and lay off the coast until there was better light and the crew was up. Later that morning the *Freeman Barnes* could be found safely moored inside Freddy's Cove.

Chapter Sixteen:
A QUICK SHORELEAVE

Most of the crew would be taking two days off before the duties and responsibilities of resupply put the crew back to work again. Susan was waiting that morning with the Suburban, ready to take those weary sailors back to Santa Barbara for some well-deserved rest. Robert and Rena would remain with the *Freeman Barnes* for the first day, and then they would be relieved by Scott and Richard. Once Robert and Rena were back in Santa Barbara, the resupply engine would be back in full swing. The two were already placing orders from the *Freeman Barnes* for items that required some lead time.

For Jack, Susan, and Josh it would be a time for family activities that all looked forward to. Both Susan and Josh would be onboard the *Freeman Barnes* for the next two-week cruise to the Channel Islands. The past two weeks of exploration had been uneventful but very productive for the crew, and the consensus was that the danger was a thing of the past. Josh had been taking scuba diving lessons for some time and had just received his certification—not bad for a 12-year-old. He was so excited about the prospects that he could barely contain himself, and the same could be said of Susan. This would be the first opportunity since

Josh was born for her to do some serious diving at the Channel Islands.

Jack, however, was not convinced that their troubles were in the past. That night he called Norm Bennett and invited him to breakfast the next morning. It was time for another briefing; and Jack wanted to know if Ramon, Juan, and James had been apprehended. If not, what were the prospects of this happening in the future? This and many other pertinent questions rattled through Jack's mind. He couldn't allow himself to believe that these three outlaws would not be back to pose another serious threat to the crew of the *Freeman Barnes*. His instincts were clearly signaling him that there were stormy times ahead, and it was with great reluctance that he agreed to allow his loved ones to be exposed to potential harm. Then again, it was only potential harm; and when the sun shines, it soon becomes a perfect world again.

This time it was Jack, Susan, and Josh who were waiting for Norm in the restaurant that morning.

"How's it going?" Norm said as he sat down at their table.

"Same table, different day," Jack responded with a smile.

"Yeah, some things never change, and you three are one of those things," Norm replied.

With greetings and social amenities completed, Jack came directly to the point. When something was on his mind he was quick to speak of it.

"So, have you picked up those three fugitives yet?" Jack asked.

"Unfortunately, we have not. These punks pulled off their second disappearing act since being picked up in the Gulf. It's not that we haven't been using all of our resources to apprehend these lowlifes," Norm said. "They've been staying one step ahead of us, as though they're reading our mail."

"That's what worries me the most. These people are smart and they have good instincts," Jack answered. "Have you considered the possibility that they may have other resources at their disposal that you are not aware of?"

"Yeah, I've thought of that, but so far we're batting zero," Norm answered.

"What about the Coast Guard?" Jack asked.

"That's the bright spot. Beginning next week there will be a cutter near the Channel Islands. That's both the good news and the bad news. A Coast Guard cutter is a very busy vessel; and if they get a call, they gotta go. You know that. But they are taking a special interest in this one, because of the killing of the seaman in Florida," Norm stated.

"Well, that's something. I do feel a little better now. For the next two weeks, Susan and Josh will both be aboard the *Freeman Barnes*," said Jack.

"Is that right, Josh? Are you a diver, too?" Norm asked.

"I just got certified." Josh gushed with excitement.

"That's truly impressive," Norm stated solemnly.

The four friends finished breakfast and said their goodbyes. Norm headed for his office, and Jack, Susan, and Josh took a drive up the coast to Santa Maria. The weather was so perfect it was difficult to stay in a glum mood for long. The three spent the day enjoying each other's company while talking about San Miguel Island and the diving on the Forbidden Reef. That night Susan informed Jack of some interesting new possibilities to be considered.

"Jack, do you remember the conversation you had with Carl concerning whether or not the *Freeman Barnes* could withstand the inrush currents of the low tide?" Susan asked.

"I certainly do, Susan. What about it?" Jack queried.

"Well, I did some math on it and then had the numbers verified at the university. The answer is yes, it is possible, provided the bow line has adequate strength to hold the ship," Susan said.

"What would be considered adequate?" Jack asked.

"The two inch rope and the chain will need to be replaced with half-inch thick case-hardened chain all the way from the underwater rock to the ship's bow. It can be done, but this is what will be needed," Susan finished.

"Thank you for that information, Susan. I'd better call Carl with this. He might want to add that extra bit of insurance, even if we leave the chain out of sight on the ocean floor and only use it in an emergency," Jack said.

Almost a thousand miles to the south of Santa Barbara, in a small natural harbor known as San Marcos, an aged freighter rested at anchor. The boat *El Chaparral* was flying the Mexican flag, but it was actually from Columbia. A little cash in the hands of the harbormaster worked wonders in Mexico. It was here that Ramon, Juan, and James could be found having dinner with the boat's captain, Miguel Mendez, while plotting their next move against the *Freeman Barnes.*

"I think it's too risky," Miguel stated flatly.

"No, it's not; it's a chance to score some gold in addition to that boat," Ramon replied. "I watched them program the ship's computer for the way in and out of the reef. The only problem was that I never got the chance to take those coordinates out of the computer. That *cabron* Jack was on to me by then."

"I don't like spending any more time than I have to, that close to the United States mainland. If they find out we're there, they'll send the Navy after us. That's more trouble than I need right now," Miguel retorted.

And so they argued that evening until Ramon finally reminded Miguel that he really had no choice in the matter. Ramon was in charge by virtue of his power and status within the cartel. Miguel eventually came to realize this and relinquished his authority to Ramon. If Ramon wanted to do this, it was his call. Miguel was unwilling to risk disfavor by refusing to follow an order given by Ramon. Tomorrow *El Chaparral* would begin another journey northward, and its final destination would be San Miguel Island.

It was early the following morning when the *El Chaparral* weighed anchor and left the San Marcos harbor. Miguel set the autopilot on a course north northwest. It was his plan to travel back to the island group in the international shipping lanes 50 miles out from the mainland. This heavily-traveled route would allow the *El Chaparral* to blend into the general traffic and arrive unnoticed at its destination. They should arrive in the vicinity of the Channel Islands within seven days.

There were 12 crew members onboard *El Chaparral*. They were mostly stevedores from Latin America, whose job it was to carry heavy loads from the holds of the ship to the main deck, where hoists would then transfer the goods to waiting craft, or vice versa. They were big and they were strong, but mostly they were a mean bunch of cutthroats, a perfect fit for this enterprise in which they all willingly participated. When these 12 were added to the captain's and Ramon's crew, there were then 16 bad hombres, all willing to do anything they felt was necessary to achieve their goals.

Although *El Chaparral* had no guns mounted above deck, it had some surprises up its sleeve, with the capability to destroy or damage any craft that challenged it. There were four fully-armed torpedoes on board that were hidden in the lifeboats. These torpedoes could be launched from the deck. Once in the water, they homed in on the noise made by the screw of the target ship. There were two ways to stop them, the first being a command from the *El Chaparral*, and the second being the launch of a torpedo from the target ship to intercept and destroy the launched torpedo before it arrived and detonated. Chances were very good that the second alternative would either fail or not happen at all.

Then there was the small-arms arsenal, well-hidden within the bulkheads of the *El Chaparral*. There were 20 M-16 fully-automatic assault rifles with 2,000 rounds of ammunition, and four air-cooled rapid-fire machine guns, also hidden on deck along with 10,000 rounds of ammo for each weapon. Every member of the crew had a handgun and knew how to use all of these weapons with expertise.

The day when the *El Chaparral* began its return journey to the Channel Islands, the *Freeman Barnes* had just returned to Freddy's Cove for supplies. Four days later the *Freeman Barnes* was en route back to San Miguel Island, completely unaware of the danger bearing down on it from the south.

Chapter Seventeen:
SUSAN AND JOSH

As the sun was rising over the Pacific Ocean from the east, the *Freeman Barnes* could be found approaching the Forbidden Reef. The low-tide currents had ended two hours earlier, and the crew was looking forward to a productive day's work. The ship's helm was given over to the computer as it flawlessly guided the ship through the channel and to the waiting moorings. As the diving crews labored to launch the diving bell and the two sleds, Jack and Carl moved unobserved to the bow of the boat. The crate resting on deck was opened, and 200 feet of case-hardened steel chain was quickly lowered onto the ocean bottom, where it would remain until the diving crews were dispatched for the day. Susan was taking Carl's position on the sled today, and Jack would not be needed until the second shift began.

The diving crew was becoming self sufficient and before long the diving bell was at the proper depth, with both sleds docked in their places. Susan and Scott would be on the sled that morning with Michael manning the diving bell. Josh would be hanging out with Jack and Carl while they went about the task of installing the reinforced chain assembly. It was not that they didn't trust the other crew members; it was just that if someone truly doesn't know something, the secret cannot be told. Both Carl and Jack considered this another card to play if it ever became necessary. These two were not yet buying the theory that the danger was a thing of the past. When you thought about it, this was their job—to anticipate dangers and provide for any possibility.

The chain was laid out to its full length and then double-wrapped and bolted to a sturdy rock outcropping. The boat end of the chain was tied to a three-quarter-inch nylon rope, which was unobtrusively tied to the mooring buoy. When they finished there were no out-of-place objects to attract attention. The rope could be reached using a rope hook from the boat and then threaded through the reinforced anchor-chain opening. From that point on, the rope could be pulled up by hand, and then the chain, which would be secured to the bow clevis with a bolted shackle also made of case-hardened steel.

Before leaving the water Jack took Josh down to the diving bell to hang out with Michael for the balance of the morning diving shift. Josh was beside himself with the wonder of it all: first the underwater seascape, then the comfortable surroundings in the diving bell with the sea creatures moving about. What could be a better adventure for a 12-year-old? Jack and Carl surfaced and went to the bridge to review the patterns emerging from the survey of the reef, now that this chain-laying chore was completed.

Josh was soon engrossed with the presence of a band of frolicking harbor seal cubs. These young sea creatures playfully nudged Josh as they swam circles around him, playing a game of tag or something like it. It was also quite a show for Michael, who had never seen anything like this before. When Josh finally re-entered the diving bell, most of the cubs followed him into the enclosure and were equally captivated with the wonder of the inside of the diving bell. Before long these pups were off to other adventures on the Forbidden Reef, as additional sea creatures came and went in the lagoon. It was an unending kaleidoscope of sea life that none of the divers took for granted. One could say that it made this job one that many workers would pay money for.

"Jack, what do you make of this?" Carl asked while showing Jack the emerging precious-metal patterns created by the data received from the sleds.

"I'm not sure what it means, but there is a familiarity here that I can't quite place," Jack said. "When it comes to me, I'll let you know."

"The most troubling thing about these patterns is that all we are seeing is barren rock formations. There is no sand, no debris from the wrecks, nothing but rocks and sea urchins everywhere you look, at the point where treasure should be located on the upper portions of the reef," Carl said thoughtfully.

"Yes, and that troubles me as well," Jack answered

"Leonard, how are the satellite images coming?" Carl asked.

"There's nothing within 30 miles to be concerned with," Leonard answered. "I'm running the satellite images continuously now, so no news is good news."

The reef survey continued on briskly and was due to be concluded by the middle of the following week. Susan and Josh were the toast of the *Freeman Barnes,* and lightened the hearts of the entire crew with their pleasant natures and their ability to find enjoyment in all things large and small.

It would be the middle of the second week when Jack finally remembered what it was that seemed so familiar to him. He woke up suddenly at three a.m., when it finally came to him what it was that he had been missing here. He wasn't quite up to waking Carl, but he thought about it. He and Susan sat up through the balance of the night going over things as the pieces of the puzzle began to fall into place.

As soon as it was reasonably permissible, Jack and Susan were at Carl's door and the three talked for the better part of an hour. When the conference was over, Carl announced that there would be no survey this day. He, Jack, and Susan would be taking one of the sleds after breakfast and would need one volunteer to man the diving bell until they returned. Although the announcement was shrouded with mystery, the crew was used to this kind of behavior; and all anticipated that something good would emerge from the change in plans. Also, it would be good to relax on deck for a while and soak up some southern California sun.

Robert volunteered to man the diving bell and offered to take Josh with him if he wanted to do some more diving. Of course Josh jumped at the opportunity to dive. He would typically swim and explore in the area near the diving bell, and then return to the bell for a respite from the rigors of scuba diving. He had quickly mastered the facemask communicator and used it almost continuously. Everything was new and exciting to him and he just had to tell anyone listening about all the things he continually observed on the ocean bottom.

Jack headed the sled to the northern edge of the reef and began slowly cruising just to the south of the first rock protrusions. The limestone here was tilted to 50 degrees from horizontal while facing the southern direction. The upper surfaces were scoured by the monster currents that ravaged the reef twice daily. What little flora was found here was both stunted and unhealthy in appearance. There had been much erosion here when this stretch of land was above the sea.

The sled cruised above some of the rocks and between many of the shallower ones on the reef as the day wore on. Jack was getting discouraged. Doubts began stretching their slender fingers through his mind. What was he missing here? Where was the similarity to one of his past experiences? Was this just another of his crazy ideas? Jack was almost ready to give up the hunt and admit to Carl that he was wrong, when in desperation he executed a gentle spiral downward below the outstretched fingers of the upper limestone appendages. He became more inspired as he continued downward, and he began to swing back to the north as permitted by the tilted rock. Finally, in 75 feet of water the sled came to a rest on one of the most amazing junk piles ever assembled. Jack had stumbled onto it by mere luck, as it was actually situated underneath the limestone cliffs by 50 feet or more. They relied on reflected light to see down here, as well as on the lights from the sled, until their eyes began to adjust to the gloom. The 50-degree tilt of the limestone cliffs effectively cantilevered over the junk pile and hid it completely from above.

Here were the remnants of almost every ship that had ever run aground on the reef, the heavy parts, that is. There were the remains of iron cannon and steel beams, but the most important thing here was the presence of gold and silver doré bars, as well as nuggets and minted coins, all scattered randomly among the rubble. It was all here for the taking, and none of this treasure could be seen from above: The riddle was finally solved. No words were spoken as Jack began a spiral up and out of the canyon and laid a course for the second tier of tilted limestone. At the bottom of this canyon there was another equally impressive pile of heavy metals similar to the first. And so it went, through seven sets of tilted limestone tiers until the ocean bottom became too deep and the tidal current to insignificant to capture more treasure.

What Jack had finally remembered was that this reef reminded him of the riffles on the eight-inch suction dredge he and his friend Freeman Barnes had worked years before on the Yuba River. What was happening here was that when the currents were flowing, the water passing over the upper portions of the limestone caused a low-pressure cell to form just below the upper face of the rock; and this low pressure caused heavy metals to drop out of the current and fall to the bottom of the ocean, just like the riffles on a suction dredge. It all seemed so simple now that the mystery was solved. Little was said as the three were silenced by the utter magnitude of the find during the trip back to the *Freeman Barnes*. Carl wanted some time to think about what would need to be done next, as this new turn of events was overwhelming for him. He asked for Jack's and Susan's silence until he had time to think about it for a while, which both readily agreed to.

The *El Chaparral* had been in the waters near the Channel Islands for almost a week now but had not been able to approach San Miguel Island because of the presence of the Coast Guard. Ramon was becoming irritable and overbearing to all of his subordinates, but until the cutter left the islands, nothing further could be done. The presence of the Coast Guard cutter bought precious time for the crew of the *Freeman Barnes,* but they were ignorant of all of this as they went about their business.

It was at dinner that evening when Carl made his announcement. Without giving too much away, Carl said that Jack, Susan, and he had located a substantial treasure trove on the Forbidden Reef and the next four days would be dedicated to the removal and storage of this treasure. The *Freeman Barnes* would then make its resupply run as usual, with another four-day turnaround to eliminate speculation by those who knew what the crew was actually doing here. As Carl spoke there was not a sound in the dining room; the crew hung on his every word. In their wildest dreams it would not have occurred to them that the result of the day's sojourn by Carl, Jack, and Susan would be this announcement.

Before Carl would allow questions he began to lay out a plan for the retrieval of the treasure, and it went like this: There would be a single shift each day with all the divers participating in the removal of the treasure. Two divers would be assigned to gather and bag precious metals, with each bag containing not more than 50 pounds of weight above water. They would be using large ore-sample bags that were sturdy and could take rough usage. If a single item weighed more than what was estimated to be 50 pounds, it was to be set aside and retrieved later. The divers bagging the metals would have their air tanks, plus two full spares each, and could expect to be relieved at the end of three hours. They would be working in 75 feet of water. There would be one person assigned to each sled for the entire day, and both sleds would be used simultaneously in this operation. Each sled could carry 500 pounds, in addition to the driver, simply by adjusting the ballast tanks. It was the driver's responsibility to secure the cargo for the return trip. Carl would be manning the diving bell throughout the day, and directing operations. Scott and Robert would alternate their duties of diving and operating the winch and bucket, with which the precious metals would be taken aboard the vessel. Tomorrow's shift would be a seven-hour marathon event, but all could see that the rewards were well worth the effort. Leonard had the most important job of all—keeping his eyes and ears on the radar and the satellite for intruders. At this point, Carl asked for questions and did his best to answer all of the concerns of the crew. Carl still had his secrets as well, by not letting the crew know that there was not one, but seven treasure locations to draw from. What they didn't know they couldn't tell anyone.

Not many of the crew slept well that night, as the possibilities of what they were about to do were overwhelming. It's funny how wealth or the prospect of wealth instantly expands the horizons of those who participate in the possibility. Lack of sleep had little effect on the enthusiasm they all demonstrated the following morning, as all had new visions of the many possibilities awaiting them in the near future.

As soon as the low-tide current subsided, the *Freeman Barnes* moved into the reef and the crew quickly set up their equipment. The first sled out was being operated by Susan, with Scott and Richard taking the first shift at loading treasure bags. Jack was also along to see that it was done properly and would be returning with the second sled, which was being operated by Michael. In less time than anyone realized, the first sled was loaded and Susan was adjusting the ballast tanks for the trip back to the ship. Once that was done, she checked the straps to insure that they were properly tightened and that the load was balanced. Susan was much like Jack when it came to details. She fully intended to deliver this cargo to its destination; and if fussing with details meant that this would happen, all the better.

She cleared the reef overhang and emerged into real sunlight again and began her trip back to the ship. Susan noticed the second sled coming and waved at Michael, who was doing a very creditable job following a compass heading to the location.

"Once you reach the tallest rock protrusion, begin a gentle spiral down the southern side of the rock. You should see the bubbles of the divers after that and know where to go," Susan relayed to Michael.

"Thanks, Susan," Michael said.

Once back at the diving bell Susan took time to wave at Josh, who was making more friends with some full-grown harbor seals, then she headed for the bucket on the ocean floor. After parking the sled, Susan filled the ballast tanks to ensure that the sled would not head for the surface when the heavy cargo was unloaded. With that completed, she unstrapped the load, and then began filling the waiting bucket. Once that task was completed, she called Carl to let those above know to raise the bucket. After three bucket loads, the sled was empty again. Susan then went to the diving bell and took two filled scuba tanks and attached them to the sled. With this done, she headed back to the reef for another load and this time was escorted by two playful dolphins. After three more trips she would need to charge the batteries of the sled, and this would allow the crew to take a break for 30 minutes while the sled was charging. Susan passed the second sled once more while en route to the treasure site and waved at Jack, who was returning with Michael and another full load.

Something should be said of the magnitude of the treasure site. From side to side it averaged 300-feet wide. No one had taken the time to measure the length of the site, but it could be as much as a quarter of a mile long. The divers were just salvaging the items lying in full view on the ocean floor; and one must remember that most of the junk on the ocean floor was just that, junk. The treasure gatherers were swimming over the ocean bottom, and when treasure was spotted in abundance, moving in and filling bags. No one had any idea of what lay at the bottom of this hole, but with the easy pickings lying around them, there was no hurry to find out. There were the twisted skeletal remains of countless vessels that unknowingly wandered into this graveyard, many of which were never reported. Jack was surprised to find a small Japanese submarine of World War II vintage, with the remains of its two occupants grinning bravely through fleshless skulls. He took the time to note the serial numbers on the hull to forward to the Japanese Embassy when time permitted. The area took on a surreal atmosphere with the indirect lighting reflecting off the limestone cliffs from above. There was no mistaking that here was a place of death and destruction. It was a place where the puny works of man were ground beneath the heel of the natural forces of mother earth. From the early 1500's until the late 1900's, this deadly reef had taken a grisly cross-section of European technology and cast it to the depths. It was as if the crew of the *Freeman Barnes* had invaded the pits of hell by coming here.

Before the first shift was completed, Scott had been forced to kill a 300-pound tiger shark that believed this area was his personal territory. These sharks grew to about the same size as the blue shark, and they were just as aggressive but not as abundant as the blues. Then later on Richard was forced to kill one of the biggest moray eels he had ever seen. This oversized bully emerged from its hole completely, with bared teeth and began stalking him.

Jack returned to the surface and directed the placement of the treasure in the ship's holds. Once he was satisfied that Robert and Rena were stowing the treasure in a shipshape manner that would not shift during heavy weather, he turned his attention to preparing for another dive. It was nearing time to relieve Scott and Richard at the treasure site, and Jack and Robert were to be their replacements for the balance of the afternoon. The two donned their gear quickly and submerged to the diving bell, while awaiting an outgoing sled to the treasure site.

And so it went, with typical Carl Webb *Freeman Barnes* efficiency. Each sled was making eight trips a day to the treasure site and returning with 500 pounds of treasure with each trip. By the fourth day of diving, the holds of the ship were filled with 16 tons, more or less, of precious metal of various kinds.

The diving bell and the sleds were quickly secured, as well as the mizzen-mast winch assembly, as the *Freeman Barnes* prepared to leave the Channel Islands. It had been an amazing four days' of treasure recovery for everyone, but now it was time to get back to the reality of visiting the mainland without tipping anyone off to the recent success of the venture. This was also a time of sobering reflection. It was a time to descend from the cloud of awaiting fortune and deal with the nuts and bolts of reality. All were affected by this, some more than others. Carl, who had recovered several treasures before, seemed to know the right words to calm the crew down, which he did on the trip back to Freddy's Cove.

The Suburban had been left on the beach in the cove, but there would be no days off during this supply run. Carl had anticipated that a treasure would be recovered and was prepared for this eventuality. He had seen to it that a building had been leased for a year in an industrial park with 24-hour access. Inside this building was a heavy-duty 2-1/2-ton dump truck and a four-ton trailer. Both were in excellent condition and were fully licensed. The name ACE Debris Hauling could be found on the building, and the truck and trailer. Only Jack, Susan, Josh, and Rena would be leaving Freddy's Cove—Jack to pick up the truck and trailer, and Rena to begin ordering and accumulating supplies for the next trip. Susan needed to get Josh back into school, and after that she was needed to run the Suburban back and forth between Freddy's Cove and Santa Barbara, as needed. She would be remaining behind for the upcoming trip to the islands.

The balance of the crew was busy moving the treasure bags from the hold to the waiting rafts, while using the same bucket that was used to pull the treasure up from the ocean. This operation would take the better part of the first day.

Once Jack arrived with the truck and trailer, the accumulated treasure was loaded by hand in both the main vehicle and the trailer. When Jack had a load, he would cover both vehicles, take two workers, and then make the trip back to the warehouse. This went on for one and a half days, until the treasure was safely stashed in the warehouse for future distribution.

Two days before the *Freeman Barnes* arrived at Freddy's Cove the Coast Guard cutter had received orders to deploy near the border with Mexico. With this ship out of the way, *El Chaparral* began making its way toward the Channel Islands once more. Finding that the *Freeman Barnes* had returned to the mainland, *El Chaparral* headed for Frenchy's Cove on Anacapa Island to lie in wait for the return of its prey.

Chapter Eighteen:
THE TRAP CLOSES

With the treasure safely secured and supplies gathered, the *Freeman Barnes* stopped briefly at the fueling dock to top off its tanks before the journey across the channel to San Miguel Island. Although Carl had been thorough and cautious with his indirect trips to the Forbidden Reef, he too was lulled by the absence of visible danger. A course set directly to Clam Harbor would have the crew in place tomorrow morning for a day's work on the reef. This roughly translated to 8,000 pounds of precious metal safely stored in the *Freeman Barnes'* hold by the day's end. In less than one week they would be coming back to the mainland with a ship filled with treasure. It was a rosy picture that the crew painted for themselves. No one thought of Ramon anymore, except Jack who could not let it go just yet. He had talked Carl into having all the crew members keep a diving mask and an earpiece in each room. It was a simple precaution, and maybe it was an over-reaction, but Jack felt better knowing that communications were possible in the unlikely event of capture.

The *Freeman Barnes* entered Clam Harbor at five a.m. and the crew tethered the boat to the moorings with routine efficiency.

The low-tide window would open in three hours, so there was time for the crew to relax.

On *El Chaparral*, Ramon had been monitoring the voyage of the *Freeman Barnes* while safely hidden in Frenchy's Cove on Anacapa Island. Now that he knew where the ship would be docking each night, a plan began to form in his head. He rightly surmised that the radar of the *Freeman Barnes* would be scanning from northwest to northeast, with all else ignored. If he moved at night, the satellites could not track him and this would give him the element of surprise, something he needed badly while up against the *Freeman Barnes*. He knew he could outgun them, but he also knew that he couldn't outrun them; Ramon needed to catch them by surprise. He decided to stay where he was for the time being and see if the *Freeman Barnes* would return to the same location the following evening.

Jack entered the bridge after breakfast to see whether Leonard had found anything suspicious, or not.

"How's it going, Leonard?" Jack asked politely.

"Everything is all right, but there are several ships I'm not sure of," Leonard said.

"Would you mind showing me those ships?" Jack asked.

"Sure, there are three boats in the yacht cove but they all look like sailboats; I'm not sure. Then there is one large craft at anchor in Frenchy's Cove that hasn't moved," Leonard said.

Jack looked at the images and dismissed the yacht cove, but the boat at Frenchy's Cove merited watching.

"Leonard, run satellite images every half hour on the craft in Frenchy's Cove. I want to know when and if it moves," Jack said.

"Will do, Jack," Leonard answered.

With that chore completed, Jack headed below to suit up for the upcoming dive.

The *Freeman Barnes* moved quickly into the Forbidden Reef with ever-increasing efficiency. The crew moved to their assignments with few words spoken. All knew what was expected of them and the tasks were now becoming routine and therefore simpler. The search for treasure had degraded into a treasure recovery in a very dangerous location. The Forbidden Reef could rank at perhaps number one of all time for the most dangerous environment to extract treasure from, but then who would rank it? Consider what would happen to the diver who was submerged when the siphon effect took place. His air would deplete in less than ten breaths. He would be in 75 feet of water, which would feel like 500 feet. His chances of survival would be very slim, and nobody really knew how this would affect him. Everything was just conjecture, a gray area that none dare enter.

The day went by uneventfully due mostly to Carl's meticulous planning. Thanks to the superb gear Carl had mustered for their use, or invented if it were not available, the assignments all seemed simple, which they were not. The hold continued to fill with treasure as the day progressed; and eventually the time arrived to leave the reef and move to the night moorings. The *Freeman Barnes* exited the reef with its usual precision and was soon on moorings once more at Clam Harbor.

Jack inquired about the ship in Frenchy's Cove and found that it had still not moved. Maybe Jack was just getting jumpy. Not long after dinner that night, most of the crew retired early, mainly because of the strenuous activities now going on daily.

Ramon weighed anchor soon after the sun dropped below the western horizon. He knew where he was going and had all night to get there. It would be five hours later when Ramon dropped anchor on the northeast side of San Miguel Island, well out of sight of the *Freeman Barnes,* but fewer than three nautical miles distant. He had handpicked the crew that would accompany him on this act of piracy. There were James and Juan because they knew the boat and the crew of the *Freeman Barnes,* and then six more of Miguel's henchmen. All were armed with AR-16s with 100 rounds each, then all had handguns of various calibers; and the six of Miguel's crew also carried nasty-looking machetes hanging off their hips. Ramon thought that *if these nameless banditos were as bad hombres as they smelled, then the Freeman Barnes was in for much trouble this night.*

He chuckled to himself while he supervised the lowering of one of the whaler lifeboats into the ocean. A small outboard motor and a pressurized gas can was then lowered and installed on the stern of the whaler. Ramon had it started and warming up as the balance of the boarding party clambered aboard. Ramon also had night-vision goggles, which he used this night. The plan was to power the whaler to within one-half mile of the *Freeman Barnes*, then stealthfully row the rest of the way in. Silence was to be maintained at all times, including while boarding the *Freeman Barnes*. There should be a stern diving ladder that was normally in place when the boat was at the islands. It could not be seen from the bridge and was the perfect place to covertly board the boat. If it were not there, Ramon had another rope ladder to use. Ramon once again reminded all that there were no weapons aboard the *Freeman Barnes*, and guns were to be used only as a last resort. He wanted all the crew alive and well for the questioning that would follow the capture.

Ramon expertly navigated the whaler around the point and directly toward the stern of the *Freeman Barnes*, a mile-and-one-half distant. All could see the lights on the bridge now and knew that their quarry would soon be in captivity. Ramon eventually turned off the outboard engine and passed the word to take out the oars. With this done, the whaler began moving slowly across the harbor to the quiet sound of the oars dipping gently in the water. There was enough residual light on the water to navigate by, so Ramon turned off the night-vision goggles to allow his eyes time to adjust before the coming confrontation.

All went as planned. The ladder was still in place on the stern and the entire boarding party silently climbed aboard. Juan and James stealthfully made their way towards the bridge. No one moved while this was taking place. James opened the door and walked in on the surprised and startled Richard, who could only stare at the gun in James' hand.

"Don't touch anything, don't utter a word," James instructed. "Lie down on the deck, face down, and put your hands behind you. Do it now, damn it!" James said with an implied threat.

Richard realized then that there was no use resisting, and quickly complied. Juan was carefully watching Richard from the outer deck and entered the bridge when Richard was on the floor.

His hands were quickly tied and a rag was placed in his mouth, and then wrapped with another foul-smelling rag to prevent him from making any noise. With this completed, James walked out and signaled to Ramon. Juan used this moment to kick Richard in the ribs. He enjoyed this part the most: when someone was helpless, Juan was always there to take advantage of them.

The hard part was now over as the pirates went into the sleeping quarters and removed the occupants one at a time, then moved them into the dining room. In an embarrassingly small amount of time, the *Freeman Barnes* was put in the hands of pirates; they had taken the ship without resistance.

Carl and Jack sat stolidly in the dining room while watching the pirates solidify their control over the ship. All seemed hopeless just then, but never underestimate the power of the human mind. The battle was won, but the war was not yet over.

Jack took a mental headcount and noticed that Rena was missing. This may or may not be a good sign. He could hear Ramon talking outside the dining room in Spanish, thinking no one could understand him. Jack had spent much time in Latin America and was fluent in both Spanish and Portuguese, something Ramon did not know. Jack wondered then what else Ramon did not know, and how this lack of knowledge could be turned against him.

"What d'you mean, the room was empty? Did you search the kitchen?" Ramon asked.

"The bed was made and there was no sign of occupancy. We searched the kitchen once and we're doing it again right now," Juan responded.

"Let me know as soon as you find that bitch," Ramon said.

Ramon walked into the room and stood in front of Jack staring down at him. Jack sat there expressionless and waited for Ramon to speak.

"Jack, you *cabron*, you tell me, where the hell is Rena? And don't lie to me," Ramon growled.

"She didn't come out with us this trip. Had appendicitis and went to the hospital instead. We're struggling along without her right now," Jack casually answered.

"If I find out that you are lying, I'll shoot you and throw you to the sharks," Ramon threatened.

Jack didn't respond.

Before long, all the crew members were accounted for, except Rena. The crew didn't know it, but Rena had been in Robert's room for the night and then went directly into the kitchen from there. The last one to arrive was Richard, who walked into the dining room spitting, having had the gag recently removed from his mouth. He tried to apologize to Carl and Jack as he held his bruised ribs, but they would not hear it.

"There was nothing you could have done," Carl said.

This conversation was interrupted as Ramon again burst into the dining room for the second time, this time with a golden goblet in his hand.

"So, you have found the treasure," Ramon stated. "How much is still there on the reef?" Ramon directed his question to Carl.

"More than you can spend in your lifetime," Carl answered.

"I don'no Carl, I can spend much money," Ramon said with a foolish grin.

Meanwhile, Rena was listening to the conversation from the safety of the ventilation ducts, a place where she quickly scampered when she heard the sound of strange voices. When the *Freeman Barnes* was boarded, Rena had been up and working in the kitchen with the intercom on. She had overheard the conversation on the bridge and had the presence of mind to grab some water and a bag of trail mix, then disappear into the air ducts. She breathed a sigh of relief when she overheard Jack explain about her illness. With any luck, these thugs would quit searching for her before long. Rena had no clue about what she could or should do next, but she knew that it would eventually come to her. Best to monitor the conversations for now, and let some water run under the bridge. Time was her friend now, and the more of it that passed the better.

Rena Schroeder had been born in East Germany at a time when Germany was still divided. Upon unification she applied for a visa to the United States, and five years later she applied for citizenship in the United States, as well. Rena was a very athletic woman who was part of the East German ski team at one time. She loved sailing and all things connected with the sea, but she had an unnatural fear of diving. Although she had signed on as the cook-housekeeper for the *Freeman Barnes,* it was her dream eventually to dive to the ocean depths and see for herself, those wonders talked about by the crew. Robert Harvey had been working with her in the evenings, and she was quickly becoming adept at scuba diving. She was a good student and was quickly overcoming her fear of the ocean depths. Knowledge was power and the more she knew, the more confident she became. She was not quite ready to speak for a position on the diving rotation, but if this expedition lasted for another month or so she would be ready.

Rena was a meticulous person and a great cook, two personal traits that endeared her to the crew. Now she found herself in a life-and-death struggle that was not of her choosing, but she was up to the challenge. As she lay there in a cramped position in the air ducts, waiting for the search to end, she swore to herself that she would unhesitatingly do whatever she must to see this piracy come to an end. Rena was not a violent woman, but for now she would become one for the impending storm that lay ahead.

Ramon had left two of his biggest and most intimidating hombres in the dining room to guard the prisoners. Jack noticed quickly that neither of the two spoke a word of English. To test his theory, he spoke to the guard nearest him on the subject of food and water. There was no response, only lack of comprehension. With that test completed, he began a conversation with Carl, while actually talking to the entire crew in a conversational tone. Neither of the guards responded, but he also knew that this would change once Ramon discovered they were talking together freely. The first subject was Rena.

"All of you remember that Rena stayed in port. Carl, this may be our best chance to communicate. Everyone monitor the facemask intercoms, and don't get caught with the earpiece hanging in your ear," Jack cautioned.

"All these pirates are heavily-armed and appear willing to use their weapons. They are acting as if they already knew that we were unarmed," Carl said.

As Carl began to think about it, a simple plan was beginning to form in his head. Maybe he could use this lack of weapons situation to his advantage. His thoughts were interrupted by the sound of a large vessel's diesel engines churning the water near where the *Freeman Barnes* was moored.

"That must be the mystery ship coming," Carl said to everyone in general.

Jack had been counting heads and knew that there were nine interlopers aboard the *Freeman Barnes,* but with the mystery ship approaching, that number could increase. All were heavily-armed, but only three spoke English. That had to count for something. The crew was also being treated exceptionally well for vanquished combatants. There had to be a reason for this, but at this point Jack did not know what it was. It was several hours' later when both Ramon and Miguel appeared in the dining room to speak to the crew members. Ramon made it clear from the beginning that it was he who was in charge of both the *Freeman Barnes* and *El Chaparral.* Miguel spoke limited English and spent the entire session glowering at the vanquished crew.

"Your lives and well-being will depend upon how cooperative you become. For now it is our wish that you should continue your treasure recovery operation, subject to our supervision, of course," Ramon finished. "Carl, Jack, give me your answers now. Whatever you decide, the rest of the crew will follow."

Both Carl and Jack could read Ramon's body language, and rightly suspected that he was there to kill some of the crew. They knew that their lives hung on a thread just then. Ramon was actually hoping that one would say no, so he could kill one of them in front of the remainder of the crew, a very effective tactic to intimidate and terrify the remaining crew members into compliance. When all of this was over, he clearly intended to kill them all anyway; but right now he needed them.

"I speak for both Jack and myself when I say that we will cooperate with you in every way possible. Isn't that right, Jack?" Carl asked.

"You bet it is, Carl. We'll do anything necessary to help you," Jack replied.

Ramon looked a little disappointed. He had a particular axe to grind with Jack and was looking forward to killing him in front of his shipmates. This simple pleasure would have to keep for another time.

Carl changed the subject, saying that it was too late in the day to enter the reef due to the shallowness of the shoals near the entry point.

"We are best to begin work tomorrow morning, early," Carl said. "What we need right now is some food and bowel relief, and then some rest in our rooms until tomorrow."

To everyone's surprise, Ramon agreed to Carl's requests. After all, he had seen the amount of precious metal gathered by the crew with just one day's work and wasn't quite ready to kill the goose that laid the golden egg. The greed gremlin was beginning to rear its ugly head, and the crew of the *Freeman Barnes* welcomed the presence of this demon, especially when they all saw him reflected in both Ramon's and Miguel's eyes.

Carl and Jack had purchased precious time, and for the chump change they would be giving up to these murderers and cut-throats, it was well worth it. The coming night would be spent thinking and planning; and by tomorrow the plan, whatever it was, would be put into action. As for Ramon and his gang of dung beetles, their days were numbered as the combined intellect of Jack, Carl, and the rest of the crew were now beginning to focus on round two of the coming tempest. The two would inventory their assets, both physical and mental, and find a way to grasp victory from the jaws of defeat—or die trying.

Chapter Nineteen:
THE NEXT DAYS OF DIVING

As the crew members of the *Freeman Barnes* were finally allowed to get some nourishment and use the sanitary facilities, the mood shifted from that of dark despair to cautious optimism. It is remarkable what those simple pleasures will do to a body, and the crew was not unaffected by this gratifying boon. Ramon now had the run of the ship, and he haughtily dismissed the threat of any future action by the vanquished crew, by allowing the captives to retire to their private rooms. This was his first mistake. After all, he reasoned, these were a bunch of unarmed pacifists and no match for him and his heavily-armed henchmen.

The sanctuary of their individual rooms gave everyone hope at a time when it was needed the most. Ramon was an incredibly intelligent man and a worthy adversary, but he also knew the value of a good night's rest, especially when he expected this crew to make him wealthy beyond his wildest dreams if he could get them to produce riches for him for the next several days. The Coast Guard cutter that had kept him at bay for over a week was still in southern waters near the Mexican border. Time was on his side and things were going even better than he had planned.

All the crew excused themselves early, saying they were exhausted from the trauma and shock they had experienced this day. Soon all were in their rooms, and when things quieted down, tuned into the crew's conferencing session. Ramon had placed three armed guards in the crew quarters, but none could speak a word of English so they represented little threat. During this session Jack was soon to point out that Ramon's success with capturing the *Freeman Barnes* so quickly was also his greatest weakness. He was an egotistical and arrogant man, with much of this attitude coming from years of dealing with intellectually inferior soldiers of the cartel. He wrongly believed that he could match wits with the likes of Carl or Jack and come out on top every time. It was also pointed out that Ramon had no knowledge of the currents or the pressures generated on the Forbidden Reef during low tide. He assumed that, as Carl put it, it was too shallow to cross the shoals during low tide. When the crew thought about it, there were many things that Ramon didn't know about the hazards and the death traps waiting for the unwary diver.

There was also a sense of urgency here because it had been made glaringly clear that all of the crew members would be murdered at the close of the treasure-gathering, or the approach of the Coast Guard. By the early hours of the morning, a plan was emerging that had a chance of working. It was contingent upon the crew's ability to focus on the budding greed of Ramon and Miguel. If this plan failed, they would be left with a frontal assault against these hardened criminals, and there would be some serious casualties taken on both sides. To a person, they were willing to do this because each crew member knew that this was a fight to the death, a view not necessarily shared by their captors. All agreed that to cause the pirates to destroy each other was the best and safest course of action.

The crew was up early the next morning showing a flair for efficiency that had even Carl and Jack impressed. During the night, Rena had acquired one of the facemasks and an earpiece, and was in contact with the rest of the crew. It could be said that if they had thought they were a team before, what was emerging now was something far beyond teamwork. They cared for each other, and the stakes in losing were unthinkable. They simply had to win.

Various plausible excuses were made for waiting until the tides were favorable before entering the reef. One of Ramon's failings was to pretend that he understood something when he really didn't. He was afraid to admit when he didn't know something, because he thought that people would think he was stupid. Carl and Jack capitalized on this, while continually assuring him just how simple it was to dive underwater.

The diving bell was submerged as usual, and then the two sleds, as the crew began their underwater efforts to gather riches. As before, Carl would be manning the diving bell. He had convinced Ramon that all divers used sign language similar to the method in use by the deaf. Nothing was mentioned about the communicators. Jack and Robert would be manning the sleds. Richard and Michael would take the first shift gathering riches, then Jack and Scott the second shift. Scott was topside operating the bucket winch in the beginning. They planned not to use the ore bags this day, except when coins were involved, but to bring up in plain sight the riches taken from the depths, and leave them on the top deck for as long as possible for the crew members of the *El Chaparral* to see. Today's event was simply team showmanship for the benefit of the pirate crew. The goal was to try to generate as much greed and envy as possible among the pirates, not only in Miguel, but in his entire crew of stevedores. The treasure was the bait and the trap would soon follow, provided that the Coast Guard could remain in southern waters.

Juan, on the other hand, was a continuing problem. Without provocation he would strike the crew members with his pistol or the butt of his machete, then stand there daring the outraged victim to retaliate. Something had to be done about this or the diving crew would be incapacitated. Carl finally went to Ramon about the problem.

"Ramon, I hate to complain; but if you don't exercise some control over Juan, I won't have a crew left by tomorrow," Carl said.

"What's he doing that I don't know about?" Ramon asked.

"He's been systematically pistol-whipping the entire crew without provocation. So far he has beaten Scott, Robert, and Richard—anyone who crosses his path is fair game for him," Carl said. "You need to put a muzzle on him before he bites someone bad."

"Just keep bringing up the gold, and I'll take care of that problem right now," Ramon promised.

Juan ceased to be a nuisance immediately, and the day went by quickly, with the majority of the crew working beneath the ocean. During the workday Scott had fabricated a pouch in the diving room that was glued to the inside of the wetsuit top, and Carl saw to it that everyone coming to the surface later in the day had one of the spear handguns, with five rounds, safely tucked inside this pouch. It would pass a casual inspection, but then these pirates were convinced that there were no weapons aboard the *Freeman Barnes* so they were not looking for any. Jack made an extra trip to bring a weapon up for Rena, although he wondered if he would have the opportunity to instruct her on its use. More than likely, the weapon would need to be left for her to claim, and the instructions would follow.

As the *Freeman Barnes* cleared the reef that afternoon, Jack overheard a conversation between Ramon and Miguel, and it wasn't pretty. Miguel and his crew were getting downright nasty about watching all that gold disappear into the hold of the *Freeman Barnes* with none of them getting any of it. After all, Miguel was at risk here as well as Ramon, and was entitled to a share in the spoils. All Carl's crew had hoped for was now coming to fruition. The visible gold on the deck had done the trick. The conversations continued to become ever-more aggressive, as the two continued to argue openly over the radio. Ramon knew for sure that no one from the *Freeman Barnes* could speak a word of Spanish; and because of this, he felt safe when arguing with Miguel.

After dinner that night, Miguel showed up unannounced and boarded the *Freeman Barnes* with the remainder of his crew. They were armed and they had been drinking. This was the critical

155

moment in the plan conceived the night before by the captive crew: to negotiate rather than to begin shooting at each other. (Although, there was also a contingency plan if they did start shooting.) Carl was standing close to Ramon, ready to offer a suggestion before the confrontation got out of hand. The antagonists were standing nose to nose, and for a short time it appeared that a gunfight was imminent.

To hell with subordinating myself to Ramon, when so much money is clearly at stake here, thought Miguel.

When a lull occurred between the shouted obscenities, Carl took the opportunity to offer a suggestion to Ramon.

"You know, what might diffuse the situation here would be to allow the *El Chaparral* into the reef alongside the *Freeman Barnes* tomorrow. We could spend the day loading up the *El Chaparral*. Then they could be on their way. Problem solved," Carl whispered in Ramon's ear.

"Yeah, but would they leave then?" Ramon asked.

"Make that a precondition," Carl said.

Without further discussion, Ramon made the proposal to Miguel, which was accepted immediately. With that finally resolved, Carl gave the coordinates to Miguel for entering the reef. He cautioned him to wait until the water was deep enough over the shoals to enter the underwater channel into the lagoon.

"Tell him not to try to enter until 10 a.m., and then he'll be all right," Carl said to Ramon.

With that accomplished, Carl exited the dining room.

"Did you notice how quickly Miguel agreed to that proposal?" Jack asked.

"I sure did. He doesn't plan to leave, once he's in there," Carl answered with a smile.

Things were beginning to come together nicely, but there were still some critical items yet to decide, and only time would tell their outcome. With all of the night before to plan, Carl and Jack had contingency plans for just about everything. But still, things could go wrong and both knew it. Both of these two had underestimated Ramon once. He had taken the *Freeman Barnes* unopposed, and that was something that neither Carl nor Jack had thought possible. It wasn't just blind luck.

Tomorrow was the day when, with a little luck and a lot of grit, the *Freeman Barnes* would be liberated and the pirates vanquished. It sounded noble when the words "liberated" and "vanquished" were used, but there would be blood on the hands of the crew before the day was finished. It always came down to that. This was fast approaching the moment when the dance would begin and the innocence of the righteous would be forever lost. The difference here was that the crew would be fighting for its personal survival, while the pirates were merely fighting for personal gain. But then, innocence once lost can never be retrieved, no matter how righteous the cause.

The crew was up early the next morning. Rena had passed the word earlier that drinking water should be taken from the system and stored. At 1:00 p.m. Rena was switching the ship's water to the emergency backup water tank. This tank had been contaminated with gypsum hours before by Rena. She used a small amount of this substance for her baking as a salt substitute and as baking powder. In large doses it caused stomach cramps and diarrhea but could not be tasted in the water. It would make a nice little going-away gift for the pirates and perhaps make some of them too sick to fight. This was the best idea Rena had come up with so far, and it was not bad.

Today was the day of reckoning, and the crew felt frivolous with excitement. All went about their tasks with a new sense of purpose, knowing that their preparations were proceeding as planned. Carl had cautioned the crew not to appear too cheerful, or Ramon would pick up on it. He then waited until close to 10 a.m. before entering the reef. Setting an example now would put Miguel at ease when entering the lagoon. The *Freeman Barnes* had just begun its preliminary work for the day's diving when the *El Chaparral* lumbered past, then swung its bow to the north and dropped anchor.

One of Miguel's issues with Ramon was his use of six of Miguel's men. It wasn't that he needed them so much as that they no longer answered to him. Ramon insisted that he needed these six men to guard the prisoners on the *Freeman Barnes*. None of this controversy really amounted to anything, but it played into the plan already put in place by the captive crew. The baser emotions such as envy, greed, jealousy, anger, and rage were being nurtured here with the show-and-tell being put on by the crew of the *Freeman Barnes*. These emotions were further enhanced with each bucket of golden objects being brought up from the deep. Two of *El Chaparral's* whalers were standing by for the transfer of the wealth as it came to them from the sea.

While the first sled was en route to the treasure site, Jack took the second sled around the lagoon and made a covert visit to the anchor dropped by *El Chaparral*. He cruised silently to the main anchor and within minutes had completed a modification to the anchor chain. With that done, Jack went back to work accumulating treasure for Miguel and his gang of thieves.

Ramon wanted to dive in the waters and see for himself where the gold was coming from. He was reluctant to do so because he feared that Carl and Jack had been less than truthful with him about the dangers. While rummaging about on the bridge, Ramon came across a book entitled "Safe Diving Practices." It was a small book, more like a pamphlet, and Ramon read through it within 20 minutes. Many of the lingering questions that plagued him were now answered, thanks to this booklet.

As the day progressed the crew made certain that all items of gold were laid out in full view of Ramon on the bridge before they were transferred to the waiting whaler for transport to *El Chaparral*. Within 30 minutes of the afternoon low tide, Ramon surprised the crew. He wanted to see the treasure site beneath the sea. Why he had waited for so long nobody knew, but his timing was still good. Had he waited five minutes more, diving would have been out of the question. Jack offered to take him on a tour. He was fully decompressed and had anticipated this moment. He only hoped that Ramon had not been drinking the water on the *Freeman Barnes*; but when he thought about it, that was Ramon's problem, not his.

Scott fitted Ramon into a wetsuit with everything but an earpiece or a weapon. He and Jack stepped off the stern of the *Freeman Barnes* together, as the diving bell and one of the sleds was being extracted from the ocean. Jack's weapon was safely tucked in the pouch of his wetsuit as he and Ramon slowly descended to the waiting sled. Carl had previously pulled up the case-hardened chain and secured it to the bow. The call to action would be the strengthening of the currents, which would start in less than 15 minutes. Jack would just have time to get to the treasure site before the low-tide currents began. What would happen to Jack after that was anybody's guess. No diver had ever survived to tell about his experiences; but Ramon would be effectively removed from the leadership of the pirates, and that was huge. The big dance was about to begin, whether everyone was ready or not.

Jack loaded Ramon onto the sled and buckled him in, then proceeded to cruise on the sled in less than 20 feet of water to prevent the buildup of nitrogen in his body. He knew that he could spend another ten minutes at 75 feet and still be good with decompression; but that was the absolute maximum he could be at that depth and not suffer permanent physical damage. He could feel the first wisps of current as he turned the sled into a gentle glide to the treasure site below. As he parked the sled, he checked his watch. Ten minutes here would give him one hell of a headache, but he should be all right afterward. But then, nobody knew for sure what would happen with this siphon effect. Jack removed the key from the sled after Ramon moved away from it. Ramon was completely mesmerized by the presence of so much potential wealth lying at his feet. He swam slowly around taking everything in, while ignoring Jack in the process.

Jack had done his work earlier to *El Chaparral* by loosening the anchor from the chain, then tying a one-inch cotton rope between the anchor and the chain. This would hold the ship at anchor without drifting; but when the currents began to flow, it would quickly weaken and break.

The low-tide currents had just begun, and the crew of the *Freeman Barnes* was waiting patiently for the show to begin, which it did sooner that anyone had anticipated. *El Chaparral* broke free of its anchor and began to drift toward the southern side of the lagoon. Miguel fired the engines up and was applying full throttle in an attempt to break free of the current, but it was simply too powerful. *El Chaparral* drifted slowly onto the waiting underwater outcropping, where the hull was breached and the craft began taking on water. More of the hull was ripped loose as the currents forced the craft onward onto the next group of rocks. After the forth encounter with the underwater hazards, the *El Chaparral* began to break apart, and soon slipped beneath the surface of the ocean. If there were any survivors, they were swept out to sea or into the depths. Half of the struggle was over now, and it was up to the captive crew to take back the *Freeman Barnes* from the pirates. It was a fight that had not yet begun.

A quick headcount of the opposition left James and Juan and the six stevedores, who were all waiting for orders from Ramon. Two of the stevedores were down with an unknown ailment.

Jack could feel the increase in pressure as he watched Ramon preoccupied with the treasure and oblivious of danger. Jack knew that the sled would be safe here, but it was time for him to go and he knew it. He swam over to Ramon and got his attention. He motioned up, then removed his scuba tank and released his weight belt, while holding on to it. He knew that Ramon had to be feeling the increased pressure. Once he was sure that Ramon knew what was expected of him if he was to survive, Jack let go of the weight belt and screamed all the way to the surface. The buoyancy of the wetsuit tossed Jack completely out of the water as he surfaced. Jack's going to Ramon, coaching him on the impending danger, and demonstrating the technique of dropping his gear before bailing out, was testimony to the basic goodness of the man Jack Morgan. He just couldn't leave a helpless man to die in a place like this without giving him a chance to live, regardless if it were Ramon or whomever.

It wasn't long before Ramon surfaced in the same manner as Jack, and he was alive and mad as hell at Jack. No one had told him to scream all the way up, but somehow he knew. Ramon was still screaming as he swam menacingly close to Jack. He should have arrived with ruptured lungs, but here he was. Jack set off swimming across the current he knew would lessen as the water deepened. He could see the headlands of San Miguel Island and struck out for it. There were still several hours of sunlight, and with luck he could be ashore before dark. As he looked back, he could see Ramon following him. Ramon was not as fast a swimmer as Jack, but he was unrelenting in his pursuit, another quality that made him so dangerous.

We were right not to underestimate him, Jack thought as he turned his attention to swimming ashore.

Rena was standing in the ship's pantry facing the door with her weapon in one hand and a meat cleaver in the other, while waiting for the signal to proceed. She had been in here for about five minutes when she heard a noise that sounded like someone breathing. Was she in here with someone else? Why did whoever was here wait so long? As she was reaching for the light switch, someone grabbed her shoulder and spun her around. As her eyes focused she could see that it was Juan. She turned around slowly with the spear gun hanging loosely in her hand pointing downward, and Juan didn't seem to notice.

"Well, if it isn't the bitch, Rena. I've hated you from the start, and now it's payback time," Juan growled. "I figured you was on board all the time."

Without warning Juan hit Rena in the temple with the barrel of his handgun, and Rena slumped to the floor dazed from the blow.

If I am going to survive this, I'd better not pass out, she thought as she raised the spear gun towards Juan. He hadn't seen it yet, but he sensed that there was something wrong. There was an explosion on his chest as the spear touched home.

"The dirty bitch shot me," he said to no one in particular. These were to be his last words as he slid down the wall of the pantry into a pool of his own blood.

Rena composed herself as best she could and quickly hid herself in the kitchen inside a cabinet. She could hear someone coming and knew from the footfalls that it wasn't a friend on his way to her rescue. She heard inquires in her earpiece about what had just happened, but she was unable to answer with one of the guards still in the kitchen. He discovered Juan's body soon after arriving, then mumbled something in Spanish as he sped off to report the death to James, who was now the man in charge.

The sun had perhaps half an hour left before it would slip into the Pacific Ocean, as Jack made his way through the tide pools towards higher ground. He could see Ramon still doggedly on his trail but a good half hour out to sea.

Maybe there is a way up these cliffs, he thought. *If I can find a way up before the sun goes down, I may be able to shake him off my trail.* With that thought in mind, Jack removed his swim fins and moved closer to the rock face. After searching for several minutes, Jack came upon another cross similar to the one he had seen before at the crest of the island. It was of the same approximate dimensions and as equally aged as the first one. This time Jack was mainly interested in getting away from Ramon, and not as interested in discovering anything profound; but if the cross would help him, then that would be good also. As he looked around he could see the indentations of an ancient trail cut in the native rock and heading upward.

I wonder if those two trails are the same, he thought as he began climbing upward on the near-vertical cliffs. The trail continued on without anything being too difficult to pass over, until he stopped to rest about halfway up the cliff face. From here he could see Ramon sitting near a tide pool and recovering from the swim in. He knew that Ramon would find the trail and would be coming up after him. It would be far better for him to find a place where he could ambush Ramon, and then wait there for him to come. He noticed a switchback in the rock trail that could not be seen from below, a perfect place for an ambush. With that thought, Jack began setting up for an ambush that would have a 100 percent chance of happening. He knew that Ramon would come, sooner or later.

Rena tersely reported the incident to the crew. The situation was now at the point of no return. The stevedore had raced to inform the others, and soon the battle would be joined. Carl was heading for the kitchen when he was stopped by one of the guards at gunpoint. There was no attempt to communicate by either party. The guard moved close to Carl and pushed him backwards into the wall. Without giving an outward sign of hostility, Carl struck the guard on the underside of the nose and drove the cartilage up into his brain. The guard collapsed on the floor and died instantly. Carl took his weapons before he left and continued on to the kitchen, where he found Rena. The two then removed the weapons from Juan and continued onward to the dining hall. The odds were improving here, but they were still badly outgunned by the pirates. Two were down too sick to move, as Robert and Richard moved quietly into their rooms one at a time, then overwhelmed them and tied them to their beds while taking their weapons from them. If the battle began to go badly, Carl left instructions to kill these two in their beds rather than allow them to recover and become a threat once again.

☃

Jack could hear Ramon coming, as he waited silently above the switchback with two large boulders resting near him on the trail. It was his plan to drop the boulders onto Ramon's head, as he labored up the trail in the darkness. Finally Jack could see the outline of Ramon as he walked slowly up the incline. Unfortunately, Jack was a bad shot with the rock, and the boulder delivered only a glancing blow to Ramon's left arm. It was good enough to break the arm, but not good enough to knock Ramon off the trail. As Jack waited quietly with the second rock, a shot was fired from below. Nothing surprised Jack about Ramon, but where did he get the gun? He must have anticipated something like this and packed a gun in a waterproof container. It was time for Jack to abandon his position; and in doing so, he covered his retreat with the second boulder, which found its mark somewhere on Ramon's body, judging from the sound of the cursing going on below him. Half an hour later up the trail, Jack found the cavern.

James was staying on the bridge while trying to hold the group of pirates together. With Juan dead there was no way to communicate to these people other than rudimentary sign language.

Damn, I wish Ramon were here, James lamented to himself. He was not the sharpest tool in the tool shed; but like it or not, he was in charge. He had witnessed the destruction of *El Chaparral* and was still in shock over the complete finality of the event. He wasn't even sure if there were any survivors at all. Now he had to deal with an insurrection, and he couldn't communicate with his soldiers. They kept coming to him for advice and he had nothing to offer them in return. Then there was Leonard, who was always fiddling with the electronic equipment. At least he didn't complain and went about his work quietly. James didn't notice him most of the time. This is how Leonard was able to walk up to James and deliver a knockout blow to the back of his head with a twelve-inch piece of pipe. With James out of the way, there were just three soldiers remaining in opposition to the crew of the *Freeman Barnes*. Leonard informed Carl of what happened to James, then tied him up soundly and carried him down two decks to the single room where the two sick hombres were now being held. They were now being held under constant guard by the newly-armed members of the crew. There were still three heavily-armed men on the prowl within the confines of the ship; and although it was looking good for the crew, it was not over yet.

❧

It was a small carved enclave on the side of the vertical cliffs with a natural cavern to the rear. There was another cross above the cavern and some writing Jack could not decipher in the starlight. He had been thinking about the coming conflict with Ramon, and he knew that come the morning, he would be at a terrible disadvantage because of Ramon's gun. It would be best to fight it out here, while Jack enjoyed some protection from the darkness. Besides, he was getting tired of running from this dung beetle, Ramon. It was a time of reckoning, and Jack had been pushed as far as he planned to be pushed in this life. When Ramon arrived, Jack would attack him with the fury of a cornered

164

foe, and would run no more. Jack knew that this was something Ramon would not be expecting; and because of this, Jack would gain a small advantage in the beginning.

Jack noticed also that there was a small upper area above the cavern entrance where someone could hide unobserved, provided Ramon had no light to see with. He knew that Ramon would come into the cavern after him, as well as he knew that he would be in there waiting for Ramon when he arrived. The chase was just about over, and there would be a finality and closure when the two adversaries next met.

ೞ

Scott and Michael had set up an ambush. They were armed with the spear guns, as well as M-16s and handguns; but Carl preferred that they use the spear guns if possible, to limit damage to the *Freeman Barnes*. This was the passageway to the sleeping quarters of the pirates, and sooner or later they would be coming back here to claim their personal belongings. The two had been sitting motionless for the better part of an hour when Michael nudged Scott.

"Someone's coming," Michael whispered. Scott nodded in return.

Down the passageway came two of the remaining antagonists, creeping stealthily to their rooms. Once they were past Scott and Michael, the two reached out and fired the spear guns at a range of less than two feet. The two nameless criminals collapsed in a heap on the floor, both dead before hitting the deck. This left just one armed foe, and it was time for Carl to come forth and offer terms of surrender.

ೞ

Jack watched Ramon enter the cavern while standing just far enough outside to prevent a clean shot. Jack was armed with the spear gun and his razor-sharpened stiletto as he scarcely breathed while waiting for Ramon to advance. For what seemed like an eternity, Ramon stood in the entrance without moving.

When he finally entered, he came in with a rush while rolling behind some rocks in the darkness. For a while Jack was unsure of exactly where Ramon was. Then he heard the small sounds Ramon was making as he adjusted his position. Jack picked up a small stone and tossed it across the cavern. Soon after the stone hit, Ramon raised himself and fired off two shots aimed at the noise. He was still out of range for Jack, who after an appropriate amount of time, launched another pebble in the same general area as before. This time Ramon fired, then changed position and moved to within range of Jack. Jack didn't hesitate a moment and fired the spear gun point blank at Ramon, hitting him squarely in the upper back. Ramon staggered backward for a step or two then fell over backward to the cavern floor, dead. The hunt was over and Jack was drained. After several minutes he went over to Ramon and made sure that he was truly dead, and then collapsed on the floor and slept the sleep of the physically exhausted for the remainder of the night.

CB

Carl made his way to the bridge with Leonard and Rena accompanying him. All three were carrying loaded and chambered M-16 rifles. With one of the pirates still remaining at large and armed, anything was still possible. Carl reached the bridge without incident and turned on the ship's intercom. He then began speaking, first in English, then in fluent Spanish, as he addressed his remarks to the remaining combatant.

"This is Carl Webb, the captain, speaking. I will soon be addressing the ship in Spanish in an attempt to allow the remaining pirate to surrender. Remember that there is one remaining and fully-armed pirate still aboard the *Freeman Barnes*. Be careful," Carl said in English.

Then in Spanish: "To the remaining pirate: You must know by now that the members of your group are either dead or in our custody. To save yourself from the same fate, you must do exactly as I am instructing you in this message. Place your weapons on the deck immediately, and begin slowly walking toward the bridge with your hands on top of your head. If you deviate in any manner from what you are now instructed to do, you will be shot immediately. Thank you," Carl finished after repeating the message for the second time. In less than a minute, Michael was on the intercom.

"We have him in custody. What shall we do with him now?" Michael asked.

"Take him to the decompression chamber and lock him inside," was Carl's answer. "Then move the rest of the prisoners, one at a time, and lock them in there as well."

And so the seizure of the ship and the subsequent counterattack by the crew of the *Freemen Barnes* came quietly to an end, much as it had begun in the early hours of the morning, three days past.

ରଃ

Jack awoke to the sun shining through the cavern entrance. He was unsure how long he had been sleeping, but he was ravenously hungry and thirsty. He went over to Ramon's body and assured himself that he hadn't dreamed the events of the past night. He knew that he needed to get back to the *Freeman Barnes* for sustenance, but he would be back later to explore this cavern, and this time he would be better prepared. Jack paused at the entrance of the cavern and looked at the inscription above the entrance. *Juan Cabrillo* was all it said. Jack had one more chore to do before he left the cavern. He walked back to where Ramon lay crumpled on the floor in a death pose. Jack lifted Ramon under the arms and began moving him further into the interior of the cavern to a place where there was no sunshine and accompanying bacteria to smell up the cavern with decay. This would be Ramon's final resting place; Jack grudgingly admired his grit.

This is a fitting place for a warrior of Ramon's caliber, Jack thought. *Rest in peace, Ramon, you fought the good fight to the end.* Jack ended his silent epitaph reverently, then turned and retreated to the cavern entrance.

Jack would be back again to solve the mystery of the island and the cave when time permitted; but for now he needed to climb to the summit and activate the cell phone Norm had given him. After that, he would try to reach the *Freeman Barnes*.

Chapter Twenty:
BACK TO CLAM HARBOR

With the conclusion of the struggle for control of the *Freeman Barnes*, Carl moved off the Forbidden Reef and back to Clam Harbor. No one had heard from Jack and all feared the worst, but there was little time for speculation: he could still show up, provided he survived the siphon effect and the death currents. No one on the crew could forget that it was Jack who had performed the most valuable service by removing Ramon from command of the pirates. Jack had not been heard from since he and Ramon left on the sled just before low tide. Norm Bennett had been notified and was on his way to San Miguel Island, along with the truant Coast Guard cutter. Both would be arriving tonight or tomorrow morning at the latest, but for now it was important that the crew solidified their control over the prisoners. Carl elected to keep them in the decompression chamber until they could be handed over to the authorities. It was a safe place from which they could not escape or cause more grief for the crew. The prisoners or more specifically one prisoner, James Grey, was quick to complain about the cramped quarters being shared by the four surviving combatants; but Carl was just as quick to point out that they could be suffering from far worse than a little discomfort. When they thought about it, they reluctantly began to agree with him.

Everyone was trying to be cheerful in the face of Jack's absence and possible demise. When the call came in, Carl announced it over the ship's intercom: Jack was alive and well and on his way back to Clam Harbor. A hearty cheer went up by the crew and a few tears were shed. Carl had been putting off calling Susan, but now he hastened to do so. He was to find out that the news of the piracy attempt on the *Freeman Barnes* was breaking on the mainland, and Susan had just viewed some sketchy reports on the local news channel. Carl gave Susan a thumbnail account of the piracy attempt and asked her to call Michael's and Richard's families to let them know that all the crew were safe and well.

Carl had a raft launched and standing by for the time that Jack would be visible on the beach. When Jack arrived there would be a crew meeting about what to do next. Carl was fairly certain that the Coast Guard would quarantine the Forbidden Reef until the location of *El Chaparral* could be verified. It could be several years before the quarantine, if there was one, would be lifted; and many hard decisions needed to be made. Including all that was in the *Freeman Barnes'* hold, there was approximately 24 tons of precious metal in the crew's possession. This conservatively amounted to $105,000,000. There were sixteen shares available, with each share worth $6,500,000 or more. The share split would be three shares for the *Freeman Barnes*, three for Carl, two for Jack, and then one share each for the remainder of the crew, which included Susan French and Roland Hawke. But for now the crew needed to be all on the same page, not that they had anything to hide other than the magnitude of the treasure they had located, and the treasure now in possession on the mainland. The fewer who knew of this, the better for all, especially considering the safety issues involved on the reef. In reality, all of the crew knew that this would be a hard secret to keep, but it was one that must be kept in light of the unusual dangers facing all who ventured to the Forbidden Reef.

ɞ

Jack left the cavern after seeing to Ramon's remains, and climbed to the crest of the island. As he reached the summit, a feeling of peace and serenity again enveloped him, and it was even a little stronger now. As he continued toward Clam Harbor to the northeast, he took Norm's cell phone out of its waterproof container. He held it so that the solar batteries could begin charging, which they did within half an hour. Once the cell phone indicated that there was enough power stored to use the phone, Jack called Norm Bennett.

"Hi, Norm, this is Jack," he said politely.

"Jack, is that really you? Carl said ten minutes ago that there was a good chance you would never be seen again," Norm gushed.

"Carl doesn't know me very well," Jack responded laughingly.

"I guess not, but you need to call him as soon as you get off the phone with me. Are you all right Jack?"

"Yeah, fine, just thirsty and famished," Jack answered.

"Where are you right now?" asked Norm.

"On San Miguel Island, walking toward Clam Harbor at the moment," Jack answered.

"OK, but call Carl right away. I'll be seeing you tonight or tomorrow," Norm said.

"I'll do that right now, and thanks," Jack said as he terminated the call.

Jack was within a mile of the harbor by the time the call to Carl was finished. He knew as well as Carl that the treasure hunt was over for now, and some serious plans needed to be made for the crew of the *Freeman Barnes*.

Jack was on the beach within an hour, and the raft was dispatched to pick him up. All met in the dining room, and each had a story to tell. The first two hours were dedicated to bringing all crew members up to speed. Jack would only say that Ramon was dead and would no longer be posing a threat to any of them. When the explanations and stories were all finally told, the crew took a lunch break, but they were back at it half an hour later. It was time to get to the heart of the meeting, because the FBI and the Coast Guard would be here in the morning, and there would be no time for group discussions after they arrived.

Jack was impressed with the fighting acumen of the crew. They had engaged a ruthless and dangerous enemy when they were both outgunned and outnumbered and had emerged victorious. Of the nine original enemy combatants, there were five dead and four in captivity, with the loss of not one single member of the crew. There were three beatings given by Juan before Ramon put a stop to it; and then finally the one given Rena, who was successful in killing Juan during that battle. It demonstrated the valor of those who fight for noble causes, as compared to those who fight for personal gain.

Carl finally called the meeting to order and the crew settled in for some serious discussion.

"As you know, we will all be under the microscope for some time, and what we do and say in the next few days will have a profound effect on how we are treated by the authorities. We have killed five persons in self-defense and caused another seven to perish on the Forbidden Reef. All of these acts will be scrutinized to determine if there was any wrongdoing on our part. Our official position is that we were doing independent research on the many disappearances of vessels near San Miguel Island, and focusing our efforts on the Forbidden Reef. We will need to reveal both the treasure site we have located, and the treasure we have on board *only*—I emphasize the word *only*. The finding of the treasure has absolutely no bearing on the piracy act committed against the *Freeman Barnes*. Although it was this treasure that saved the lives of the crew initially, it was incidental to the research we were engaged in. The presence of treasure should remain confidential, and due to the extreme danger, it must not be revealed to the public. Once the initial investigation is completed, we will make one more quick trip to Freddy's Cove, and then the *Freeman Barnes* will be heading back to San Diego to the Kona Kai Yacht Harbor. We will be berthing in the yachts-in-transit section as before. We need to remain together on the

Freeman Barnes as a cohesive unit until this investigation is completed," Carl continued.

"A quick calculation on the conservative side gives each crew member $6,500,000 or more for their efforts on the Forbidden Reef. I will begin liquidating as soon as the smoke clears from the investigation. One more thing: don't plan to work in the reef for at least a year, maybe more, and don't forget, never mention the treasure to anyone. Finally, this is not a tax-evasion scheme, and all of you will be responsible for your own taxes later when the treasure money is divided up," Carl finished. With this having been said, Carl called for questions and there were many aired before the session was finally concluded.

Susan, on the other hand, was being assailed by the media. Somehow it had been leaked that she was part of the crew and possessed inside information that no one else had. Susan finally had to quit answering the door and the phone due to the volume of solicitations she was receiving from the media. She called the *Freeman Barnes* and got Jack on the phone to let him know what was happening on the mainland. This was deteriorating into a category-five media blitz, and the crew could expect to be visited by news helicopters and assorted journalists in speedboats. Carl once again calmed the crew with his good advice. He had been through similar brouhaha's in Florida, so this wasn't new to him.

Carl's rules were quite simple and easy to understand, and they went like this: "Always smile and never be rude to anyone connected with the media. Answer all questions politely and as honestly as is necessary," and finally, "Never volunteer information. These are rules to live by, both for the media and the coming investigation," said Carl. There were several flybys by news helicopters that afternoon, but they didn't stay long due to the 70-mile round trip from Santa Barbara to San Miguel Island.

The Coast Guard cutter pulled into the harbor just before sunset and dropped anchor near the *Freeman Barnes*. The cutter stayed away from the ship until it was visited by another helicopter from the FBI. It wasn't long after that a launch was dispatched from the cutter. There were three Coast Guard officers with four military police and three FBI agents present, with Norm Bennett being one of them, as they boarded the *Freeman Barnes*. All could see that this would be a very long night for everyone, and Carl was thankful that the crew had been briefed.

The prisoners were turned over to the Coast Guard immediately and there were some good-natured comments made about the high-priced holding cell Carl had detained them in. It was good to be clear of these meatheads, and the crew breathed easier with them now in the custody of the United States Coast Guard. There would be no danger of the Coast Guard repeating the lax security that indirectly launched the crime wave of Ramon and crew. The prisoners would be interviewed aboard the Coast Guard cutter and were finally gone for good from the *Freeman Barnes*. With the removal of the bodies and the accompanying cleanup, the pirate attack would be brought to a fitting close. Now it was time for the grueling interviews from the FBI that would continue late into the night. No one looked forward to this, but all knew that it was necessary and all were willing to do their part.

It would be two days later when the *Freeman Barnes* was finally cleared by the initial investigation and was given permission to leave Clam Harbor. As expected, the Coast Guard quarantined the Forbidden Reef, but allowed Carl time to remove his sled and his moorings both on the Forbidden Reef and at Clam Harbor. This was done before leaving for the mainland. Someone had found Carl's satellite phone number, and the incoming calls were so constant and intense that the phone had to be shut off. The media flap was still in full bloom and created some mild problems for the crew. Freddy's Cove and Ace Debris Hauling were still secure, and there were eight tons of precious metal aboard the *Freeman Barnes* still needing to be secured.

Carl decided to enter Freddy's Cove after dark and rely completely on Leonard's programming. It was three a.m. when the *Freeman Barnes* entered the cove, then executed a 180-degree turn and backed to the stern mooring. Within minutes the ship was secured and the crew went to work preparing the precious metal for transport to the shore. Jack had left with Susan in the Suburban to bring the truck and trailer into the cove. Jack was back in three hours and loaded up in half an hour. By 10:30 the next morning, Susan dropped Jack back at Freddy's Cove.

The plan had gone without a flaw, and within 30 minutes the *Freeman Barnes* was heading out to sea. The following day the ship moved into a berth at the yachts-in-transit section of the Kona Kai Yacht Harbor in San Diego. Within hours the media got wind of the whereabouts of the *Freeman Barnes;* and whether they wanted the publicity or not, they were all making the six o'clock news nationwide. This was the first reported act of piracy within the United States maritime territory in over 100 years and the media was milking it for all it was worth. As the personal interviews progressed, the media gravitated to Jack Morgan. His rugged good looks and his easy manner made him the most sought-after member of the crew. Jack was no media ham, but he knew the value of making a good impression and followed Carl's advice to the letter. Within a week or so, the media finally had other windmills to charge, and the crew of the *Freeman Barnes* finally got a measure of their privacy back. On another note, because of all the publicity, Jack Morgan's family members were able to re-establish contact with him. He, Josh, and Susan were treated regally by Jack's brothers and sisters at some speedily-organized family reunions.

Chapter Twenty-One:
TIME TO COUNT YOUR MONEY

The dealin' was done and all the members of the crew knew it.
The media flap had subsided to a livable level, and the entire
crew was able to participate in the inventorying and handling of
the treasure. Carl and Jack decided to divide up the coinage
among the crew, rather than get into a controversy over which
coins were the most valuable. The selections were made by blind
choices after lots were randomly drawn, and all choices had the
same weight and same gold-to-silver ratio. This eliminated any
bickering over who had the most or least valuable coin, and it
also saved Carl and Jack from risking the publicity of having the
coins appraised.

The majority of the treasure was Spanish doré bars both gold
and silver. These bars averaged 46 pounds each and contained a
little better than 60 percent precious metal. Carl had buyers flying in from around the world to visually inspect and place bids
on the items. Artifacts made of gold or silver, such as statues or
chalices, were viewed but not placed for sale at that time. Carl
paid a share to the crew for all of these items, after all agreed
upon their worth. A windfall in favor of the crew occurred when
it was determined that some of the gold doré bars were extremely

rare and attracted special attention. There were 65 bars with a feather and a crown cast into the metal; the bids went as high as ten times over spot price for these rare artifacts.

Carl had done business with all of those buyers present and knew that they were all reliable and well-heeled. The buyers were evenly split between principals and agents, and all were versed on the various values of the treasure offered for sale. Within two weeks the treasure was completely liquidated. Carl's original estimate was $105,000,000 for the value of the treasure. As it turned out, the actual net amount received was close to $125,000,000. This raised the value of each share to the amount of $7,812,500. Carl had been paid in green cash, checks, direct money transfers, cashier checks, and irrevocable letters of credit. It was his intention to begin paying dividends as soon as all the instruments of credit had cleared his bank. This also gave the crew some time to get acquainted with their new wealth and become comfortable with it.

Robert Harvey and Rena Schroeder were planning to pool their resources and buy a yacht, and then cruise to the South Pacific. Leonard Smith was going back to New England to open up his own electronics company. Scott Shepherd would remain with the *Freeman Barnes* and in Carl's employment. He enjoyed the job and it wasn't like work to him. He also liked to socialize with those who shared the same love of sailing as he, and this was the right place to do that. Richard Mitchell and Michael Munson were heading back to school in Santa Barbara and intended to remain there until they received their degrees. Roland Hawke was still in shock about his good fortune and hadn't had time to think and decide what he would do, now that he had some real options. Jack was still an unknown entity, a mystery within a mystery. No one knew for sure what motivated him, including himself. For now he was with Susan and Josh, but how long that would last no one knew. He had never revealed what he would do with his newfound wealth, perhaps because he didn't know yet.

There was another piece of magic that the entire crew had in common now: there was a bond among them that could not be broken. What they had gone through had forged a relationship beyond friendship. They would always be there for each other, and they would always stay in touch. Carl saw to that when he gave them all satellite phones with a lifetime of service, at his expense. He knew a good thing when he saw it, and this group of people was exceptional. When the quarantine was lifted on the Forbidden Reef, he would be calling them back and they knew it. Then if another project should develop in the meantime, they were all still available. They were now treasure hunters to the core, and they all knew this as well. The thrill of the hunt and the sweet taste of success had seduced the lot of them.

One might ask why someone with six million dollars after taxes would want or need anything more. It is a good question and one that deserves an answer. There are theorems of life, just as there are theorems in mathematics. (Theorem: an idea accepted or proposed as a demonstratable truth, often as a part of a general theory). One of the most famous ones would be the Pythagorean Theorem: The sum of the squares of the sides of a right triangle are equal to the square of the hypotenuse; or more simply put, A squared plus B squared equals C squared. Using the same logic, one such life theorem is: One is never thin enough, and another life theorem is: There is never enough money. These are absolutes and unquestionably correct. When you think about this you will know that it is true, and this is also the reason that all the crew, with the possible exception of Jack Morgan, would be back for another treasure hunt. For Jack Morgan it was never about the money, it was always about the hunt and the life experience.

Chapter Twenty-Two:
JACK AND SUSAN

Jack expertly guided the inflatable raft through the pea kelp and up to the sandy beach at Clam Harbor. He and Susan had borrowed Norm Bennett's 30-foot *Islander* for this trip to San Miguel Island. This was something that Jack needed to share with someone; but more than that, he needed to complete the unfinished business that began here over 20 years ago. He had told Susan very little about this experience because he did not want to prejudice her judgment.

The two left the Santa Barbara Yacht Harbor the day before and spent a leisurely morning sailing to Santa Cruz Island and on to the yacht cove. They spent the afternoon diving and sightseeing in the cove, both above and below the water's surface. Two good-sized lobsters were taken that afternoon and made a delicious meal for the two in the evening. Susan was still in mild shock about what to do with her new wealth. For a woman who had always lived comfortably but frugally, this represented a dramatic lifestyle change. Not so for Jack, however, who had never felt the call of wealth. When he thought about it, what more could he want that he didn't already have? It was nice not to have to scratch for money in times like these when jobs were scarce, but to Jack, jobs were all part of the life experience. This marvelous obsession of Jack's to live his life and experience it to its fullest was what motivated and drove him. He would have done many of the same things for free, just for the experience.

The couple leisurely climbed the steep slopes to the crest of the island while holding hands most of the way up. As they crested the island, Jack could feel the serenity and peace enfold him. He glanced at Susan and was rapidly assured that she was experiencing the same spiritual gift. Susan gave him a knowing look that said that now she finally understood the attraction Jack had always felt towards this island.

It was a gorgeous morning with a slight breeze drifting across the upper reaches of the gentle valley located at the crest of the island. The two walked slowly westward without talking, as each was enveloped in the experience of San Miguel Island. It was enough to know that they had each other, and both were having the same spiritual experience. As they continued westerly through the myriad wildflowers that seemed to be everywhere now, the feelings intensified. The seabirds seemed to know that this was a special moment and flew with muted calls while going about their business. Both Jack and Susan knew that they were approaching the source, and before long their questions would be answered, but neither wanted this experience to end.

Jack located the cross and then began showing Susan the narrow trail that wound downward towards the jagged rock-strewn cliffs below. It looked far more intimidating in the mid-morning's light than it had in the recent past when Jack had climbed up this trail on his way back to the *Freeman Barnes*. Once Susan found that there were substantial hand- and foot-holds to supplement the trail, she quickly became comfortable with the climb downward. About one-eighth of a mile from the upper cross trailhead, Jack and Susan entered the alcove. Jack hadn't noticed before but, below the name *Juan Cabrillo* were the numbers 1543: *The year this trail was carved from the stone no doubt,* Jack thought.

Jack had remembered to bring light this time, and handed one of the two flashlights to Susan. They entered the anteroom of the cavern and paused there for a time to allow their eyes to adjust to the gloom. As they began to slowly work their way through the cavern, it wasn't long before they passed the remains of Ramon, still and unmoving in his death pose. Susan shuddered at the sight of the body; she knew that it could just as easily have been Jack lying there instead of Ramon. They continued on past Ramon, still feeling gently drawn to the interior of the cavern. As they rounded a corner in the cave, they saw before them a massive iron door with an equally massive lock fully 18 inches long and 12 inches wide. For a moment it appeared that this would be as far as they could go this day. Susan noticed that the hinges for the door had been bolted into wooden posts, and the wooden posts had been badly eaten by some animal or insect. The hinges were loose and partially hanging because of the condition of the posts. With a little prying and a lot of praying, the iron door began to move from the hinges outward. Before long there was enough room for both Susan and Jack to wiggle in behind it.

As they turned their flashlights to the interior of the room, they were stunned by the amazing array spread before them. On a stone bier in the center of the room lay a figure in full Spanish body armor; his skeletal hands still gripped a Spanish long sword with gem stones encrusted on the handle. Next to the wall to one side was an ancient chest, partially open, and both could see that it was filled with hand-drawn charts and maps and a sundry of ancient navigation devices. On the wall opposite the open chest was a small pile of what first appeared to be bricks. Once Jack and Susan took a closer look they were surprised to find 70 neatly-stacked gold doré bars weighing between 50 and 70 pounds each. There was another chest larger than the first one, and it was closed. An ancient lock holding the hasp fell to the cave floor in a rusty pile.

"This cavern must get a lot of moisture at times to cause such massive oxidizing," said Susan to no one in particular.

Jack opened the chest and discovered the Cabrillo family coat of arms, neatly folded and in excellent condition after all the intervening years. Under that were personal items originally belonging to Juan Cabrillo, and priceless now due to their age and condition. In a flash of insight, Jack now knew why he had been drawn here. He had a small service to perform for Juan Cabrillo. Once he explained this to Susan, she agreed with him completely.

The two left the cavern while sharing a heavy load, and began the upward journey to the crest of San Miguel Island. It would be late that afternoon when Jack and Susan stood once more on the beach at Clam Harbor. It had been a tiring trip down from the crest, but their toils were now just about over. They would be leaving tomorrow morning for the Santa Barbara Yacht Harbor.

Jack sat in the first-class section of the American Airlines jet as it taxied down the tarmac at the San Diego International Airport. The Spanish Embassy had been quite helpful in locating the Juan Cabrillo heirs for him. When he had spoken to Roberto Cabrillo, the twelve-times-removed direct descendant of the Spanish explorer Juan Cabrillo, earlier that week, Jack had informed him that he would be arriving in Madrid, Spain on this flight with something of value for the Cabrillo family. Jack could discern the distrust and disbelief in Roberto's voice, and he didn't blame him. After all, why would a stranger go to such lengths to bring the family a gift while receiving nothing in return? Even Jack had a hard time with that one.

Jack had done some research in the Santa Barbara library about Juan Cabrillo and was surprised at who this man was. He is credited with the discovery of California and died while mapping the California coastline. The year of his death was 1543 and he was interred in full body armor together with his gem-encrusted sword. It has always been thought that he was buried on one of the Channel Islands with San Miguel Island being the generally accepted burial site. As for the gold bars, both Jack and Susan got the feeling that this was a gift to them for this small service. Both agreed that the bars were to remain there in the burial chamber until such time as there was a need for them. Neither Jack nor Susan could think of a compelling reason to take them now, but things change over time, and who knew what the future would bring.

Jack met Roberto in the lobby near the baggage checkout, and a friendly conversation soon blossomed. Jack spoke fluent Spanish and before long had given Roberto an account of the grave where his ancestor lay interred. Jack left his personal luggage in the terminal for the return flight and proceeded to customs with a large and heavy piece of luggage. Within half an hour Jack had cleared customs and moved the luggage to the front of the terminal where Roberto had a small transport vehicle waiting. Before loading it in the van, Jack opened the luggage. Inside was the original chest containing the personal belongings of Juan Cabrillo, but the most important item was the family coat of arms. This pennant had been taken off the wall of the family's ancestral home in Madrid by Juan Cabrillo and had remained missing since that time. It had been made by an unknown artisan sometime during the first Crusades, and it had been missing for over 450 years. Roberto was overwhelmed. He reached over to shake Jack's hand but gave him a heartfelt hug instead. The two parted soon after. Jack's plane was leaving for San Diego, California, and he didn't want to miss it.

Epilogue

There really is a reef to the west of San Miguel Island that encompasses ten square miles, give or take a mile or so. There really was a Freddy Steele who enjoyed Irish whiskey a little too much, but he was never the dedicated hunter gatherer as depicted in the book (I took that character from my friend Dan Huffman). He was a simple abalone diver who gave two teenage boys a chance to live a dream one summer in the year of 1959. He drank too much and he was grumpy and hung over every morning, but we didn't care. The good outweighed the bad, and that magic summer was worth more than anything I have ever done or experienced since.

Freddy was terrified of the reef and neither I nor my friend Bobby Landers could get him to go near it except once. He said that the currents were so strong there that they would sweep the diver away into the depths, never to be seen again, or something like that. Just once when the ocean was calm, he got the nerve to venture into the reef and it was almost a disaster. Yours truly was at the helm as we gingerly moved into the reef area. We had not gone in more than 300 yards when the seas began to rise. When that happened, the surrounding water began to boil because the rocks were so close to the surface. I did the only thing I could think of to do, which was to reverse the engine and back out the same way we had entered the reef. I didn't dare even to turn the boat around. Our luck held that day, but I was never again tempted to enter those uncharted waters. It was a lesson learned without having to pay the piper, and I never had the inclination to do the same thing again.

The Island of San Miguel and Point Arguello both line up as depicted in the book, and the Japanese current does pass this way on its journey through the northern hemisphere. Juan Cabrillo was real also and is thought to have been buried on San Miguel Island: no one knows for sure.

The Forbidden Reef is an enigma itself. There are five acknowledged shipwrecks attributed to this reef, and 17 attributed to the Channel Islands in general; but these are the shipwrecks where some witnesses lived to report the tragedy. One could safely assume that triple the number of ships perished with the entire crew; it would be within the realm of possibility. Of course there is no way of knowing the actual number, which gave yours truly the idea of creating this fictional account. The low-tide currents and the siphon effect were added to give the heroes and heroines more challenges to strive against. One thing is certain, and this is not fictional: the Channel Islands are very dangerous to the unwary. They have been so since the first Europeans arrived, and they are dangerous even now to the uninformed sailor.

❧

I will leave the reader now with the Freddie Steele story taken from my previously published book **Reflections.** It is an account taken from the memories of a 15-year-old boy, and the basis on which this fictional work was created.

I wish you good reading, and May God bless you all.

FREDDIE STEELE

It was in the summer of 1959 and I had not yet reached my six-teenth birthday when I first met Freddie Steele. Summer vacation was just beginning and I was staying at a place called Avila Beach, California with one of my uncles. I had never seen the Pacific Ocean before coming here and I was fascinated by it as well as a little intimidated of its awesome power. Unlike the lakes I had seen before, the Pacific Ocean was alive and I knew it with certainty from the first time I saw it.

Freddie Steele had mentioned to my uncle that he was in need of a *line-tender* for his Abalone Diving Boat and I was soon summoned to their mutual *watering hole* to apply for the job. Freddie was glassy eyed and jovial and hired me with a cavalier wave of his hand. I did not have a clue then as to just what the duties of a *line-tender* could be, but I was willing to give it a try. Freddie asked me to report to *The Fisherman's Pier* the following morning and I happily agreed. *The Fisherman's Pier* was well over a mile from the main street of Avila Beach. To reach it one must cross an ancient bridge to the north of town then follow the winding dirt road that closely tracked the natural terrain until it ended at the peer. I left for the peer that morning in plenty of time to walk this distance and be there when agreed.

I arrived at the appointed time and spent the better part of an hour wandering around the rotten timbers and dilapidated structures that served as *The Fisherman's Peer* while waiting for Freddie Steele to arrive. Freddie finally showed up almost an hour late and was in a spiteful mood. It took me a little while, but I finally learned that Freddie was not to be trifled with in any way in the early mornings. Freddie suffered from *world-class* hangovers and was best left alone if at all possible. On the positive side, Freddie was a good teacher and I learned many things from him when he was not being a grump. Although I did not know it then, Avila Beach was one of those places where people who *march to the beat of a different drummer* tended to congregate and live. I have experienced this kind of a community on various occasions through the years and I have always found them extremely friendly and comfortable, much like an old pair of tennis shoes. I mention this because Freddie Steele would surely qualify as one such of an individual as does yours truly. I have never met anyone quite like him in my journey through life and I would have to say with deep conviction that the mold was broken after Freddie Steele was born. If Freddie had been born sixty years earlier he would have participated in the Alaska Gold rush of the 1890's. If he had been born one hundred years ago, Freddie would have been here for the California Gold rush, I have no doubt. Freddie was the last of the swashbuckling pirates who choose to live on the outer fringes of the law. Freddie did everything his way while he slipped through the cracks or evaded all of those who would refuse to let Freddie Steele be what he was born to be. Freddie was one of those people who lived his life larger than life itself, and I am sure that he will go to his grave kicking and screaming that he is not yet ready to go there.

We boarded Freddie's skiff and I commenced to row out to his fishing boat using the double oars that were hanging off the sides of his ugly little rowboat. Freddie's fishing boat was anchored several hundred feet out from those aging and dilapidated ruins called *The Fisherman's Peer*. As we approached Freddie's boat I noted that it shared the same homeliness as Freddie's skiff.

There was a large sign on both the port and starboard (right and left) sides of the boat that said (A21) in twelve-inch black letters on a blue background. Freddie explained that this was his *California Commercial Fishing License Number for Harvesting Abalone*. There were no other markings on the boat other than a small stenciled sign on the upper port side that simply said TOILET in one-inch letters. Although there really was a toilet there, Freddie Steel's boat became known from that moment on as "THE TOILET ". It was a name that once given could never be taken back no matter how annoyed Freddie became over his boat's anointed surname. What was worse was that his bar room buddies soon got wind of it and never passed up an opportunity to remind Freddie of his boat's new handle.

Although the boat was homely, it was sturdy and sea-worthy as I eventually discovered. Today was to be a test day to see if I could do the work assigned me without getting Freddie Steele or myself killed in the process. Freddie fired up the engine and before long we were lifting anchor, or rather I was lifting anchor while Freddie manned the helm. The anchor was pulled without incident and soon *The Toilet* was heading south along the coast between Avila Beach and Pismo Beach, California. As Freddie explained it, we were in route to some Kelp beds to begin work. The Kelp beds when we found them were of a variety known as "Pea Kelp", a more warm water plant that has many small flotation sacks as opposed to "Bull Kelp", a cold water lover that has only a single large flotation sack. Freddie explained that Avila Beach was the unofficial dividing line and to the north we would find only the "Bull Kelp" growing from the ocean floor. I was to learn later that the "Pea Kelp" was the more hazardous of the two species because it was much easier for the diver to become entangled with it while working the Abalone beds beneath. Freddie also explained that Kelp was the natural food of the Abalone and it was here in the Kelp beds that we would find those mysterious shellfish. I had never tasted Abalone or most other seafoods for that matter, so I had an open mind about this venture. Somebody somewhere must like Abalone and wanted to buy them I thought, or we wouldn't be harvesting these critters from the depths of the ocean.

Freddie picked a spot he thought might be productive and we dropped anchor. The motor was left idling to power up the air compressor that would be needed for breathing while working on the ocean floor. Today we would be working "Dead Boat" as Freddie called it and how it worked is like this; *The Toilet* would be at anchor and Freddie would descend into the depths, then start out from the boat. He would move until he came to the end of the air hose, then return to the boat and head out another direction. Upon each approach, I would send down an empty basket and Freddie would remove it and attach the filled basket to the rope. I would then pull up the basket by hand and empty the contents onto the deck. It was also my job to check each Abalone for legal size and send back all those which were too small. While doing all of this, I needed to keep my eye on the air bubbles and play out the air hose or pull it back in depending upon which way the diver was moving. The hose needed to be coiled in a specific manner to prevent tangling and the air pressure must be watched constantly. Freddie also explained that this hose was known as "semi-floating" in that it hung about six to ten feet off the ocean floor and therefore had less of a tendency to entangle on the rocks or the Kelp below. This was a whole lot of stuff for a fifteen year old to remember but it beat farm work and that was good enough for me.

After the anchor was safely in place and the air compressor tank drained of condensate water, Freddie went below and began to dress for the days diving. First he put on three pairs of thermal underwear, then climbed into his dry suit from a hole on the front of the suit. This had to be sealed with elastic similar to rubber bands only far more substantial. It took a joint effort to do this. Freddie would carefully roll up the rubber material into a watertight ball then I would apply the elastic to hold this ball in place. This is not nearly as complicated as it sounds. I can never remember a leak in any dry suit after it was sealed in this manner. Next came the bottom boots which were war surplus ski boots with big treads and easy to take on and off. Then finally came the weight belt and facemask after being lightly soaped on the inside face from a bottle of *Liquid Joy*, which Freddie said kept the facemask from fogging up. Both the weight belt and the facemask were attached to the air hose. The weight belt was secured to the hose by several loops of nylon material. This was done to hold the air hose safely while preventing it from pulling the facemask off the divers head in the event of tension on the hose.

Once all of this was in place it was *Showtime* for Freddie. Freddie would pick up his Abalone pry-iron and fasten it to his wrist with a nylon loop, then with his empty hand he would grasp the Abalone basket. Typically, Freddie would climb down the ladder into the water, then adjust his suit buoyancy using one of the valves on his facemask. After this was done he would slowly descend while using a rope to control his submersion. This would allow him to clear his ears, (equalize the pressure) until he finally reached the ocean floor. Once there, Freddie Steele did not let algae grow under his feet. He moved out immediately at a brisk pace for several hundred feet to the end of the hose, then back to the boat and off once more in another direction. At each pass, Freddie would attach a full basket of Abalone. There were primitive signals that were used between us. Simply one tug of the hose meant that Freddie was coming up to the surface while two tugs meant that Freddie needed an empty basket, three tugs was my signal to him to surface as soon as possible or his signal to me that he was coming up immediately.

Within two hours Freddie was up and we were underway to another dive location in the same kelp bed. This would be repeated once more before Freddie had ran his race for the day and we pulled anchor for the last time that afternoon and headed *The Toilet* back in to port. Freddie explained that a diver could work only for a period of four to six hours under the water because of the physical exertion needed to work at that depth. I found this to be true at a later date when I also began diving. After four hours beneath the surface of the ocean, I would come up muscle weary and spent from the constant effort.

Freddie pulled *The Toilet* in close to *The Fisherman's Pier* and between the two of us; we managed to unload the days catch from the boat using an ancient electrical winch that somehow still functioned in spite of its pathetic appearance. This was all new to me, and Freddie had little patience when it came to the mooring of his boat to the peer or the unloading of the catch. After the first day, this process went smoothly but there was much uncertainty on my part as well as some harsh words from Freddie in the beginning.

Freddie Steele was in a much better mood as the day progressed. The catch had been substantial and my performance had been adequate although I still had much to learn. Freddie explained to me how the pay worked and that I would need a commercial fishing license which could only be obtained in Morro Bay, California. Because Freddie would be driving there that afternoon to deliver the days catch to *Breebes Seafood,* it would be an ideal time for me to acquire the necessary license if I tagged along. As I remember, the license cost $15.00 at the time. In 1959, that was a lot of money for a fifteen year old to have in possession. Freddie came to the rescue and advanced me the money on the days catch. According to Freddie, the Abalone were sold by the dozen and our price would be between eight and ten dollars per dozen after processing. *Breebes Seafood* would be paying only twice per month and that is when I could expect to be paid as well. A *line-tender* was entitled to one sixth of the catch for each day. We had taken eight and one half dozen Abalone on our first workday and could expect to do about the same the day following. I quickly calculated that I had earned at least $12.00 if one did not count the fishing license. This was not a lot of money but in 1959 it was half again more than farm labor paid, plus there were no deductions. Then there was always the chance of earning more money if we located a more productive area to harvest those slimy shellfish. I had to admit that this experience was very stimulating to me and I enjoyed being on the ocean with all the new sights and smells to be experienced, as well as observing the varieties of animal and bird life to be found there. At the time, I do not think I could have found a better summer job that paid as well and was filled with so much adventure. Putting up with Freddie's *acid tongue* each morning was a small price to pay for such an amazing experience.

My seamanship and *line-tender* skills continued to improve and soon Freddie Steele approached me with a proposal of sharing the diving responsibilities with him. It sounded good on the surface but I knew nothing about diving or the hazards that lurked beneath the ocean surface. Freddie explained that when diving I could claim three sixths of the catch as opposed to the one sixth I was now receiving. In addition to that, we could work three to four hours longer with a fresh diver and gain productivity each day. I knew that there was more to diving than merely donning a facemask and going to the ocean floor so before I committed to this I wanted to know something of the hazards I would be facing in that alien environment.

The first and greatest danger was called "*Air Embolism*" which was normally fatal if one attempts to swim to the surface while holding compressed air in ones lungs. The expanded air would rupture the lungs and the diver would soon suffocate from lack of oxygen. The way to combat this was to remember to exhale *all the way* to the surface if one found it necessary to "bail out" on the ocean floor (drop ones weight belt and mask and swim for the surface) for any reason. As Freddie explained it, one could perish in three feet of water while breathing compressed air, simply by trying to hold ones breath and coming to the surface. The second most dangerous hazard was known as "*Nitrogen Narcosis*" and how it effected one was like this. When diving in depths in excess of forty feet, the nitrogen in the blood system would accumulate and if one surfaced too quickly, the nitrogen would begin boiling and form bubbles in the blood stream, causing severe cramping and muscle spasms. Although this could be fatal or permanently disabling, one could simply decompress by hanging off at certain depths for a period of time to allow the nitrogen to stabilize. In the event of an emergency, one could come to the surface and be taken later to a decompression chamber ran by either the Coast Guard or the Navy. The sooner this took place, the less likelihood of permanent disability.

So now I understood the <u>basic</u> dangers but what if going below the surface terrified me? And what about the gear that Freddie used? I knew nothing of the adjustments or tuning required to stay submerged for a reasonable time. In the end, I agreed to give it a try. Who knows? I might even enjoy it.

My first dive was reasonably successful and Freddie was giddy with excitement over the prospect of having someone to share the diving duties with. I, on the other hand, still harbored some serious reservations about diving in general. There were still many unanswered questions rattling around in my brain about diving hazards. Most of these reservations came from lack of knowledge of what to do in an emergency. Of the myriad possibilities of emergencies that included equipment failure and shark attack, Freddie Steele dismissed with a wave of his hand. He said to "just go down to the bottom and go to work and all would be fine." Even when I was only fifteen years old, this cavalier dismissal did not ring quite true but I agreed to go forward with Freddie's scheme anyway.

My first actual diving day I submerged into about thirty-five feet of water and I did it slowly until I reached the bottom. Then I just stood there on the ocean floor and looked around until I was certain that I would not be devoured by a giant fish. Soon I discovered some Abalone less than ten feet away and hanging off a rock as if waiting for me to harvest them. I moved over and popped them off the rock and into the basket while seeing several more to harvest further on. It wasn't long until I had reached the end of my hose and began my return journey to the boat with a filled basket of Abalone in tow. This was how the afternoon went and after two more dives at different locations, we were on our way in to port with a sizeable harvest of which I had a good share of profits to look forward to. This was pretty much the way my days went most of the time but there were some really scary moments that I remember quite clearly.

In the first week of my newly acquired skill, I had just descended to the depths when my facemask began filling up with water and I hadn't a clue of what to do about it. In desperation, I dropped my facemask and weight belt and headed for the surface while remembering to exhale *all the way* up. Freddie Steele was mad as hell about my *bailing out* and acted as if I should have known how to clear my mask without resorting to such extremes. This was only one example of the many things that Freddie neglected to tell me and as I sit here writing this story, I wonder how I survived the early part of that summer. The solution to *water in the facemask* was easy when it was finally explained by Freddie. One simply puts pressure on the top of the mask and blows air into the mask through the nose thereby forcing the unwanted liquid out the bottom of the facemask. The solution was simple and it was the same method used to clear one's ears when descending into the depths. I faced similar hazards like this, sometimes on a daily basis without the experience or the knowledge to alleviate those situations that could become life threatening. One would have thought that Freddie Steele would explain in detail the diving hazards and their remedies or maybe it just never occurred to him to do so. Then there was the possibility that perhaps there were simply far too many dangers for Freddie to remember. Who can say? Maybe he simply didn't want to scare me at the time. All things had to be learned *the hard way* with Freddie Steele. After each near death experience, Freddie would act as if my lack of knowledge was my fault and not his, but I never complained.

Then there was the Basking Shark incident. I had been diving for less than two weeks and I was down in the Kelp beds between Pismo and Avila Beach one afternoon when a shadow passed over me. The visibility was very good that day and I could see clearly for about thirty feet in the murky depths. I looked up and saw the biggest fish I had ever seen in my life and I could tell instantly that this fish was also a shark. The shark turned and slowly swam toward me and I knew with certainty that I was about to be eaten by this monster. By some miracle this behemoth only gave me a passing stare, then swam off in another direction. I was too terrified to move for some time, then I signaled that I was coming up, which I did with all haste. As I remember, that Basking Shark was at least forty feet long and its eye when it passed me was the size of a dish. When I related my story to Freddie Steele he laughed and pointed out that what I had seen was *only* a Basking Shark. He also explained that Basking Sharks eat plankton and had no taste for creatures like me. Freddie then pointed out that this particular shark had been around this part of the ocean for a number of years and was well known by all the divers in the area, all but me that is. This was *just another day in paradise* for this fifteen-year-old boy learning everything the hard way. When one is that age and without much life experience, it was easy for Freddie to manipulate me, which he did constantly. I found out later that a Basking Shark is considered to be the biggest fish in the ocean. Whales do not count because they are mammals not fish.

Perhaps a little history of those shelled mollusks we were harvesting would be appropriate at this juncture. Abalone were first introduced to the American palate by Japanese fishermen in the early part of the twentieth century. It would be the Portuguese fishermen however, who first began diving for this tasty sea creature and developed the industry. Abalone were also the food of choice for the Sea Otter and with the massive slaughter of the Otters by the Russian Fur Traders, the Abalone were left without natural enemies. The balance of nature had been interrupted and there occurred a massive proliferation of these shellfish. This was how the Portuguese divers found them in the thirties and forties. Abalone literally covered every rock on the ocean floor along the California coast to a depth of over one hundred feet. As for Freddie Steele, he was a hanger-on from the glory days of Abalone harvesting. Freddie was just happy to be making a comfortable living while pursuing this dangerous occupation. In 1959, both Freddie Steele and I would occasionally spot Sea Otters along the coastline and frequently came upon signs of their feeding off Abalone in the ocean depths. We knew with certainty back then, that these sea creatures were not extinct as so many naturalists led us to believe. In retrospect, I was witnessing the death-throws of the Abalone fishing industry. With the regeneration of the Sea Otter in later years, these once abundant shellfish became scarce and no longer economically feasible for commercial harvesting. In 1959, Freddie Steele was one of maybe ten commercial Abalone Diving Boats remaining and operating out of the Avila Beach and Morro Bay area. I think that I am being kind with the numbers when I say this.

Freddie Steele purchased his fuel from the docks in Morro Bay, as there were no commercial vendors in the Avila Beach area. It was always a pleasurable trip to Morro Bay that consumed the day and was simply a lot of fun for this fifteen year old. I enjoyed tagging along for the many unusual sights, sounds, and smells. There were plentiful Sun Fish, Seals, Pelicans, Porpoises and Seagulls to occupy my time, not to mention the rugged coastline and the reefs.

There was one large rock that comes to mind that was well over one mile out from the shore. Freddie called it *Seal Rock* due to the large population of Harbor Seals that called it home. There were also large numbers of Seagulls and Pelicans as well as many lesser-known sea birds living there and it was fun to cruise close to it during our forays for petrol. On one such occasion we were visited by two Orcas as we cruised northward toward Morro Bay. We spotted them at the same time they spotted us as they changed their course to intercept *The Toilet*. Soon they were cruising beside our boat, one on each side and were within two or three feet of the boat rail. The dorsal fins of these magnificent animals towered eight to ten feet up from their backs and we guessed that these two whales were between twenty-five and thirty feet in overall length. The Orcas cruised effortlessly with us for a while then abruptly veered off in the direction of *Seal Rock*. Freddie changed course as well and we followed these animals as they fluidly pulled away from our lumbering craft. In the meantime, the Harbor Seals had spotted the Orcas and a din of distressful howling rose from all of the Seals who recognized the danger lurking so close at hand. Freddie stood off about five hundred yards while slowly circling the rock as the drama unfolded. Meanwhile, the Orcas went into action circling the rock close in while waiting for the panic-stricken seals to come to them. It did not take long for those terrified sea creatures to flee for the safety of the open water. This was when the feeding of the Orcas began. Seals and parts of Seals were being thrown through the air as these deadly hunters gorged themselves taking only one bite out of each Seal caught, then turning to catch still another. This slaughter continued for almost one half of an hour until the mighty appetites of these Orcas was finally sated. The two Orcas moved away from the rock simultaneously as if some signal had passed between them. They headed out to sea and soon faded into the ocean mists. I had never seen anything even remotely like what I had just witnessed nor do I think that Freddie Steele had either. Neither of us spoke as Freddie turned *The Toilet* toward Morro Bay once more. I think I was in a mild state of shock from that savage display of nature at one of its more graphic moments. Later on that summer, I would see little difference between the Orcas and the Harbor Seals while observing the Seals feeding upon Smelt in much the same manner as they themselves were fed upon by those two Orcas.

I had been working for Freddie Steele for less than three weeks when he came up with another one of his incredible plans. Freddie asked me if I had ever heard of the *Channel Islands* and the answer was absolutely not. As Freddie explained, the *Channel Islands* were a group of uninhabited islands off the coast of California at roughly the same latitude as Santa Barbara, California. Freddie went on to say that these islands had not been worked for several years and we should consider going there for the balance of the summer.

The names of these islands are as follows; *Anacapa Island,* the closest, and more like two large rocks than an island, then *Santa Cruz Island,* the most scenic underwater wonderland and most diverse landscape of all the islands, then *Santa Rosa Island,* the largest and most inhospitable, also said to be a private hunting preserve, then finally *San Miguel Island,* the most distant and also the most enchanting of all the Islands. These islands were roughly twenty to thirty miles off the California coast depending upon one's destination. Freddie Steele stated that we could go there for the remainder of the summer and work if I could find another worker to train as a *line-tender* for the two of us. He explained that the Abalone beds were far richer out at the

Channel Islands and less picked over than the beds we were working here on the central California coast. In retrospect, I think that Freddie suffered from *the grass is greener* mentality but my enthusiasm for this new adventure was unbridled. We would be picking a "Pink Abalone", about half the size of the "Red Abalone" we were now harvesting. Needless to say, I was mesmerized at the prospect of these Islands and with the new adventure of going there, so I promised Freddie Steele that I would, without fail, recruit one of my friends the following weekend and have him here and ready for work on the coming Monday morning.

I left for the *San Joaquin Valley* that evening and after hitch-hiking for many hours, arrived at my friend's house a little after one AM in the morning. Bobby lived with his parents at a farm labor facility known as *Linnell Camp, California*. A place that I am unsure if it still exists today. His name was Bobby Landers and he was currently picking Peaches for one dollar per hour. It didn't take much persuasion to convince him to abandon his farm labor job and come with me on the escapade that I was proposing. This new summer job now promised to be one filled with adventure which was far better than picking peaches in the hot *San Joaquin Valley* sun. Bobby would have come along if only for the fact that a *line-tender* made one and one half times more money than his current farm labor job paid. We sat up the rest of the night talking about what we were about to do and the excitement was undiminished as the sun finally rose that morning. I think that Bobby would have left immediately that same night when I arrived if his parents would have let him.

Bobby Landers and Freddie Steele hit it off immediately and it wasn't long until we were operating like a well-oiled machine. I became the boat operator and after a lot of practice, I became quite proficient doing it. This new method of Abalone diving was known as "Live Boat", and it worked like this; the diver would descend to the Ocean floor and the boat followed him through the water as he worked the depths for these elusive shellfish. The *Line Tender's* duties consisted of keeping the hose clear of Kelp by the use of a long pole with a sharpened scythe type knife attached to the end. Typically, the *line tender* would hold the hose in one hand and use the other to cut the Kelp away from the diver's hose. Freddie had changed the hose to a floating variety that aided the *line-tender* in keeping the air hose safely free for the submerged diver. The *line tender* would send empty baskets to the bottom, then pull the full ones to the deck while emptying their contents and sorting the legal ones from those still too small to be taken. The *line tender* helped the diver both in and out of the boat and assisted him with his gear as well.

The boat operator, on the other hand, had one job, to operate the boat safely. While at the helm, the boat operator had total responsibility for the safety of the diver as well as the boat and could call the diver up at any time when he felt that the safety of the boat or crew was in jeopardy. This was somewhat of a heady responsibility for a fifteen year old but I took it in stride. I had just received my driver's license six months prior but operating a boat was completely different. All boats turn from the stern and must be backed out and away from any mooring or dock to a place where the operator can safely maneuver the boat forward. Then the wind was a constant variable that must be compensated for continuously with the throttle during these close-in maneuverings. I never took my responsibilities lightly as I knew from the start that I could endanger both the boat and the crew simply by making a bad judgment call. The *boat operator* held the craft in position with the diver's air bubbles just visible from the bridge at the port bow. From this vantage point the operator could observe both the divers directional movements and the *line-tenders* work.

During this training period Freddie managed to talk me into diving into seventy feet of water. I think that Freddie wanted to know if Abalone could be found there and was unwilling to go down himself to find out. Just like the fifteen year old know-it-all that I was at the time, I agreed to make the dive. Let me tell the reader that seventy feet of water versus forty feet of water is a big step to take even for an experienced diver. It has been said that *ignorance is bliss* and I was surely blissful when I descended to that depth that fateful afternoon. I was working *dead-boat* at that time and was well over one hundred feet from *The Toilet* when disaster struck.

I had been on the bottom for less than ten minutes and I had found it barren of the shellfish we were searching for. The rocks were strewn with Sea Urchins and little else. Sea Urchins are red spiny creatures that always seemed to contest for rock space with the Abalone. I had just begun my return trip to the boat and back to the surface when the air regulator stuck in my facemask. Simply put, there was no air coming through the hose. As I had done on numerous occasions, I dropped my weight belt and facemask and then to my horror, I had too little buoyancy in my dry suit to rise to the ocean surface from this depth. I could see my facemask and weight belt lying within a few feet of me on the sandy bottom, although retrieving them would not have helped at this point. There was one slim chance and it was all I had. I ran up some rocks that protruded about ten feet off the ocean floor and from the top of that rock pile I jumped upward with all my strength while kicking and swimming and trying to get to the surface before I drowned. Eventually, I could feel myself moving slowly upward and after forever, it seemed, I emerged from those depths to the ocean surface. This *redneck* had taken in water on the way up and I coughed and choked for several minutes afterward. The most difficult thing I had ever done that summer would be to put on another set of weights and facemask then descend to the ocean floor once more to retrieve the gear I had left behind in my haste. As much as I hated it, I was still terrified by my latest near death experience as I clung to the rope and very slowly descended once more. Upon reaching the bottom I simply stood there for several minutes afraid to let go of the rope. Then familiarity began to set in and my fear diminished to the point where I was finally able to move over to my downed gear and attach it to the rope for retrieval. I allowed the *Line-Tender* to pull the rope up with the gear, then after several minutes I signaled for the rope to begin my own ascent. I could now see the wisdom in Freddie's insistence that I *must* be the one to go back down into the ocean depths to conquer my fear or I may never have had the courage to dive again. Giving this a positive spin, and after this latest incident, I insisted that Freddie acquire a CO2 inflatable life preserver that could be activated when needed. We had never experienced this problem before but even Freddie agreed that he also would have perished that day by being unable to inflate his suit at that depth without incoming air. The two of us always wore this safety device from that point on when diving to any depth.

Finally, the day arrived for our trip to the *Channel Islands* to begin. The three of us left from *The Fisherman's Pier* in the early morning hours. Freddie was actually up and dressed at 4:00 AM and for once he was not biting our heads off with each breath he took. A heading was set to clear *Point Sal* to the south and we settled in with three-hour watches at the helm. That afternoon found *The Toilet* still north of *Point Arguello* and close to the same latitude as *Vandenberg Air Force Base*. While in route that same afternoon, we were hailed by a Coast Guard Cutter and asked not to proceed any further south until after a missile was launched from the Air Base. Freddie turned *The Toilet* toward the shore and dropped anchor in a Kelp bed with about thirty feet of water beneath. We did not have long to wait until a missile streaked across the sky to the south of us, then over the horizon to its appointed target in the South Pacific. The incredible speed at which this missile traveled amazed us even in 1959. It took less than five minutes to race from horizon to horizon then disappear completely over the western Pacific Ocean.

We enjoyed a leisurely dinner that afternoon, then Freddie noted that we still had three hours of sunlight left. Why not take advantage of this and get some diving in? Who knows, there may be Abalone below just waiting for us harvest. Somehow Freddie convinced me to put on the gear and go check out the ocean floor. Freddie had a knack for doing this. I did not mind however, because this always meant a larger share for me.

There was a gentle warm breeze wafting from the shoreline then, not the usual northwest wind with its chilled bite. That afternoon, I dropped into one of the most scenic underwater panoramas I had witnessed to date. The water was clear as compared to the usual coastal waters and there was little wave activity to stir up the bottom. On the ocean floor there was a new specie of Kelp growing amongst the Pea Kelp that was truly a visual treat. It was known as Palm Kelp and it was amazing. It grew from six to eight feet tall and had leaves that resembled palm trees. This Kelp was growing from rocks that were about three to five feet tall. These rocks were emphasized dramatically with the whitest sand I had ever seen. It could have been the angle of the sun or the unusual clarity of the ocean that afternoon, but that glistening white sand was strewn like a series of interlocking footpaths between the rocks throughout this underwater forest. I spent some time enjoying this moment as I had done many times in the past since I had begun diving. It was simply one of my secrets to stop work for a moment or two and respectfully observe something I had never before witnessed. After pausing for a while to *smell the roses*, I then turned back to the task at hand, harvesting Abalone. These rocks were loaded with Red Abalone and in a short period of time I had sent up multiple baskets of these shellfish.

I had been down less than thirty minutes when I received an emergency signal to come up immediately. I inflated the dry suit and quickly rose to the surface. To my dismay, the gentle breeze I had experienced prior to diving had turned into a raging *Santa Ana* blow. *The Toilet* was being driven out to sea and dragging me along with it. If this situation continued, my airline would eventually break because I was hopelessly entangled in Pea Kelp. Bobby Landers was pulling on the hose as hard as he could and Freddie Steele was at the helm. Freddie soon had the boat turned into that howling tempest and was even making small progress at coming back to where I was stranded in the Pea Kelp. When I first began diving, I always took one additional tool with me, a very sharp knife held on my left wrist by a nylon cord. It was a stainless steel stiletto with a six-inch blade and I had sharpened both sides to the sharpness of a razor. With the combination of Bobby cutting Kelp and my own efforts with this knife, I finally made it back to the boat and climbed aboard totally exhausted from the effort. I had never let go of my Abalone basket during this ordeal because it was mostly under water and did not weigh very much. I had extended my right arm through the webbing of the basket while grasping the air hose with my right hand, leaving my left hand free to cut Kelp. After this crisis was over, I was briefly ribbed by Freddie for failing to let go of the basket in the face of an emergency. I did not mind the ribbing because I knew that secretly Freddie was happy that I was able to salvage it. The truth of it was that I just didn't think of letting the basket go at the time when all the other events were clamoring for my attention. I had never heard of *Santa Ana winds* before this incident took place, but after my firsthand experience of how seductive these winds could be for one moment, then how incredibly destructive the next, I gained a new respect for these off-shore winds that I have never relinquished.

After freeing me from the Kelp entanglement, Bobby Landers raced to the bow and began lifting the anchor. Once the anchor was safely aboard the boat, Freddie set a new course toward *Point Arguello*. There would be no peace for us this evening with that raging offshore *quartering tailwind* at our backs. It would be far better to travel through the night than suffer the pounding that these *Santa Ana winds* would administer if we remained there. Freddie Steele's seamanship and experience blossomed that evening and I began viewing him with far more respect now that I knew that Freddie had the *right stuff* in an emergency. Freddie Also inspected the knife that I had used to cut the Kelp with during the emergency and asked me to make him one when we reached Santa Barbara. I took this as an extreme compliment and I was happy to do this for him.

With the coming dawn, *The Toilet* would be found south of *Point Conception* lumbering along at a steady seven knots through calm seas. The *Santa Ana* gale subsided soon after rounding *Point Arguello* and the balance of the night was uneventful with the exception of the occasional passing of cargo vessels. I got the impression right away that these large ships would stop for no one, and shame on the unfortunate mariners who happened in the path of these behemoths. These ships moved at three times the speed of *The Toilet* while never varying their appointed direction by one degree. They seemed to be completely indifferent to everything but their own selfish interests. We learned on the first day to avoid these ships immediately wherever they were encountered.

Freddie Steele's plan was to first reach the harbor of Santa Barbara, then load supplies for a four-day trip to the *Channel Islands*. We would then be returning to Santa Barbara for resupply and delivering our catch. This would be a two-day turn around with *The Toilet* leaving in the afternoon of the second day and cruising all night to the island of current choice. It was a busy schedule but we did not mind as we were beginning to trust Freddie's judgment in all matters pertaining to seamanship. Also, Freddie had been here before and knew the ins and outs of Santa Barbara and more importantly, the *Channel Islands*.

It would be late evening when *The Toilet* rounded the breakwater and cruised into the *Santa Barbara Yacht Harbor* access channel. It would also be in this access channel where we would drop anchor both now and at each additional visit to the mainland. Freddie had me pull *The Toilet* up to the Harbor Master's dock that first evening, both to announce our presence and also to let them know that we would be anchoring in the access channel from time to time. The Harbor Master was not pleased with this ugly little commercial fishing boat amongst those expensive yachts but he had little choice in the matter. He was legally bound to provide a *safe harbor* to all who entered this facility. He simply became extremely helpful in the accurate assumption that we would not tarry here long once supplies were obtained. The following day was uneventful with the filling of gas and water storage tanks. Freddie and Bobby went to the grocery store and loaded up with the supplies we would need for the next four days as well as visiting the *Fisherman's Pier* to the south of the yacht harbor. I am pleased to report that this *Fisherman's Pier* was in a state of good repair, unlike the one at Avila Beach. Freddie informed us that day, that this *Fisherman's Pier* also maintained a small fleet of 'hardhat" (full head helmet) diving boats known as the *red fleet*. We were warned to always be on the lookout for these boats but never once did we spot them at the *Channel Islands*. Later on that year, seven of these *red fleet* boats were seen working out of Morro Bay for a short time, not that it mattered then to either Bobby Landers or myself.

Once our supplies were safely stowed on board and needful business conducted, it was time to raise anchor and depart the safety of the *Santa Barbara Yacht Harbor*. Our first destination would be *Santa Cruz Island* and once again Freddie set a course to a little known natural harbor that once contained a Gambling Casino and Hotel in the early part of the twentieth century. According to Freddie, the Casino and related buildings burned to the ground at some later date but were never rebuilt.

This channel we would be crossing multiple times is worthy of note. At mid-crossing for a distance of roughly ten miles there always occurred extremely rough weather with high seas and strong winds. The swells were high (usually ten to fifteen feet) with deep troughs and all things aboard ship needed to be firmly secured during this passing. Freddie said that this was due to different ocean currents being funneled into such a confined area of water. That was as good of an explanation to me as any but the crossing was always rough and I was happy to get through it at each passing. It was also infested with *Blue Sharks* which are very aggressive scavengers. During this time period, the city of Santa Barbara was dumping its garbage in the channel and large *garbage barges* could be seen on most days coming and going from Santa Barbara. I am sure that this garbage dumping is no longer an acceptable practice but in 1959, this accounted for the large number of sharks in these waters. The *Blue Shark* grows to between eight to ten feet in length and those sharks in the channel would actually follow the boats passing through in large numbers, while occasionally nudging the boat as if begging for food. At one time I counted twenty-three of these blue devils closely following *The Toilet*. Freddie Steele pointed out that these *Blue Sharks* were known to engage in feeding frenzies with little provocation and we should be vigilant at all times. Freddie had little use for these *Blue Sharks* and he specifically requested to be called up if a *Blue Shark* was spotted in the area of our diving.

It should also be noted that during this time there was an intrusion of warmer water from the South Pacific. The water temperature was at least fifteen degrees warmer here than at Avila Beach to the north. With the warmer water there were also varieties of marine life not normally seen here. We commonly spotted schools of *Bonita* which is a smaller member of the *Tuna* Family, and flying fish abounded. Then there were *Langustina* hatchlings, a salt-water variety of a small lobster or a crayfish found normally in Latin America. These critters clung to the Kelp by the thousands near the surface of the ocean, while using the Kelp to give them cover from lurking predators. The warmer water was an unexpected bonus for me as I was planning to leave the dry suit to Freddie and begin using a wet suit once we began work at the islands. I had a cold-water wet suit which Freddie had provided, and a *demand regulator* similar to the type scuba divers use. Unlike the full-face mask that was part of Freddie's gear, the *demand regulator* controlled both the airflow and the pressure and had a soft rubber mouthpiece. The diver needed to bite down on the device and breathe both inhaling and exhaling through the mouth. I planned to swim with fins instead of walk the bottom during this work adventure, and I also had two hundred feet of new floating hose to work with. Freddie would be working the stern of the boat and I was to work the bow area. We had never actually done this before and both of us hoped that it would work well in actual conditions. It was completely untested but we were all optimists then. We also hoped that the air compressor would be adequate for the two of us when diving because the divers expend tremendous energy when below and the demand for air increases in the lower depths.

When we arrived at Freddie's secret harbor on Santa Cruz Island we were surprised to find four other boats at anchor there. This must have been a popular destination for the yachters from the mainland. There were two fairly substantial *ketch rigged* (double masted) yachts anchored close to shore, then two small, single masted sailboats that were no doubt launched from boat trailers. These two smaller boats cannot carry much in the way of supplies but the people on them appeared to be having a wonderful time. The yacht people were all out of sorts when *The Toilet* lumbered in and dropped anchor next to them. The following morning only one boat remained in the harbor other than *The Toilet*. The other three yachts had vanished silently in the night.

This small protected harbor was absolutely beautiful with evergreen trees growing down almost to the shoreline and crystal clear water that had unclouded visibility from forty to fifty feet in all directions. This would be the first and last time we would visit this marvelous little harbor however, because it had been picked clean by countless scuba divers over the years. The old Casino foundation could still be seen as well as some concrete stairs and a large iron ring embedded in rock at the waters edge. Bobby Landers and I would have enjoyed going ashore and exploring the area but time was not on our side just then. This was to be the only time we would see other boats, either pleasure or fishing boats like ourselves at the *Channel Islands*. I am absolutely certain that this lack of interest in the *Channel Islands* by the public is no longer true but that was the way of it back then. These islands had not yet been discovered by the yachting public. Just getting there was a minor achievement for a small craft by *running the gauntlet* of the channel crossing, and I do not think that this part of the voyage has ever changed.

The following morning was our first actual work day and we raised the anchor soon after breakfast and cruised to the south along the leeward side of *Santa Cruz Island*. We discovered cove after cove of calm water and crystal clear visage. We randomly picked a cove to begin work and set about our business of collecting Abalone. Fortunately, our plan of Freddie to the stern and myself to the bow worked flawlessly. I enjoyed my new freedom of swimming instead of walking and it was actually an advantage over Freddie Steele. The island dropped away quickly into the murky depths below but Freddie could only work where he could walk. I, on the other hand could swim down those vertical faces and pick Abalone until my basket was bulging. I was working at sixty to eighty feet then so after each foray into the abyss, I would work in thirty feet of water or less for a period of time. The second advantage was that I could move back and forth from the boat to my picking area with less effort and in less than half the time it took Freddie to cover the same ground and I could do this while carrying a bulging basket of Abalone.

The most amazing thing was the remarkable underwater oceanscape that glistened in the sunlight and abounded with marine life of an incredible variety. There were corals of many bright colors, Scallops, and schools of friendly curious fish above, below, and on all sides. The Kelp grew like trees in a forest and lent shadows and light to the drama below. There were lobsters to be found everywhere and on a more sober note, Tiger Sharks and Moray Eels. The water was always thirty to fifty feet deep or more but it never felt deep like it did in Avila Beach because of increased vision. There was sunlight and shadows and the most amazing array of dramatic colors flowing one into another as the sun moved across the summer sky. There were many Tiger Sharks everywhere we dove while at *Santa Cruz Island*. These fish had tiger stripes that served them as a good camouflage when they were not moving and they grew to about five to seven feet in length. The *Tiger Shark* was aggressive when on the trail of Abalone and would make continual attempts to remove Abalone from our baskets. A well planted thump on the top of their head with an Abalone Pry-Iron was usually enough to limit their aggression but they would then follow us around sulking while never quite giving up their quest for Abalone.

Then there were those *Moray Eels* who are extremely territorial and had a nasty habit of flaring out at you when you happened too close to their lair. Usually it would mean a mouth full of razor sharp teeth only inches from your face while you backed away as quickly as possible. I was never comfortable with these Eels because they always surprised me and gave me a good scare at each of the many confrontations I continually had with them. On one of our trips to *Santa Cruz Island* Bobby Landers and I brought a Spear Gun along with the thought in mind of bagging one of these Eels. So confident was I that I could simply swim down and shoot one of these *Moray Eels* that when the first one was located I immediately returned to *The*

Toilet for the Spear Gun. Although I had never used one of these before, it seemed like a simple task. With Spear Gun loaded and in hand I headed straight for that troublesome Eel. When the Eel flared out from its lair and was only inches from the Spear Gun, I launched the spear. The spear missed the Eel's mouth and penetrated about six inches from its neck closer to its midsection. If I were to say that metaphorically speaking, *the minions of hell were unleashed upon the world* that morning; I would not have been far from wrong. I can tell the reader with conviction, that the only thing that saved me from the wrath of that Eel was its inability to determine where its real antagonist was located. I immediately released the Spear Gun and headed for the surface, coming onboard *The Toilet* and staying there until the death throws of this sea monster finally subsided. It would be over an hour later when I finally had the courage to timidly move into the area where I had left this maddened creature while it was biting and attacking anything and everything close to it. The Eel was dead when I arrived and I retrieved the Spear Gun and headed back to *The Toilet* with the Eel safely impaled on the spear. When Bobby Landers pulled the Eel aboard, we were both stunned at the damage the Eel had inflicted to the spear. The shank of the Spear was bent in corkscrew fashion and there were teeth indentations on the Spear Gun where softer metal could be found. The speed and power of this Eel was awesome and I knew that I was lucky not to have been severely bitten by this rampaging fiend. I felt then that I had surely dodged a bullet by taking this *Moray Eel* so casually and I vowed never to be so foolish as to spear another of these sea monsters again. This is a vow that I have never broken.

Then there were those amazing lobsters with no pinchers (Pacific Ocean Variety). When they were spotted on the ocean floor, it was a simple task of coaxing them out from under their rock hide-e-holes and into our hands. Both Freddie and I wore white welding gloves with black rubber spots on them that the foolish lobster always got confused with food. One simply laid one's hand down near the lobster and wiggled ones fingers. The lobster would soon charge out and jump on your hand thinking it was dinner and it actually was, only not for the lobsters. Once caught, they were tied to the Abalone basket and sent to the surface with the full baskets. There were so many lobsters that we limited our catch to the amount we would consume that day, then only taking them when a taste for Lobster was upon us. There was another colorful fish called a *Sheepshead* that seemed to be one of the more plentiful fish throughout the *Channel Islands*. These fish also liked Abalone and were suckers for a head smack with the Abalone pry-iron. Those unfortunate ones would be sent to the surface where Bobby Landers would filet them for the evening's meal. We were always careful then, not to *chum* the water where we were working for fear of attracting a larger predator. The fish and lobster parts were always saved on board until the day's diving was completed before disposal. The *Sheepshead* is fairly large by fish standards and grows from eighteen to twenty-four inches long. It has an ugly flat face and two short fangs protruding from the lower jaw. They were quite colorful with reds, blues, and silvers and they were more of a nuisance than anything else. One of these fish of medium size would provide all that the three of us could eat for a day and they were actually quite good when freshly caught.

As we migrated south along the leeward side of *Santa Cruz Island* I noticed how the land changed on the island itself. The rich growth of trees and shrubs at the northern tip of the island gave way to prickly pear cactus and other arid climate plants. From time to time *Moreno Sheep* could be seen on the cliff's edge, always unsheared and equally of both genders. Freddie said that these animals were the remnants of a sheep ranch that flourished here at one time. I was struck by the bounty of the marine life that existed in such profusion beneath the surface of the adjoining ocean while on the barren cliffs above, life was struggling to survive. *The Toilet* worked for four days in the coves of *Santa Cruz Island* before returning on the evening of the forth day to Santa Barbara for re-supply. Freddie had brought holding containers along on the trip and each days catch was transferred to these boxes which were then dropped onto the ocean floor with a buoy and attached line marking their location.

The catch had been very generous to us then and after transferring the Abalone to *the Toilet's* hold, the freeboard to the stern was less than two inches above the water as we began our return crossing. Freddie was optimistic that *The Toilet* could take the pounding in the channel and deliver both our cargo and ourselves safely to Santa Barbara. I was never that confident but Freddie's prediction came true and from that point on, I ceased to worry about the sea worthiness of *The Toilet*. Two days in port then departing on the afternoon of the second day for the *Channel Islands* became routine and Bobby and I were always too busy with boat chores to do much exploring in Santa Barbara that summer. Our next destination would be *San Miguel Island,* the farthest and most mysterious of all the *Channel Islands.*

The Toilet approached *San Miguel Island* from the Northeast as the morning sun dazzled upon the Kelp beds below. There is a phenomenon there that Freddie Steele called *The Sand Spit* and it ranged from one tip of the island out to sea for at least one or maybe two miles. It was whitish –yellow in color similar to the color of a swollen stream at springtime and there was continual agitation there caused by opposing waves breaking over the sandy bottom and meeting in the center of this Sand Bar. Freddie claimed to have gone through it once before in the darkness and he said that it was not as dangerous as it appeared. The mists created from the crashing waves rose to well over several hundred feet that morning, and it was truly a sight to be observed as it sparkled in the morning sun. I never got the feeling that this *Sand Spit* was anything but dangerous. The *Sand Spit* to me was similar to seeing *Niagara Falls* for the first time, it was spectacular but it was also very dangerous just the same.

The Toilet was headed for a harbor that Freddie Steele knew of, and of all the harbors we visited on the *Channel Islands*, this one was the best protected and deep enough for an Ocean Liner to drop anchor there. In this harbor the *Langustina* abounded in such profusion that they gave a reddish tint to the kelp beds by their presence. There was an inviting sandy beach where Bobby Landers and I dug clams from time to time or just relaxed when time permitted. This Island was small by *Channel Island* standards but Bobby and I made many trips across it during our Abalone excursions. The upper portion of this island was rolling hills and easy for us to get around once the summit was made. *San Miguel Island* was the home of sea birds and foxes; no other animals lived here except for the Harbor Seals at certain times of the year. If one enjoys solitude, this island mountaintop would be the perfect place to meditate or feel the imminence of nature. I have never been to any place quite like *San Miguel Island* before or since, where one is immediately struck by the reverence of the sounds of the wind the surf and the sea birds blending together in amazing harmony. It should be noted that the Spanish explorer Juan Cabrillo, the man who is credited with discovering California, died in 1543 and his crew buried him on one of the Channel Islands. It is believed that the island was *San Miguel* but I do not remember seeing anything resembling a gravesite during my wonderings there.

Something should also be said about the Shoals to the northwest of *San Miguel Island.* On the charts this area was clearly marked *shoals, danger, uncharted hazards.* It was an area roughly the size of *San Miguel Island* itself and beginning at the western shoreline, it extended westward for three to five miles. I had inquired to Freddie Steele about this area on several occasions while wondering why we never entered the *Shoals* for diving purposes. It seemed to me that the harvest there should be excellent because no one had worked or entered this forbidden sea in recent history. Freddie dismissed the region as incredibly dangerous with strong currents that would sweep a diver away with little warning. I could see that Freddie Steele was clearly afraid to enter this uncharted danger zone and nothing I could say or do would change his mind. In retrospect, I am certain that Freddie's wisdom was superb here because when I researched *San Miguel Island* in later years, I discovered that not one but a total of seven ships had perished on these shoals beginning with the Spanish Galleons and ending with American Steam Ships. This was, and still is, a very dangerous area for the unwary mariner to wander into. *Fools rush in where wise men fear to tread,* and when I was just fifteen years old I was sufficiently qualified as one of those fools, armed with both the optimism of youth and the bliss of ignorance. I just wanted to go in there and see for myself what it was like.

San Miguel Island was to be the place where *The Toilet* would spend much time due to the bounty of the harvest. Our diving was with two exceptions, incident free here. One afternoon when diving at *San Miguel Island,* I had a minor encounter with young *Orca.* I was fortunate enough to have seen the whale as it turned in my direction. It was <u>only</u> about twenty feet in length but obviously looking for dinner. The beaches at that time were inhabited by *Harbor Seals* and that must have been what attracted the Orca in the first place. This critter had me confused with dinner and as it approached, I did the only thing I could do which was to wiggle back into a crevice where the *Orca* could not reach me. Freddie Steele had previously warned both Bobby Landers and I about attempting to swim to the surface if either an *Orca* or a *Great White Shark* were encountered while below. According to Freddie Steele, both the *Great White* and the *Orca* like to catch their dinner on the run and both have little time for things that wiggle into crevices. I can remember thinking that I really hoped that Freddie knew what he was talking about as that big whale made two passes at me before losing interest and moving on. I still had vivid memories of the feeding frenzy exhibited by those two *Orcas* at *Seal Rock* south of Morro Bay, California. Needless to say, as soon as it was safe I scampered to the safety of *The Toilet* and I remained there for some time. Our diving ended abruptly for the day as several larger Orcas were spotted in the area. I am also happy to report that neither of we three divers ever had a confrontation with a *Great White Shark* either at the *Channel Islands* or back in Avila Beach earlier that summer.

Bobby Landers had acquired and interest in diving and I would let him use my equipment at the end of each day. His skill quickly improved and his diving rewarded him with a larger share of the summer's profits. It was on one of Bobbie's diving excursions where the other incident took place. It was minor but it could have been fatal if not for blind luck. Bobby Landers had just donned my equipment and was submerging toward the bow of The Toilet to the reef below. While crossing the anchor chain the boat tightened due to an unusually large surge and Bobby was lifted approximately four feet upward almost instantly. The only thing that saved him then was that he was exhaling when the lift occurred. Bobby spoke of the instant tightening in his chest as he increased the volume of released air. It was a subtle reminder to all, of the myriad dangers encountered when entering an alien environment. It was incidents such as this that have caused me to say with conviction that *I have always preferred luck over skill in all of life's endeavors.*

It would not be fair to allow the reader to think that our days were filled with near death experiences due to equipment failures or attack by sea monsters. As our diving skills increased, our incidents of equipment failure or lack of knowledge decreased to the point where the days became routine in many respects. I am guilty of highlighting the most memorable events of that magic summer and I hope the reader will forgive this small indiscretion with the telling.

On one of our trips out to the *Channel Islands*, Freddie mentioned that there was a shipwreck off the coast of *Anacapa Island* that could be seen from the ocean surface on a clear day. Both Bobby Landers and I badgered Freddie to show us this wreck and eventually he succumbed to our collective whining and reluctantly agreed to take us the wreck. Actually, it was more like quieting a child by giving into them, but we didn't care because actually seeing a shipwreck was exciting for the two of us. According to Freddie, the wreck was in ninety feet of water and it went aground in the eighteen hundreds while loaded with forty-niner gold and many passengers. As far as Freddie knew, no salvage work had been done. He also said that some of the timbers of this ship could still be seen, strewn upon the ocean floor. The best viewing would be when the sun was at its zenith and the ocean was calm. Freddie knew exactly where this wreck was located and soon we were peering into the ocean with facemasks and snorkels at the sunken wreck. I asked Freddie why he had never tried to salvage this ship and his reply was that the water was simply too deep for safe diving and the costs were prohibitive. I had the occasion to research this wreck in later years and to the best of my knowledge it was The Steamship *"Winfield Scott"* loaded with miners and millions of dollars in forty-niner gold. The ship was said to have wrecked off the rocks of *Frenchy's Cove, Anacapa Island* in 1853. This diversion to see the shipwreck would represent the only time *The Toilet* would visit *Anacapa Island* during our tenure at the *Channel Islands* but I have always been fascinated by the history of this tiny rock. It has been said that *Anacapa Island* was once the home of pirates and smugglers at various times in the turbulent history of early California but that would be the subject of another story.

We also made several trips to *Santa Rosa Island* and did reasonably well there. *Santa Rosa Island* was far larger than *San Miguel Island* but there were few trees to be seen from the ocean anywhere on this island. It was merely rolling hills and grasslands much like an extension of the rural Southern California coastline. Bobby Landers and I visited it only one time while diving there. We encountered herds of scraggly deer and Elk but we never crossed a road or saw a building when hiking there. I am sure that there must have been roads and dwellings somewhere on this island but we never found them with our one visit. This island had nothing compelling for teenagers like us to return for, unlike *Santa Cruz* and *San Miguel Islands*.

To the south of *Santa Rosa Island* was a long reef that extended for several miles along the southern shore. The water there was twenty five to thirty feet deep and there were abundant Abalone to be harvested. This is where *The Toilet* spent much time working when at *Santa Rosa Island*. There was also an impressive surf that rolled across this reef and built to a crashing crescendo upon the sandy beaches at the shore. This wave surge had the effect of clouding the water by its surge action (back and forth), and the visibility here was never as good as the friendly waters we encountered at the other islands. As a bonus however, the water surrounding *Santa Rosa Island* was warm and the harvesting of Abalone was always good.

This shoreline hosted two types of seals, the Harbor Seals and some super huge *Elephant Seals* both lived here in harmony. The *Elephant Seals* were truly amazingly graceful animals while submerged on the reef and I never tired of watching these curious mammals when time permitted. *Harbor Seals* were everywhere on the reef as well, and sometimes it was a busy place to be. Then there were the sea birds that actually flew under water. I would look up and see a sea bird flapping its wings as it passed by, only it would be twenty to thirty feet under water while searching the reef for food. Diving at *Santa Rosa Island* could be compared to working under water at *Sea World* I think, although I admit that I have never worked at *Sea World*, ever.

I mentioned before that Freddie Steele was a world-class grump in the mornings and both Bobby and I steered clear of him whenever possible at that hour. I mention this only because Freddie's temper got the best of him one morning while diving on this reef. After the incident with the *Moray Eel*, I was far less inclined to smack any sea creature with my Abalone pry-iron when a gentle push would do as well. Freddie on the other hand, wielded his pry-iron like a sword especially in the early mornings when his grumpery was at its zenith. Perhaps I should explain just what the pry-bar looked like and why it could deliver such a hurtful blow. Freddie fashioned these tools out of car leaf-springs flattened at the front to wedge under the Abalone, then a handgrip on the other end. What Freddie used to inflict pain on the sea creatures that crossed his path was a measuring tip that extended out on the side of the pry-bar. One could quickly measure the length of the Abalone to see if it qualified as a legal take, or if it must be placed back on the rock from which it was taken.

On one morning when Freddie was in one of his foulest and ugliest of moods, I had been submerged for less than a half hour when I received an emergency signal to surface. As I approached *The Toilet*, I witnessed Freddie Steele fighting with a *Harbor Seal* as he struggled to board the boat. As Freddie climbed up the ladder, the enraged seal came up with him while catching him on the back of his heel. The powerful jaws of the

Harbor Seal bit through Freddie's Ski Boot and came close to severing his Achilles tendon before reluctantly releasing Freddie's foot. In defense of the Seal, as it finally drifted away, I could see blood clearly weeping from the top of its head. Ole Freddie had brought this incident entirely upon himself by his hatefulness that morning and this event clearly taught yours truly a life lesson that has never been forgotten. Although I attempted to appear appropriately saddened by what had happened to Freddie Steele, I was secretly happy that the *Harbor Seal* had whipped Freddie's ass so thoroughly, as he so righteously deserved.

This incident curbed our diving by one day as we made the boat ready for its return to Santa Barbara. For a time it appeared that our summer would end with this tragedy but that was not to happen. As we set a course for Santa Barbara and Freddie Steele's much needed medical attention, Bobbie Landers and I put our heads together to find a way to continue our diving at the *Channel Islands*. We both had a month of summer vacation left and neither of us was willing to call it quits just then if an alternative could be found.

During the channel crossing, Bobby Landers first broached the subject of diving to Freddie Steele. What he proposed was that he would be willing to take Freddie's place and continue diving with the dry-suit gear for the remainder of the summer. It surprised even me at how fast Freddie embraced this plan. I think secretly, he was planning to offer the same suggestion himself but it was better if we thought of it ourselves. Bobby Landers had been diving extensively for a month using my gear and was becoming quite proficient at harvesting Abalone. Freddie Steele was just happy to have someone else diving so he could stay where it was safe on board *The Toilet* and drink alcohol whenever he felt like doing so, which was every day starting around noon.

Soon after Freddie's wounds were taken care of, both he and Bobby Landers were in route to the diving store to purchase another dry-suit. Bobby also insisted upon some fresh thermal underwear because Freddie never washed his. After a two-day turn around we were once more making the channel crossing for another four-day diving adventure at these remarkable islands. Bobby Landers had little trouble adjusting to the dry-suit as he had the benefit of my knowledge to draw upon. There were much fewer life threatening emergencies as we settled in for the remaining summer. Freddie Steele was still a complete asshole in the early mornings but we could quickly remedy this situation by getting into our gear and submerging into a world where Freddie Steele's *acid tongue* could not penetrate.

Bobby Landers had only one accident that would be worthy to report only that it demonstrates the lack of safety precautions practiced by the few remaining Abalone divers of this era. While down in forty-five feet of water, the nylon twine holding the hose to the weight belt gave way and Bobbie's facemask was ripped from his face. Thinking clearly, Bobby activated the CO2 inflatable harness and quickly rose to the surface. I should add that Bobby remembered to exhale all the way to the surface. I went down and retrieved his gear as Bobby was unfazed by the incident and was willing to continue with the day once repairs were made. There was a complete lack of safety precautions or procedures back then. Diving gear was used until it failed then repaired if it was possible or replaced if it was not. The diver would simply carry on with his work if he were lucky enough to survive the equipment failure. This was what was expected of him.

As for Freddie Steele, he began to enjoy his newfound freedom where he could sit on the deck and use the hoist to pull up filled Abalone baskets for Bobby and I. All too soon this summer came to a close and I finally turned sixteen when we had less than two more weeks of work left at the *Channel Islands*. It was with great sadness for all when *The Toilet* crossed the channel for the last time, then headed north the following day to Avila Beach, California. It had been an astounding summer but soon after we arrived at Avila Beach, reality once more reared its unattractive head. Bobby Landers headed back to *Linnell Camp* and Mt. Whitney High School in Visalia, California for football practice. I, on the other hand, elected to stay with my uncle and enrolled in San Luis Obispo, California, High School for my junior year of studies.

I saw very little of Freddie Steele after that summer. The bite from the Harbor Seal never healed properly and before long I heard that Freddie had sold his boat and moved on to other endeavors. Freddie Steele was in his late-forties when this adventure took place and I am sixty-three at this writing. If Freddie were still alive today he would be in his early nineties. I still think of him occasionally and wonder what he is doing and how life treated him after the *summer of 59*. Bobby Landers and I rarely talked about that summer to anyone except each other out of fear of ridicule or non-belief. Both Bobby Landers and I owe Freddie Steele more than we can ever repay not only for this amazing adventure but also for treating us like men as well as helping us to become better men later on in life. He taught us how to conquer fear and how to do our job in spite of our fears. Freddie gave us respect and dignity at a time when the more affluent members of the community we lived in treated us as if we had leprosy. Wherever you may be Freddie Steele I give you a heart-felt thank you both for myself and for Bobby Landers (now deceased).

THE END

LaVergne, TN USA
05 February 2010
172146LV00002B/1/P